P9-DMJ-040

JANICE PRESTON

Cinderella and the Duke

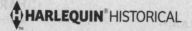

HARLEQUIN®HISTORICAL

Recycling programs
for this product may
not exist in your area.

ISBN-13: 978-0-373-29937-9

Cinderella and the Duke

Printed in U.S.A.

www.Harlequin.com

Janice Preston grew up in Wembley, North London, with a love of reading, writing stories and animals. In the past she has worked as a farmer, a police-call handler and a university administrator. She now lives in the West Midlands with her husband and two cats and has a part-time job with a weight-management counselor (vainly trying to control her own weight despite her love of chocolate!).

Books by Janice Preston

Harlequin Historical Romance

The Beauchamp Betrothals
Cinderella and the Duke

The Governess Tales
The Governess's Secret Baby

Men About Town
Return of Scandal's Son
Saved by Scandal's Heir

Linked by Character
to *Men About Town* duet
Mary and the Marquis
From Wallflower to Countess

Visit the Author Profile page at Harlequin.com.

To Dad—with much love.

Chapter One

February 1812—Buckinghamshire

'For pity's sake!'

The sheep darted on either side of Rosalind Allen, ignoring the open gate into the field where the rest of the flock grazed. Rosalind whirled around to see them scatter up the lane.

'Stupid ani—'

Her jaw snapped shut at the sight of an approaching horse and rider: a stranger. Instinctively, she tugged her shawl tighter around her head and body. But at least the sheep had wheeled around on spying the horseman and were dashing back in her direction. Rosalind threw her arms wide and waved the stick she had been throwing for Hector, to try again to divert the sheep through the open gate. This time the sheep swerved through the gateway and galloped, baaing loudly, to the far side of the paddock to join the rest of the flock, who were being discouraged from joining the runaways by Hector, Rosalind's dog, still sitting on the spot where she had commanded him to stay.

Rosalind trudged to the gate, which listed drunkenly on its solitary hinge. She tucked the stick under one arm as she hefted the gate up and struggled through the mud to

close it. Only when it was latched did she recall her hoy-
denish appearance. Conscious of the approaching rider, she
pulled at her skirts, silently cursing. When she had set out
on her walk, she had hitched her skirt to mid-calf level,
using a belt, to keep the hem from soiling. Apart from old
Tom the shepherd, she had never seen anyone else on her
walks, but now—too late—she recalled a hunting party of
gentlemen from London was staying at the nearby recently
sold Halsdon Manor. She'd heard the huntsman's horn earlier in the day, but had forgotten it until now... This man
must be one of that hunting party.

'Oh, no, don't cover up those pretty legs, dear heart.'
The voice slithered through the silence. 'Does a man good
to see such an enticing sight after a hard day.'

Rosalind stiffened as, behind her, the squelch of his
horse's hooves ceased. A worm of fear wriggled in her
belly. Nothing would surprise her about the so-called *gentlemen* of the *ton* after her family's experience with Nell's
guardian, Sir Peter Tadlow, and his cronies. Thank goodness Nell—her stepsister—was no longer at Stoney End;
she had departed early that morning in their family coach
to stay with her aunt, Lady Glenlochrie, in London to prepare for her debut into society. Hopefully she would be safe
in her aunt's care until the start of the Season.

The visitors to Halsdon Manor would not recognise
Rosalind or Freddie, her brother, for they had never been
welcome in society circles, but Nell was a different matter.
Heaven knew who she had come into contact with whilst
staying with various family members over the years.

Willing herself to stay calm, Rosalind finished fixing
her skirts and only then did she turn to face the horseman,
Hector's stick hidden in the folds of her skirt, the rough
bark reassuring against her palm. The gentleman was tall
and dark with classically patrician features. His skin was
unusually swarthy and he sat his sweat-stained black hunter

with insolent grace. His finely moulded lips were stretched in a smile that did not touch his eyes, the darkest Rosalind had ever seen. He raked her from head to toe with a gaze full of cold calculation that left a trail of wariness and vulnerability in its wake.

'Good afternoon to you, sir.'

Head high, Rosalind moved to pass the horse and rider, to head back up the lane in the direction of her home. Her attempt to brazen it out failed. The man backed his horse sharply around in front of her, blocking her path—so close the smell of the animal filled her nostrils and waves of heat from its sweat-soaked skin washed over her face.

'Not so fast, m'dear.' The rider's tone was sharp, his eyes intent. 'I simply wish to introduce myself.' He raised his hat. 'Anthony Lascelles, at your…*service*.'

Rosalind's stomach clenched at the oily insinuation in his tone.

'I am the new owner of Halsdon Manor,' Lascelles continued. 'And you are…?'

'Mrs Pryce.' Thank goodness she'd had the foresight to adopt the guise of a widow when they moved to Buckinghamshire. Her false identity boosted her courage. 'Now, if you will excuse me…' She attempted once more to bypass Lascelles's horse.

Again, he reined the black round to block her path. Rosalind gritted her teeth and glared up at him, then jerked away as he reached down to tug at her shawl. She brandished the stick, ready to do battle, then recalled Hector— no doubt still patiently awaiting her call. She smiled inside at the thought of Lascelles's shock. She put two fingers to her mouth and whistled.

Behind her came the scrabble of claws on wood, then Hector was by her side, hackles raised, snarling in defence of his mistress. A dog of the type developed to hunt wolves in Ireland many centuries before, Hector was a magnificent animal, his head level with Rosalind's hip. Lascelles's horse sidled and plunged, throwing his head in the air, tail swishing in agitation as his rider paled, his eyes wide and lips tight. A skilled horsewoman herself, Rosalind sensed the black's reaction was due as much to the tension of his master's hand on the rein as to Hector's appearance.

Surely Lascelles would detain her no longer?

'Quiet, sir!'

The sharp voice sounded above Hector's growls and the silence was sudden and absolute. Amongst the confusion, Rosalind had failed to notice the arrival of three more riders. Her nerves strung tighter. Even Hector could not withstand four men if they were intent on harm. Rosalind grasped his collar, more for her own comfort than by the need to restrain the dog, for he had responded to that autocratic command and now stood, mute but alert, his gaze locked on to Lascelles. Rosalind concentrated on breathing steadily and maintaining her outward calm, despite the tremble of her knees.

'How much further back to the Manor, Anthony?'

It was the middle of the three—chisel jawed and broad-shouldered, with a haughty, aristocratic air—who spoke, his voice clipped. He sat his huge bay with the grace of one born to the saddle, his mud-spattered breeches stretched over muscled thighs, his gloved hands resting casually on the pommel. The hard planes of his face were relieved by his beautifully sculptured mouth, his eyes were an arresting silvery grey under heavy lids and straight dark brows, and his hair, glimpsed under his hat, was very dark, near black.

Rosalind's racing heart thundered in her ears as her palms grew clammy. She swallowed past a hard lump in her throat and raised her chin, still fighting to hide her panic.

'A mile or so down there.' Lascelles pointed with his whip.

'In that case let us proceed. It is getting late and I for one am tired and hungry. If you really wished to spend your time on *that* sort of hunting, I suggest you should have remained in London. I've no doubt the quarry there is less well protected.'

With that, his gaze swept over Rosalind, who experienced an instant tug of attraction despite the arrogance of his perusal—he had not even bothered to glance at her face. His indifference as he viewed her muddy boots and shabby attire stirred her resentment, but his words, and his tone of voice, had reassured. Surely this was not a man to turn a blind eye to a woman in jeopardy?

Then the man's attention moved to her face. Rosalind sensed a subtle shift in his bearing as his silvery eyes narrowed, boring into hers with such intensity her insides performed a somersault. She felt a blush creep up her neck to her cheeks. Despite her aversion to his kind, she could not deny his magnetism. Try as she might, she could not tear her gaze from his, even though the slow curve of his lips in a knowing smile made her blood simmer.

The spell he cast was broken when Lascelles, who had finally brought his horse under control, manoeuvred it between Rosalind and the other men, blocking her view of all but the man on the right of the three, who had removed his hat to reveal thick, brown hair and chocolate-brown eyes.

'You three ride on to the Manor,' Lascelles said. 'I won't be long: I simply wish to reach an understanding with the charming Mrs Pryce.'

The brown-haired man threw a look of disgust at Lascelles. 'Leave her alone, Lascelles,' he said. 'I'll wager there are willing women aplenty around here, but she don't seem to be one of them.'

'Ah, but therein lies the attraction, my dear Stanton. I find I enjoy a spot of resistance in my wenches—it adds spice to the chase and makes the ultimate reward all the sweeter, don't you know?'

He made her skin crawl. How dare he talk about her like this, as though she were not even present? Wench indeed.

Lascelles swivelled his head, assessing Rosalind with his chilling black gaze and a humourless smile. 'And I always do get my reward, you know,' he added.

'Get him out of here, Stan.' Quiet words, spoken with menace, by the man with those hypnotic silver eyes.

Stanton spurred his horse alongside Lascelles, jostling the other man's horse so it faced in the direction of Halsdon Manor as Rosalind sidestepped out of their way, tugging a still-alert Hector by the collar.

'Let us go, Lascelles. You lead the way.' Stanton shot an apologetic look at Rosalind as he rode past her, tipping his hat.

But Lascelles, with a snarl, hauled his horse round to confront the remaining two men.

'You have no right—'

His venom was clearly directed at the silver-eyed man, but it was the third man who kicked his horse into motion. He was handsome, with green eyes and chestnut-coloured hair, and bore such a striking likeness to the first newcomer and, to a lesser extent, Lascelles that Rosalind could not doubt all three were related.

'Don't be a fool, man,' he muttered, placing his hand on Lascelles's forearm. 'You know how Leo feels about such matters. Leave well alone.'

Lascelles hesitated, his lips a thin line, his brows low. Then he gave an abrupt nod, wheeled his still-fretting horse around and followed Stanton down the lane. The green-eyed man hesitated in his turn, glancing at the man called Leo, who ignored him, his attention still fixed on Rosalind. The other man shrugged, raised his hat to Rosalind and gave his horse the office to proceed.

Leaving Rosalind facing Leo.

She met his gaze, suppressing the quiver that chased

across her skin as he looked deep into her eyes—his expression impassive—for what seemed an eternity. Finally, goaded, she tilted her chin and raised her brows.

'I am grateful, sir.'

His lips flickered in the ghost of a smile and he tipped his hat as he nudged his horse past Rosalind.

'Good day to you, madam.'

She watched him go. Unfamiliar sensations swirled through her, provoking a sense of loss she could not begin to explain. Unbidden, her hand lifted to her chest. There, outlined beneath the wool of her gown, her fingers sought and found the oval shape of the silver locket made for her by Grandpa for her sixth birthday. Her most treasured possession, representing her father's world, and her only link with his side of the family. Her mother had severed all links with the Allens after Papa was killed.

The gentleman riding away from her was of the world that had moulded her mother: a world of entitlement ruled by strict codes of behaviour and an unshakeable belief in class—a world that neither accepted nor acknowledged Rosalind and Freddie, even after their widowed mother had been welcomed back into its folds.

A hateful, unforgiving world that Rosalind wanted no part of.

But the emotions those silver eyes of his aroused in her paid no heed to reasoning. Those emotions picked her up and tossed her around until her head whirled as giddily as her stomach. Those emotions hinted at possibilities—they raised the promise of pleasure, disturbed a desire for the touch of a man's hand and lips.

And not just any man.

This man.

She should be shocked at herself for such scandalous thoughts, but she was intrigued. Never before in her thirty years had a man aroused such feelings in her breast. Those eyes. They penetrated, seemingly, into her soul and, for the first time in her life, she had the inkling of an understanding of passion.

A nudge at her hand shook her from her reverie.

'You're right, Hector. It is of no use mooning after a handsome face.'

She was unsettled with being forced to leave Lydney Hall, that was all. It would pass. All things did pass, given time.

'Come, let us go home.'

Hector trotted up the lane ahead of Rosalind, stopping at intervals to investigate an interesting smell. Rosalind tramped in his wake and contemplated her future with little enthusiasm.

Thirty years of age, and the past fourteen years of her life spent raising Freddie, their stepsister, Nell, and stepbrother, Jack, after their own mother died of childbed fever. Rosalind had long accepted she would never marry or have children and she had always been content with her lot until her beloved stepfather had died quite unexpectedly last spring, leaving chaos in the wake of his passing.

Step-Papa had made his will, leaving pensions for both Rosalind and Freddie and making provision for a generous dowry for Nell. The title and estates now belonged to fourteen-year-old Jack, Eighth Earl of Lydney, and those estates were held in trust for him until his twenty-first birthday. But the late Earl's younger brother—named in his will as guardian to his children—had predeceased him by three short months and the Court of Chancery in London had appointed Nell and Jack's maternal uncle, Sir Peter Tadlow—their closest male relative—as their guardian.

Yes, Rosalind had been content, until Sir Peter had descended upon Lydney Hall to 'fulfil my obligations to my dearest nephew.' It had not taken long for his true nature to emerge. Lydney Hall was soon plagued by visits from Sir

Peter's friends and acquaintances, with Jack's inheritance paying the bills. Sir Peter did not hide his utter contempt for Rosalind and Freddie and their humble parentage—their father had been a soldier, the son of a silversmith, who had eloped with the granddaughter of a duke—and he and his visitors viewed Rosalind as 'fair game' and Freddie as an object of ridicule. They would have remained at the Hall and tolerated any amount of unpleasantness, however, had it not been for Sir Peter's plans for Nell.

Rosalind swallowed down her impotent rage at the thought of seven long, frustrating years with Jack's estates and future under the control of that...*wastrel.*

As she arrived at the gate of Stoney End, the modest house they had called home for the past fortnight, Rosalind tore her brooding thoughts from her long-term future, directing them to the next few days instead. Immediately, a handsome face with a mesmeric gaze and sensual lips invaded her thoughts and that peculiar blend of yearning and curiosity swirled through her once more.

Leo.

Would they meet again? Should she fear such a meeting? Should she fear *him*?

Her intuition told her no...at least, not in the way she might fear another meeting with Lascelles. But there remained a thread of unease. Even as an innocent, she sensed the danger of a different kind that he posed.

To her. To her heart. To her peace of mind.

Chapter Two

Leo Alexander Beauchamp, Sixth Duke of Cheriton, reined his horse to a halt and twisted in the saddle to peer back along the lane.

The woman—back straight, head high—continued on her way, her shawl wrapped tightly around her form, accentuating the provocative sway of her hips as she walked. Her face materialised in his mind's eye. Not a predictable youthful beauty, but a hypnotically attractive woman. She had met his gaze with challenge but, more enticingly, with a welcome lack of calculation and coquetry—two traits he had become adept in recognising in the ladies of the *ton* in the thirteen years since Margaret, his wife, had died. A titled, wealthy widower—even one who was a father of three—was always of interest to the fairer sex.

Mrs Pryce. Presumably there must be a Mr Pryce somewhere. He should put her from his mind, then.

And yet…there had been a definite spark when their eyes had locked, as when a hammer struck stone. He huffed a near-silent laugh—an apt metaphor, perhaps: the clash of a mighty force against an unyielding substance. She had certainly exhibited a steely resistance to Lascelles. The thought of his cousin triggered the sudden awareness that he was sitting on his horse in the middle of a country lane, staring after a stranger. He squeezed Conqueror into motion.

And there was Vernon, waiting for him, a wide smile on his face.

'Whatever you're about to say…don't.'

'Me?' Lord Vernon Beauchamp—Leo's brother and his junior by four years—feigned a look of innocence. 'I am only concerned you may not find your way back to Halsdon without my guidance.'

'I'm not in my dotage yet,' Leo growled. It was something of a sore point, as he had recently passed his fortieth birthday. 'My homing instinct is as keen as it ever was.'

Vernon glanced over his shoulder, then quirked a brow at Leo. 'I can see that.'

Leo narrowed his eyes at his brother. 'She's married.'

Having been in the position of cuckolded husband himself, Leo was not about to inflict that indignity on any other man.

'Besides,' he continued, 'we are only here another ten days. *If* I stay that long.'

'Still fretting about Olivia?'

'I do *not* fret.'

He was a duke: head of a large extended family, wealthy, powerful. Nothing could threaten him.

'Cecily is wise to Olivia's wiles and tricks,' Vernon went on, in complete disregard of Leo's obvious wish to be done with the topic. 'Lord, that girl is a minx, Leo.'

Leo knew it. His only daughter and youngest child, eighteen-year-old Olivia was on the brink of her introduction to polite society. Her upbringing alongside her older brothers had instilled in her a deeply felt sense of injustice at the unfairness that allowed them so much more freedom than she could now enjoy. Leo had left her in London in the care of his sister, Cecily, who had raised Leo's children after their mother was murdered.

'I *said* I do not—'

'And Beauchamp House is more secure than the Tower of London,' Vernon went on, seemingly oblivious to Leo's growing irritation. 'They will be safe without you for a couple of weeks.'

Leo curbed his exasperation. Families! They saw too much and they understood too much. He might have no need to fret, but that did not stop him worrying about his children, and Vernon knew it. 'And Alex?' he said. 'Who will keep a tight rein on him?'

The younger of his two sons, Alexander was twenty, and growing more sullen and secretive by the day.

'Avon will keep him out of trouble…at least *he* gives you no cause for concern.'

Dominic, Marquess of Avon, was Leo's eldest son and the heir to the dukedom, who indeed gave Leo little cause for concern. In fact, he was almost too serious for such a young man. Leo's heart clenched. Was it because his children had lost their mother so early in life that he worried so about them? An unusual feeling stirred, deep in his gut.

Fear. No, not fear. Vulnerability. That was it. He didn't like the feeling. Not one bit. How he wished he could keep them all—particularly Olivia—shut away safely at Cheriton Abbey for the rest of their lives, even though the Abbey hadn't proved a place of safety for Margaret, who had been violated and strangled in a summerhouse. The impossibility of completely controlling his family's surroundings was a constant worry. Leaving London to come to Halsdon Manor—against his natural instincts to stay put and to *protect*—was how he proved to himself he would not succumb to this irrational fear.

Uncomfortable with such feelings and thoughts, he thrust them aside.

'Come, let us catch up with the others,' he said and nudged Conqueror into a trot.

They soon caught up with Richard, Lord Stanton, walking his horse on a loose rein, a preoccupied look on his face. A look, Leo guessed, that had everything to do with his new wife, Felicity—Leo's cousin and former ward.

'Where's our esteemed host?' Vernon asked.

'Rode on ahead,' Stanton said, with a curl of his lip. 'That poor animal of his won't last another year if he carries on riding him so hard. He can't even be bothered to walk him home to cool him off gradually. Mind you...' he slanted a look at Leo '...it'll give him a chance to get that temper of his under control before you two meet again.'

Leo shrugged. 'Anthony always had a nasty streak and it seems he hasn't improved since he's been away, not if that little interlude is anything to go by.' His cousin had spent several years in the Americas, returning to England only a few months previously. 'I suspected this trip was a bad idea, but I thought I owed him the benefit of the doubt when he invited me.'

Plus—although he would not admit it to the other men— he was a little relieved to leave London behind for a while. He could not bear yet another simpering young miss being thrust in front of his nose by ambitious parents keen to ally themselves with the house of Beauchamp. He did not want, or need, another wife. His first marriage had cured him of any desire to wed again.

'You owe him nothing, Leo,' Vernon said. 'It's hardly your fault Uncle Claude refused to marry his mother.'

'But if he *had* married her, Lascelles would be the Duke now.'

'He was right not to marry her,' Stanton said. 'An actress and a whore for a duchess? And can you imagine a man like Lascelles with that amount of power and wealth?' He shook his head. 'It doesn't bear thinking of.'

'We can always go home earlier than planned if Anthony becomes too obnoxious,' Vernon said. 'There'll be nothing else to keep us here once Stan's had a look at those ponies for Felicity.'

Leo grunted in agreement as they rode through the gates of Halsdon Manor.

Stanton had been searching for a pair of ponies suitable for Felicity to drive and Lascelles knew of a suitable pair for sale by his neighbour, Sir William Rockbeare, a renowned horse breeder and trainer, prompting Stanton to join the hunting party. Unfortunately, on their arrival two days before, they had learned Sir William was away from home and not expected to return for almost a week.

Nothing else to keep us here...

The memory surfaced of the woman, stick in hand, facing up to Lascelles. Leo found himself hoping that there was indeed a Mr Pryce. There was no sense in getting entangled in anything unnecessarily. No sense at all.

'You were gone a long time, Ros. Did Hector run you ragged?'

Rosalind hooked her shawl over a peg by the back door and smiled at Freddie, who was scratching Hector's shaggy ears.

'He tried to,' she said. 'Then, on the way back, the sheep were out in the lane again and it took an age to put them back into the field.'

She thrust the encounter with the gentlemen from Halsdon Manor to the back of her mind, determined not to trouble Freddie with what had happened. It would only worry him to no purpose, for there was nothing he could do. Hopefully Lascelles would remain occupied with his guests and then the Season would start, the hunting party would return to London to continue their lives of idle pleasure and Lascelles would forget all about their meeting.

'I hope Sir William appreciates you keeping his sheep safe.' Freddie lurched awkwardly down the passage, leaning heavily on his crutch, and disappeared through the door leading to the main rooms of their temporary home.

Rosalind followed her younger brother to the front parlour, where a welcoming fire flickered, lending a homely charm to the shabby room. It could not match Lydney Hall for comfort and space, but at least it was somewhere to call home.

'It's the least I can do when he refuses to accept any rent for this place,' she said. 'I do not know what we would have done had he not offered us sanctuary.'

Sir William Rockbeare was an old friend of their late stepfather—the Earl of Lydney—and it was to him they appealed for help when forced to flee Lydney Hall two weeks before, together with their stepsister, Nell, Lady Helena Caldicot. Thankfully their young stepbrother, Jack, the new Lord Lydney, was safely at school. Rosalind was still petrified Sir Peter would discover Nell's whereabouts before she made her come-out.

Would he...*could* he...force Nell to marry that awful toad, Viscount Bulbridge, to whom—Freddie had discovered—Sir Peter was deep in debt? When Sir Peter had bartered Nell's dowry against those debts without a care for the future happiness of his niece, Rosalind had seen no other option but to remove her from his control immediately. She had written to Step-Papa's eldest sister, Lady Glenlochrie, to beg her to come down from her home in Scotland to take Nell under her protection and present her to society. And now Nell was safely in London and Rosalind and Freddie were here—for the time being at least. What a messy situation it was to be in...and how precarious.

Freddie had turned at her words, and, as he did so, he stumbled. Rosalind darted forward and clutched his arm to prevent him falling.

He shook her away. 'I can manage.'

Rosalind bit her lip. Would she never learn? But she

could not help herself: with Freddie, her instinct always was to help and to protect, as she had done his entire life. 'I am sorry.'

As usual, when his lameness was mentioned, even obliquely, Freddie ignored it. He returned to their previous conversation as he lowered himself on to a chair.

'We would have coped. Jack is safe at school and we could have continued straight to Lady Glenlochrie in Scotland, if necessary. Sir Peter will not dare to flout her: she might be widowed, but she still has influence. And as for you and me, my dear Ros…as usual, we are of no interest to anyone. That is one benefit of being the product of such a shocking mésalliance,' he added, with a wry smile.

After Papa and Mama had eloped, Mama's father—Lord Humphrey Hillyer, youngest son of the Duke of Bacton—had disowned her, refusing to relent even after Papa was killed in the same carriage accident that had maimed one-year-old Freddie for life. Rosalind's hand crept to her locket, her throat aching with the memory.

'Indeed,' she said. 'The only benefit, as far as I can see.'

Freddie shot her a sharp look and she cursed her loose tongue. Five years older than her brother, Rosalind had always shielded Freddie from the truth of their parents' marriage, with its vicious quarrels and their mother's frequent tears. The last memory Rosalind had of their mother and father together had been of their bitter argument as they travelled home from a visit to Grandpa, a visit her mother had hated.

Her sixth birthday. The day her darling papa was killed.

Her mother had bloomed after Papa's death. Confused and distraught, Rosalind had mourned alone. She had lost Grandpa, too, that day. She had no idea if he was even alive still…no idea how or where she might find him. Mama had made certain of that.

'Are you envious that Nell will have the opportunity denied to you?' Freddie watched her intently.

'No, I am not, if by opportunity you mean marriage to a gentleman of the *ton*.' She could think of nothing more likely to bring her misery. 'Besides, the opportunity was not denied me, Freddie. Step-Papa offered me a Season when I was nineteen, with the idea of finding a husband, but I declined. And I am happy I did so.'

Or I might have ended up with an unequal union such as Mama and Papa's.

Love had not been enough for her mother. Papa had tried to keep her content and happy, but Mama had hankered after luxuries poor Papa could not afford. Mama's second marriage, to the Earl of Lydney, had been much happier than her first and that, to Rosalind's mind, proved that no good comes of marrying outside one's own class.

The late Lord Lydney had been a generous and loving stepfather and, when Mama died of influenza, he had continued to support Rosalind and Freddie as if they were his own children, even though their maternal relatives continued to disown them. When his second wife had died after giving birth to Jack, Rosalind, then sixteen, became a replacement mother to Freddie, eleven, Nell, four, and baby Jack and, three years later, when presented with the chance of a Season in London in order to find a husband, she had opted to stay at home with her family. She had never regretted her choice. The thought of facing her maternal relatives and their censorious friends, with their contempt and their snubs, filled her with dread even now.

The poor relations. The nobodies. The spinster and the cripple.

No, she held no envy in her heart for Nell and her forthcoming debut into polite society.

'Well, with any luck,' Freddie said, 'Nell will find herself a husband during the Season and he will keep her safe.'

'I do hope so.' Rosalind sank on to the sofa with a sigh. 'I cannot be easy that we have left Sir Peter in sole occupation of Lydney, Freddie. Heaven knows what havoc he will wreak. If only Step-Papa had realised the danger of him being appointed guardian, I am sure he would have altered his will as soon as his brother died.'

Her fingers were twisting together in her lap and she forced her hands to lie still. The weight of responsibility lay heavy upon her. Her stepfather would expect her to protect Jack's inheritance, but although she and Freddie had both tried to stand up to Sir Peter, in the end they'd had to admit defeat.

'We couldn't have stayed there, Ros,' Freddie said. 'We were right to leave. If we had not, poor Nell would be married off to Bulbridge by now. But I agree. If Tadlow is left on a free rein, Jack won't have much of an estate to take over when he reaches his majority.'

Rosalind silently cursed their lack of power. 'Maybe I should ask Sir William's advice on it all?'

She had been reluctant to burden their benefactor with more of their troubles. They did not know him well, though he had been a lifelong friend of the late Earl.

'I will consult him as soon as he returns from his visit to his daughter,' Freddie said.

Sir William had left Foxbourne the day after their arrival, on a long-planned visit to his widowed daughter and his grandchildren, who lived in the north.

Freddie's quiet statement penetrated Rosalind's thoughts. 'You need not bother yourself, Freddie. I will deal with it.'

Freddie had his sketching, his insatiable appetite for books and his interest in politics to occupy him. She did not want him troubled. He had enough to contend with and the mockery he'd endured from Sir Peter and his friends had only increased Rosalind's determination to protect him from the harshness of life.

She stood up. 'I will go and ask Penny to make some tea.' She caught sight of Freddie's scowl, prompting her to add, 'Unless you would prefer something stronger?'

'No. Tea is fine.'

Rosalind was distracted by the door opening before she could question his brusqueness.

'Oh, how lovely. Thank you, Penny. I was about to come and request tea. You have saved me the bother.'

Penny—who had been Freddie's nursemaid and had agreed to accompany them to Buckinghamshire to keep house—smiled as she placed the tray on a table. 'Shall I pour, ma'am?'

'No. I shall do it.'

By the time she handed a cup and saucer to Freddie, and sat down with her own cup, Freddie had resumed his customary expression of good humour. When they had drunk their tea, Rosalind worked on her embroidery whilst Freddie picked up his book and opened it.

As Rosalind set her stitches, she tried to ignore the slow, uneasy coil of her stomach. That anxiety had been present ever since they had arrived at Stoney End, but today there was a different edge to it. A foreboding. Was it because Nell had gone to London, leaving the future for herself and Freddie even more uncertain? She would love nothing more than to go home to Lydney Hall and to live out her days there in obscurity, but would that be possible with Sir Peter in residence? Surely not.

Or was it that meeting with Lascelles that had increased her apprehension?

Leo's face materialised in her mind's eye—handsome, strong, assured—and a very different feeling stirred...tension of a sort she had never experienced before today, as though something deep within her had recognised him and now stretched out...seeking...yearning.

Humph!

'Is there anything amiss, Ros?'

Startled, she looked up to find Freddie regarding her with raised brows. Her cheeks heated, realising she had allowed her snort of exasperation to sound aloud.

'I am quite all right, thank you.'

Rosalind bent her head to her embroidery once more, pushing all thought of Leo's lean face and silver grey, penetrating eyes from her thoughts. He might be the most attractive man she had ever met, but he demonstrated a remarkably poor choice of friends and, worse, he was obviously a member of the conceited and condescending world of the *haut ton*. The world she detested.

Chapter Three

Three days later, Leo strode into the local village of Malton, leading one of Lascelles's hunters, a fine gelding, his coat as black as Leo's mood. The horse—recommended to him *particularly* by Lascelles—had thrown a shoe within half an hour of the hunt starting and a swift examination of the animal's remaining shoes had revealed their sorry states. Leo cursed himself for not examining the horse more thoroughly before they left Halsdon Manor. His cousin was doing a fine job of pushing Leo's temper to the limit, the bad blood between the two smouldering beneath the surface urbanity.

This trip to Buckinghamshire had been a mistake. The days were just about acceptable, with outdoor pastimes to occupy them, but the evenings were a trial, the atmosphere fraught. More than once Leo had been within ames ace of leaving and returning to town, but Stanton had arranged to view those ponies the day after tomorrow, and Leo was damned if he would give Lascelles the satisfaction of believing he had driven him away. No. He would stay put and return to London with Vernon and Stanton in a week's time as previously arranged.

Disinclined to wait for a fresh horse to be sent from Halsdon, Leo had instead elected to lead Saga the mile and a half to Malton for reshoeing, savouring the solitude. It was a bright morning, with frost still lingering in pockets where the sun had yet to reach and a chilly breeze. As he waited in the February sunshine, Leo felt his irritation dissipate as he watched life in the quiet village of Malton unfold before him. The farrier—Benson by name—chattered nonstop as he worked, calling out greetings to passers-by, regaling Leo with their life histories once they were out of earshot. During a lull in the man's discourse, Leo's attention was drawn by a light grey Arabian, complete with side-saddle, tethered a hundred yards or so down the street. The horse had exceptional conformation and a flowing snowy-white mane and tail.

'That is a spectacular animal,' he said, thinking how much Olivia would love the Arabian.

Benson peered along the street before fixing his attention once more on Saga's off fore. 'Ah, yes, a fine beast, sir, a fine beast indeed.' He placed the red-hot horseshoe on the animal's hoof, removed it and deftly pared the scorched areas level before nailing the shoe in place. ''E belongs to Mrs Pryce, so he does. Poor young lady. A widder, sir, so they say.'

Mrs Pryce? Leo kept an eye on the horse and, before long, a figure dressed in a peacock-blue riding habit and matching hat emerged from a nearby doorway, followed by a man who laced his fingers for Mrs Pryce to step on to in order to mount the Arabian. If Benson had not already identified her, Leo would never have recognised her. She looked very different to the shabbily clad woman of a few days before.

A widow. Anticipation rushed through his veins, stirring his blood…except…so they say? Gossip and conjecture, not fact.

'Has she not long lived here?'

'Only a couple of weeks, sir. She rides in most days to

fetch a newspaper and the post, but the others keep themselves to themselves, they do. Living out at Stoney End, they are. That's a house on the Foxbourne estate, sir, seeing as you's a stranger yourself to these parts.'

Foxbourne. That was Rockbeare's place, where they were due to go on Thursday to inspect that driving pair for Stanton.

'They?'

'She lives with her brother and sister, sir. Or so I'm told—no one's seen a hair of their heads since they moved in.' Benson filed the wall of Saga's hoof, sweat dripping from the end of his nose. 'There.' He put the horse's foot down, and straightened his back, wiping his forehead with one sweep of his beefy forearm. 'All done.'

The Arabian stepped daintily down the street in their direction and Leo retreated into the gloom at the rear of the forge as Benson raised his voice in greeting. 'Good day to you, Mrs Pryce, a fine day it is, is it not?'

Mrs Pryce responded to Benson with a stunning smile that slammed into Leo with the force of a kick from a horse.

'Good morning, Mr Benson.'

She cut a graceful figure, her skirts draping elegantly to conceal her legs and feet. Her appearance and manner proclaimed her a lady—unlike her former attire—but she did not move in Leo's circles. He would not have overlooked such a female, with her clear, direct gaze and her full soft lips. His body responded to the memory of the provocative sway of those rounded hips with the spontaneity of a youth. It was too long since he'd had a woman. A dalliance with a comely widow might be just the remedy for his boredom and help lessen his exasperation with Lascelles.

Mrs Pryce disappeared from view, and Leo swung up on to Saga and set off in pursuit. Her reaction the other day suggested she might not welcome his company, but he enjoyed a challenge. He recalled his cousin's words with a twist of disgust. Most definitely *not* the kind of challenge Lascelles had hinted at. Vernon had been right—Leo could not stomach any kind of coercion, but neither did he particularly relish bedding the readily available widows he came across in society. They had no interest in him as a man. As a *person*. Their avaricious eyes fixed on his title and his wealth and rendered them oblivious to all else.

Mrs Pryce presented a rare opportunity. The true identities of the guests at Halsdon Manor had been concealed in an attempt to keep the matchmaking mamas of the county set at bay and Leo was visiting as Mr Boyton, Viscount Boyton being one of his many minor titles. Most parents of marriageable-age daughters were unable to resist the lure of an unmarried duke in their midst and it was easier not to receive invitations to hastily planned balls and parties than to offend the local gentry with refusals. So Mrs Pryce would have no idea of his true identity.

He could play a part.

Leo Boyton the man—not the Duke with a vast fortune and extensive estates to gild his appeal.

Saga's ground-eating trot carried them around a blind bend, beyond which was a river spanned by a bridge. Leo was so deep in conjecture he failed to notice the Arabian had halted as, in the absence of any contrary instructions from his rider, Saga trotted on until they were almost upon the smaller animal. The Arabian let out a shrill neigh and, half-rearing, plunged away from the oncoming threat, causing its rider to lurch violently to one side. As Mrs Pryce scrabbled to gather the reins, a sheet of paper flew from her hands, helped on its way by the breeze. Her hat tilted and slid from the crown of her head, carried on a heavy fall of soft golden-brown waves that spilled over her shoulders and down her back. The hat, with its white feather, came to rest at a lopsided angle at her nape, seemingly hanging by a single pin.

'Oh!'

That breathy half-squeak triggered a visceral reaction deep inside Leo, setting his pulse pounding. He watched in admiration as Mrs Pryce expertly brought the skittish Arabian back under control. She stared at Leo for several seconds, her eyes wide, then her brows snapped together and she turned her horse, urging him towards the bridge. Before they reached it, however, she halted again, wildly scanning the surrounding area.

'*No!*'

She lifted her right leg clear of the pommel and slid to the ground, revealing a glimpse of slim calf as her skirts rode up.

'Stand, Kamal.'

She hoisted up her skirts and ran to snatch up the letter the breeze had deposited on the riverbank, where she teetered for a few seconds before regaining her balance. Her back to Leo, she straightened her shoulders and shook out the skirt of her riding habit. She then attempted to bring some order to her hair as it wafted around her head in the breeze, but in doing so she dislodged her hat. It whirled into the air, raised on a sudden gust that promptly dropped it straight into the river.

'Oh!' Mrs Pryce bent to gather the draping skirt of her habit again and then hesitated on the bank, one foot raised. She stamped her foot back to the ground, dropped her skirts and whirled to face Leo, narrowed eyes shooting sparks. '*Now* look what has happened. That…' she waved towards the hat, floating off downstream '…was my *favourite* hat.'

She was all womanly wrath, full breasts heaving.

She is magnificent.

Leo tore his attention from her, leapt from Saga's back and ran along the bank until he was level with the blue hat, whirling in the current, feather fluttering. A nearby sapling grew close enough to the water's edge to provide an anchor so Leo removed his own hat, locked one arm around its trunk and leaned over the water, stretching towards the hat with his hunting crop.

There. Almost. He snagged the hat, pulling it close to the bank, then released the trunk and stepped forward to fish it from the river. He registered the subtle shift of soil beneath his foot too late. Before he could retreat, the bank gave way and his right leg plunged knee-deep into the bone-chilling water of the river.

'Hell and damnation!'

He grabbed the hat, dropping his crop in the process, and hauled himself back on to the bank. Thank God it was just the one foot. He looked back at the river, hoping to retrieve his crop, but it was already several feet away, spinning in an eddy.

A splutter assaulted his ears and he turned slowly. She must have followed him, for she was closer than he expected, her full lips pursed tight, her eyes dancing. Leo straightened to his full height. How dare she laugh at him? He had done her a favour by rescuing her hat...was it too much to expect a little gratitude...concern even? He'd wager she would soon sober up if she knew his identity.

Coming the Duke again, Your Grace? Vernon's jibe—thrown at Leo whenever he was in danger of becoming pompous—whispered in his brain. What was the point in travelling as Mr Boyton if he flaunted his title the minute he was treated with less than due deference?

'Oh, dear.'

Mrs Pryce's gaze locked on Leo's boot, which squelched as he walked towards her. Her brows shot up, her lips quivered and another laugh gurgled forth. Leo's irritation melted away as his own lips twitched in response.

He stopped in front of her and bowed. 'Your hat, Mrs Pryce.'

He proffered the hat and she took it, holding it away

from her as it dripped. She smiled up at Leo, a dimple denting one cheek, her eyes—a beautiful golden-brown, exactly the same shade as her hair—sparkling.

'I thank you, sir. That was most…er…*chivalrous*. But I am afraid you have the advantage of me, for I do not know your name.'

'Boyton, ma'am. Leo Boyton, at your service.'

Her expression clouded. 'At your service…' Her voice dripped scorn.

She spun on her heel and marched towards where their horses now cropped the grass side by side. Halfway across the intervening gap, she stopped and whirled around to face Leo. 'Do not imagine I am not grateful, Mr Boyton, but I cannot be easy here with you, in view of the company you keep. Your choice of friend, sir, does you no favours.'

Friend? Leo followed Mrs Pryce who, having reached the grey, now hesitated. She bent her head, looking down for a second or two, then sucked in a deep breath, her shoulders lifting as her lungs filled.

'Would you be so good as to assist me, sir?' The words sounded as though they were forced between gritted teeth.

Leo grinned, safe in the knowledge she could not see. 'Of course…but…first, allow me to defend myself.'

She turned, her narrowed gaze that of a lioness about to pounce. 'I am pleased you find my predicament *so* amusing.'

Leo sobered. How could she tell, from those few words he had uttered?

She crossed her arms. 'Pray, continue.'

'You claim, justifiably, that my choice of friend does me no favours, but will you so readily condemn a man for his family, over whom he has no choice?'

'Family? You are related to my neighbour?'

'Yes. We are cousins. We are not close, however.'

A wry smile curved her lips. 'I, of all people, cannot

judge you by your relations. As you say, one has no choice to whom one is related. But, nevertheless, you *have* chosen to accept your cousin's hospitality.'

'That is true. My cousin has lived in the Americas for many years. He returned to England only a few months ago and invited my brother and me to enjoy a few days' hunting. It seemed churlish to refuse.'

'And your other friend? Mr Stanton?'

'He is searching for a safe pair of ponies for his new wife to drive and there is a pair for sale locally.'

'I see.'

'And what of your family?' he asked. 'It sounded as though you also have relatives you do not care for.'

'My *immediate* family is delightful.'

'So you do admit to some less than agreeable kin?'

'One or two.'

She half-turned from him, towards Kamal, then glanced over her shoulder and raised a brow. He ignored her silent command and indicated the letter she held.

'Is that letter from one of them?'

The paper crackled as her fingers flexed.

'Not from one of the less than agreeable members or I should have happily relinquished it to the river and we...' she faced him again '...would not be having this conversation.' Her gaze travelled—lingeringly—down the length of his body, leaving a fiery trail of desire in its wake. It came to rest on his boot. 'Should you not remove your boot to drain the water from it?'

His foot and lower leg were numb with cold and he would dearly love to do as she suggested, but...

'I fear I would struggle to remove it without help. Unless, of course, you care to offer your assistance?'

Her brows rose, as did her gaze, which locked with his. 'That would hardly be appropriate, sir. Why, I hardly know you.'

'That can soon be remedied.'

He stepped closer, effectively trapping her between his body and that of her horse. A faint gasp—intrinsically feminine—whispered past his ears and his heart responded with a lurch and a yearning he hadn't experienced for a very long time. He studied her: her fine, creamy skin, the peachy blush of her cheeks and her straight yet delicate nose, the lush pink lips, the fine golden-brown threads of her brows. Her eyes, framed by long lashes, gleamed as they held his gaze. There was curiosity in their depths. No hint of fear or apprehension.

Leo stripped off his glove and touched his fingertips to her jaw. Her skin was silky-smooth, soft and warm. The scent of jasmine and warm woman weaved through his senses and blood surged to his loins. Then, on a swiftly indrawn breath, she looked down and away.

Leo stepped back and her lids flew open. Her gaze sought his again, questioning, and he smiled reassuringly. There was no hurry. She might be a widow, but he had no intention of rushing her. Over the years, he had found the preliminaries—the intricate dance and the anticipation— almost as enjoyable as the act itself. Delay only served to enhance the pleasure.

There was only ever one first moment of recognition.

Only one first kiss.

Only one first time to lie together.

They were times to savour.

He slid his hands either side of her ribcage, then smoothed his palms down her sides to the indent of her waist. He tightened his grip and lifted her, the narrowness of her waist and the womanly flare of her hips imprinting in his memory as he raised her to the saddle. She hooked her leg around the pommel, settled her skirts, placed her sodden hat upon the Arabian's withers and finally tucked her letter inside her bodice. She cast him an unfathom-

able look, then nudged Kamal towards the bridge. Before
they had taken a dozen paces, however, she halted him and
reined him around.

'My home is not far, Mr Boyton. Would you care to
come with me and dry your foot? You must be frozen and
I should hate for you to catch a chill after so gallantly rescuing my hat.'

Her smile radiated, feeding his lust, but he was conscious of a ripple of disappointment that she had cut short
the fun of flirtation. Still…mentally, he shrugged. He
wouldn't refuse her. She was a lovely woman and it appeared she was willing.

'Thank you. That would be most welcome.'

Chapter Four

Rosalind watched Mr Boyton mount his black gelding. The flex of his shoulders within the fine cut of his hunting jacket and the bunch and flex of his thigh muscles as they propelled him into the saddle made her mouth go dry. She could still feel the secure grip of his fingers at her waist, the effortless power with which he'd lifted her on to Kamal's back, his gentle fingertips along her jaw, the intensity of that silver gaze as it penetrated deep into her soul.

He had been going to kiss her.

She had almost allowed it.

She had *wanted* him to kiss her.

Strange sensations swirled deep inside, the same sensations as before but stronger, more intense. Nervy, intoxicating waves that washed through her—promising, enticing, persuasive—feeding her regret that she had stopped him and feeding her regret that she had never experienced a kiss.

And now she wondered—how *would* it feel? To feel a man's lips on hers? No. Not any man. *This* man. To feel *his* lips upon hers?

She swallowed, suddenly unsure. Why had she issued that invitation? She had ridden away. She had *intended* to keep going. He would not be in the area long and prudence dictated she should avoid him, but with every step Kamal had taken the stronger the urge had become to snatch more time with him whilst she might. That urge had swelled until it was near undeniable.

Flustered, she turned Kamal once more for home. Even though Leo was behind her and out of her sight, every tingling inch of her skin was aware of his presence. The black hunter soon ranged alongside Kamal and Rosalind peeked sideways at its tall, straight-backed rider. Above all else, she sensed she must conceal the confusion he aroused within her. She would not relinquish all control of this—whatever *this* might be—to a man who was clearly used to authority. She cast around for a neutral topic—anything that would prevent him studying her too closely.

'I am surprised you are not hunting today, sir. It is the perfect weather for it, is it not?'

'It is and I *was* with the hunt, until Saga here threw a shoe,' Leo replied.

He removed one glove and slowly smoothed the horse's neck with his bare hand as he spoke. Rosalind followed his movement, gooseflesh erupting across her back and down her arms, as though it were her skin he stroked. Her pulse quickened and her lips tingled. She risked a quick glance at her companion's face. She caught the gleam in his eyes, and guessed his action had been deliberate…designed to provoke such a reaction.

Take care. Compared with him you are as unknowing and as inexperienced as Nell.

The thought of her sister steadied her.

I might be inexperienced in matters of the flesh…and of the heart…but I am no green girl.

Unconsciously, she raised her chin and, from the corner of her eye, she saw Leo's lips twitch again. After a couple of beats of silence, he continued.

'I elected to walk him to the farrier in the village rather than send to the Manor for a replacement.'

Rosalind studied the lane ahead of them, determined to give him no further opportunity to distract her. 'I, too, was in the village earlier. I recall seeing a black horse in Mr Benson's forge as I passed. That must have been you.'

He glanced down at himself, then at Rosalind, his lips curving. 'Not me precisely,' he said. 'The last time I looked, I was not a black horse.'

Rosalind bit her lip against the urge to giggle. 'My apologies, sir. I shall endeavour to select my vocabulary with more care in future.'

He grinned. 'I find it does help to prevent misunderstandings. That is a remarkably fine animal you have there, Mrs Pryce.'

'Thank you. He is beautiful, is he not?' Rosalind patted Kamal with pride and affection. 'He was a gift from my father.'

He had actually been a gift from her stepfather, but the less anyone knew of her connection to the late Earl of Lydney the better. It could only harm Nell's reputation if it became known that she had not moved straight from her guardian's protection to that of her aunt.

'I assumed he must be a gift from your late husband,' Leo said.

'No.' The less she said about her fictional dead spouse the better.

'Have you been a widow for long?'

Rosalind shot a swift sideways glance at Leo before answering. 'I would prefer not to talk of it.'

'You are not in mourning, I see.'

She tweaked the peacock-blue skirt of her riding habit. 'You are correct.'

She was uneasily aware that Leo was studying her closely. She kept her attention firmly on the lane ahead.

'Have you lived here long?'

'We moved here two weeks ago.'

'We?'

'My brother and I.'

'Just the two of you, then?'

'Yes.'

Thankfully, Leo fell silent. A sideways glance revealed a thoughtful expression. His questions... Rosalind's nerves jangled. Why *had* she invited him back to Stoney End? For the sake of a wave of longing that had temporarily robbed her of her wits? None of the gentlemen at Halsdon Manor must connect her and Freddie with Jack Caldicot, the new Earl of Lydney and, through him, with Lady Helena Caldicot, on the brink of making her debut in society. Who knew what lords and knights and so forth Leo was acquainted with? Without doubt he must know Sir Peter. All these society people knew each other, or knew *of* each other.

Donning the mantle of a widow had seemed a sensible precaution when they fled Lydney Hall, in fear of pursuit from Sir Peter and Lord Bulbridge and, for the same reason, both Nell and Freddie had stayed hidden at Stoney End. They were far more memorable than Rosalind, with Freddie's lameness and Nell's silver-blonde beauty. One careless word and all their plans could come to naught. If it became known Rosalind had taken Nell from her legal guardian's care to live here under assumed identities—even for so short a time as two weeks—it would surely create a scandal, which could ruin Nell's chances of making the splendid match she deserved.

At last, the chimneys of Stoney End came into sight. Rosalind led the way into the stable behind the house.

'You can tether Saga in there.' She pointed to an empty stall. 'There is an old blanket at the back, to stop him catching a chill.'

Leo loosened Saga's girth as Rosalind led Kamal into his stall and started to unsaddle him.

'Where is your groom?'

'We do not have a groom at present, but a lad from Fox-bourne Manor comes in twice a day to help.'

Before she knew it, Leo was inside Kamal's stall, setting her nerves tingling again as he brushed past her to take over the unsaddling.

'I can manage.'

'I make no doubt you can, but a lady should not have to do this sort of work,' Leo said, removing the saddle and starting on Kamal's bridle. 'Could your brother not take over during the absence of your groom?'

'No. Freddie is... He is not strong.'

She moved back to give Leo space, still jittery over her reaction to his touch.

'Does he not ride?'

'Not at present. He took a fall shortly before we came here and he has not ridden since.'

Yet another thing she could thank Sir Peter for...him and his cronies...mocking poor Freddie and deliberately spooking his horse until it bolted in sheer terror. Pure rage at that memory burned in Rosalind's heart. She hated that Sir Peter had won...had driven them from their home... She had failed to protect Freddie, deserted their loyal servants, abandoned Jack's inheritance. But at least she had protected Nell from marriage to that lecher Bulbridge. Her come-out had been all planned for last year, before Step-Papa became ill. Surely Sir Peter could not object to Nell coming out with her aunt as chaperon?

Rosalind gradually became conscious of stillness and silence, and refocussed on the present to find Leo standing in front of her, Kamal's bridle and saddle in his arms. He was studying her face and she quickly schooled her expression.

'The harness room is at the back,' she said, pointing.

'So you only have Kamal to care for?' Leo spoke over his shoulder as he went to the saddle room.

'Yes.'

Rosalind turned to leave, but Leo lingered, gazing around at the empty stalls.

'No carriage horses? No vehicle of any kind?'

'Not at present.'

The Lydney carriage and horses were now at Nell's disposal in London. She sensed Leo's attention on her.

'Come.' She gestured to the stable door, eager to forestall more questions. 'Let us go indoors and dry your boot.'

She felt him on her heels as she crossed the yard towards the back door. 'I hope you will not object to entering the house this way?'

'Not at all. Before we go in, however...'

Hard fingers gripped her upper arm, pulling her around to face him. Rosalind's breath grew short as Leo gazed down at her and her cheeks heated. She swallowed and tentatively tugged her arm from his grasp. He released her immediately, but she remained pinned in place by the command of those silver-grey eyes. Up close, she could see the shadow of dark whiskers on his jaw and cheek. It gave him a dangerous, almost piratical, air and yet her fingers twitched with the urge to feel their rasp.

Leo touched the tip of her nose—gently, fleetingly—with his forefinger.

'What is your name?'

His voice was low. Husky. Rosalind caught the faint scent of cologne—musky, with a trace of orange and cinnamon—beneath the smell of fresh air, horse and leather. Her insides swooped like a swallow in flight and her breathing hitched.

'Rosalind.' It emerged as a croak. She frowned, cleared her throat and spoke with more force. 'Rosalind.'

'Rosalind...' The mellifluous way he rolled the syllables of her name created shivery waves over her body. 'It is a beautiful name.'

His eyes darkened and Rosalind felt another quiver run through her, as though he had gently tugged on an invisible cord attached deep within her core. It was as though she were a musical instrument and a mere look, or the sound of his voice, could tease a tune from her body as surely as a harp would respond to the plucking of a string.

This will not do. This is dangerous.

The thought that she was out of her depth swam through her thoughts. She squared her shoulders, spun on her heel and marched over to the back door. She would dry off his boot and then send him on his way.

Her steps faltered. Was that a chuckle? *Arrogant rogue.* Exasperation flamed at her involuntary responses to him and her inability to hide them. More than ever she wished she had left him standing by the bridge, wet foot or no wet foot.

'Penny,' she called as soon as she set foot over the threshold. 'Penny, where are you?'

He was right behind her. She could *feel* him. She cast her still-wet hat on to the kitchen table and then crossed to the fireplace, where a lazily steaming kettle hung to one side. She swung it over the centre of the fire and bent to grab the poker to stir up the coals, conscious the entire time of his eyes upon her. Where was Penny when she had need of her?

'Take a seat, sir.' Rosalind indicated the Windsor chair set to one side of the hearth, keeping her attention on the fire. 'I will help you—'

The door flew open, interrupting her, and she glanced round as Freddie came in, Hector at his heels.

'Ros, have you seen my—' Freddie fell silent. His brows lowered. 'What the devil are *you* doing here?'

Chapter Five

Roused from his appreciation of Rosalind's beautifully rounded derrière, Leo twisted to find a scowling young man of slender build standing in the kitchen doorway. There was enough resemblance to Rosalind for him to guess this must be Freddie. The swish of fabric and her jasmine scent told him Rosalind now stood next to him. The dog he had seen the other day in the lane padded around the table. He appeared not to share Freddie's misgivings, for he swaggered over and thrust his wet nose into Leo's hand.

'Freddie! That is no way to speak to a guest.'

'And I,' said Leo, scratching behind Hector's ear and curbing his instinct to slap down the young man's presumption, 'cannot imagine what I have done to arouse such… er…*vitriol*.'

Freddie's scowl lifted, but only slightly. He moved away from the door, rounding the table awkwardly, supported by a crutch jammed into his right armpit. Was that the result of the tumble from his horse Rosalind had mentioned?

'My apologies,' Freddie said as he approached Leo. 'For a moment, I thought…that is, you have the look of our new neighbour, Mr Lascelles, but I see now you are not him.'

A gasp, quickly stifled, whispered past Leo's ear and

he sensed the woman by his side stiffen. She was right to be wary of his cousin.

Leo smiled at Freddie. 'Ah…in that case, I shall excuse your caustic welcome. I am Boyton. Cousin to your new neighbour, although I hope you will not hold that against me.'

'I shall endeavour not to do so.' A fleeting smile crossed Freddie's face. 'We all have family connections we should prefer to forget.'

Almost the exact same words his sister had used. Leo tucked that knowledge away for the future. They shook hands.

'Allen. Frederick Allen.' The younger man's cheeks flushed. 'Of sound mind, if not body.'

'Fr-e-e-ddie…'

Rosalind's protestation suggested this was not the first time her brother had used self-mockery in such a defensive way. A mixture of hurt and anger flashed across Freddie's face. Sympathy for the young man bloomed as Leo concluded Freddie's impairment was of longer standing than the recent fall of which Rosalind had spoken. At close quarters the lines of stress on Freddie's face were visible. They made it hard to guess his age, but Leo would lay odds he was younger than his sister.

'I am pleased to meet you, Allen,' he said, 'and I apologise for this intrusion, but my boot is full of river water and your sister kindly offered me the opportunity to dry off.'

Freddie's brows rose. 'River water?' He surveyed Leo's buckskin breeches, one knee of which was noticeably wet. 'Dare I ask what you were doing in the river? It is hardly the weather for paddling.'

'Mr Boyton very kindly rescued my hat.'

'That is a great deal of kindness for one day,' Freddie observed. 'And your hat, dear sister? Might one enquire exactly how it ended up in the river?'

'Never mind that, now, Freddie. Where is Penny? Mr Boyton needs help removing his boot.'

Rosalind's brusque dismissal of her brother's question again set Leo wondering at the relationship between brother and sister. He contemplated his own sons' reactions if he should speak to them as though they were boys rather than the young men they now were, and he bit back a smile at the likely result. Alex, in particular, would take immediate affront.

'She is not here. The cook at Foxbourne sent her a message inviting her to raid the herb garden and offering her surplus preserves from her larder. I do not believe I have ever seen her move with such speed. She could be heard muttering about rosemary and pickles as she bobbed up the path.'

Leo remained quiet, observing as brother and sister shared the joke. It was obvious they were close, despite Rosalind's tendency to take the reins. Freddie appeared an easy-going young man who accepted her assumption of control rather than cause a fuss.

'Oh…well…it appears I have no choice but to assist you myself, Mr Boyton.'

A blush tinted Rosalind's cheeks. Was she, like him, remembering their earlier, similar conversation? At the memory of that almost kiss, blood pounded Leo's veins, pooling in his groin. How long since his body had reacted with such unruly eagerness? She was so near, almost touching him, her scent weaving through his senses…the very air seemed to crackle between them. Freddie would have to be blind not to notice the frisson.

'Perhaps your brother might help?'

Rosalind's eyes brimmed with sympathy as she caught her brother's eye. Freddie's lips twisted and Leo cursed his own insensitivity.

'Would that I could,' he said, after a moment's fraught silence, his tone suspiciously airy, 'but with my appalling balance…or lack of it, I should say… I should end up on the floor.'

Rosalind again indicated the chair by the fire.

'If you would care to sit, sir?'

A gentleman, surely, should at this point decline the offer and be on his way. But Leo was not ready to leave: he was intrigued by both Rosalind and Freddie. He sat.

'Please raise your leg.'

She was close enough that her scent again wove its enchantment around him. He could hear her breathing, surely faster than it should be? She could not conceal her body's reactions—she was as affected by their nearness as he. She moved to stand by his extended foot and grasped his boot at the ankle. Leo smiled at her fierce determination as she heaved until the boot came off with a slurp and a splatter of drops on to the flagstone floor. Rosalind looked up and their eyes met. She touched her upper lip with the tip of her tongue and he responded with a surge of lust so powerful he could barely stop himself from reaching for her there and then.

Her blush deepened and her lashes lowered.

'There. Now, if you care to remove your stocking, sir, I shall hang it by the fire to dry.'

Leo did as he was bid. Freddie's scowl had returned as he looked from Rosalind to Leo and back again.

'Do you care to partake of some refreshments whilst your boot dries?' Rosalind asked. 'A cup of tea, or perhaps something stronger?'

'Thank you. Tea would be splendid.'

'I will fetch the tea caddy and brew the tea,' Freddie said.

'There is no need, I can do it.'

Again, Leo caught that flash of irritation from her brother as Rosalind hurried to a door at the other end of the kitchen and then emerged with a caddy and a teapot.

'Would you show Mr Boyton to the sitting room, please, Freddie? I will bring the tray through when it is ready.'

'Might I trouble you to remove my other boot, in that case, Mrs Pryce?'

About to add a jest about having to hobble to the sitting room, Leo caught his words, having no wish to add to Freddie's discomfort and, again, his heart went out to him. How must it feel to a young man to be unable to do the things others took so much for granted?

'I will find you a pair of slippers to prevent your feet becoming chilled.' Freddie started towards the door.

Rosalind, who had positioned herself to tug at Leo's other boot, almost snatched it from his foot. 'I will do it, Freddie.' She rushed across the room to forestall him. 'There is no need for you to struggle up the stairs. If you show Mr Boyton to the sitting room, I will bring the slippers there.'

'If you would care to follow me, sir?'

Freddie's wooden expression and voice revealed his resignation. Could Rosalind not see how damaging her cossetting ways were to the young man's self-esteem? Leo could not doubt it was kindly meant, but was she really so blinkered as not to recognise the effect upon her brother?

Freddie led the way to an over-furnished, old-fashioned sitting room and gestured to one of a pair of chairs by the fire before sitting on the other. Hector, who had followed them, flopped in front of the fire and stretched out on his side with a sigh.

'You mistook me for my cousin before,' Leo said, when Freddie seemed disinclined to begin a conversation. 'I feel it incumbent upon me to apologise for the offence he caused.'

The preoccupied frown lifted from Freddie's face and he grinned. 'You do not doubt he caused offence then, sir?'

'I do not. Quite apart from your reaction upon your first sight of me, I know my cousin and his…shall we say, quite unique way of endearing himself to others.'

The frown returned. 'I cannot say I am overjoyed at the prospect of having Mr Lascelles as a neighbour.'

'Was he intolerably rude?'

'Not quite intolerably. I consider myself something of an expert in the art of exercising tolerance in the face of others' unthinking comments.' A smile lit Freddie's countenance and then was gone. 'Name-calling cannot, after all, hurt.'

Leo had never believed the truth of that statement. Name-calling, thoughtless comments, sly looks: they could hurt as much as physical pain.

'I should have anticipated he would discover your sister's whereabouts after our previous encounter.'

Freddie sat forward. 'Previous encounter?'

So Rosalind had not told her brother, presumably protecting him.

'Mrs Pryce did not mention our meeting the other day?'

'No, she did not. Will you tell me what happened?'

Leo would not patronise the other man by shielding him from the truth. 'My cousin was, I fear, quite objectionable to your sister. Although, to be fair, we all thought she was perhaps a farmer's wife or daughter. She was rounding up sheep when we came upon her in the lane.'

'Ah. Now, she did tell me about *that*.'

'My cousin had ridden ahead of the rest of us—'

'Rest of you? How many?'

'Four in total. We are visiting for a couple of weeks. Next week we return to London.'

'Lascelles, too?'

'As far as I am aware...yes, Lascelles, too. It might set your mind at rest to know he is not a country lover. He purchased Halsdon Manor for its nearness to London, to enjoy the occasional hunting and shooting trip. He is un-likely to pay frequent visits.'

'I doubt we shall be here much longer anyway,' Freddie said. 'What did he say to my sister, Mr Boyton?'

'I did not hear his precise words, but suffice it to say that when we came upon the two of them your sister had raised a stick to my cousin and your dog appeared on the brink of attack.'

He should have found out exactly what had passed be-tween them. Knowing Lascelles had taken the trouble to find out where Rosalind lived did not bode well. The past few days had revealed more of his cousin's character than he would wish to know.

Freddie's hands clenched into fists. '*I* should be able to protect her.' The words sounded as though they were wrenched from him. 'Rosalind has spent her life helping to raise us, but even though I am older than the others, it is I who will continue to be a burden upon her.'

The others? Who else was there? Where were they?

'I am sure your sister does not view you as a burden.'

Freddie's eyes glittered, and he blinked rapidly. 'She is too selfless to think of me as such, but that does not stop me feeling useless.'

'You mentioned others—have you more brothers or sis-ters?'

Rosalind had spoken only of Freddie, but Benson had mentioned another sister.

Unease flickered across Freddie's face. 'There are two others, but it is just me and Rosalind now.'

Leo did not pursue the subject. He had quite enough to ponder as it was.

* * *

'Why did you not tell me you had already made the acquaintance of our new neighbour, Ros?'

Bother! Why did I not warn Leo not to mention our previous meeting?

Rosalind took her time before replying, putting the tea tray on the table and handing the slippers, which she had tucked beneath her arm, to Leo. He took them with a smile and a deep murmur of thanks that melted through her like butter on warm toast.

Only as she poured the tea did she say, 'I did not wish to trouble you.'

As she handed Leo his cup and saucer, she could not miss the knot of muscles on either side of Freddie's jaw.

'It is not about troubling me, but about sharing your worries.' His words rang with bitterness. 'Can you not accept that I can provide moral support even if I am unable to protect you physically?'

Rosalind paused in the act of handing her brother his cup of tea. When had he become so irritable?

'Oh, Freddie.' The ever-ready guilt flooded her. Why had it not been she who was injured? Why had she escaped with mere bruises whilst Freddie's life had been altered beyond measure? 'I am sorry. You are right. I am thoughtless. I am so accustomed to... I simply do not think at times... after all this time it is hard to remember you are a grown man and not just my younger brother. And after all that has happened—'

With a lurch of horror, she bit off her words. What was she thinking, running on so in such an ill-considered fashion?

'I apologise, Mr Boyton. What must you think of us?'

Freddie took his cup from her with a look of reproach. Well, she deserved that. She forced a laugh.

'That is more than enough about our family. Tell me,

Mr Boyton, are you familiar with the countryside around here?'

They indulged in stilted small talk whilst they drank their tea, Rosalind painfully aware of the speculation in Leo's eyes every time they alighted upon her. Thankfully, it was not long before he rose to his feet.

'I have trespassed upon your hospitality long enough.'

'Not at all,' Rosalind said, but stood up and led the way to the door lest he changed his mind. 'It was the least I could do after you rescued my hat. I am certain your stocking will be dry by now.'

Leo made his farewells to Freddie, who made no attempt to follow them from the room.

As soon as she entered the kitchen Rosalind hurried over to the fireplace and snatched at the stocking. 'Yes, this is dry.' She bent to scoop Leo's boot from the floor. 'And although your boot is still damp, it is an improvement, I am sure. And it is not so far to Halsdon Manor. I am sure you will—oh!'

Leo had followed her across the room and, as she straightened, he was right beside her. He lifted her chin with one finger, tilting her gaze to his.

'I understand you are anxious, Rosalind, but there is no need to fill every second of silence. You may tell me "all that has happened" if you wish, but I shall not interrogate you.'

Conversely, his words fuelled her apprehension. He saw far too much with that keen silver-grey gaze.

Leo released her chin and sat down to pull on his stocking and his boots. 'Your brother mentioned, though, that you are unlikely to remain here much longer. Where will you go?'

'Oh. I do not… That is, I am not certain.'

She had avoided thinking beyond their immediate future. She had not planned much further than ensuring Nell was safe. She and Freddie could not impose on Sir William's hospitality for ever, but where were they to go? Back to Lydney? The idea was unpalatable, with Sir Peter—as far as she knew—still in residence, and yet she could not leave him in sole charge, and what of the school holidays? Jack must return in the summer and she would have to go back then. She could not leave him to Sir Peter's care.

She sighed. Indecision. It had plagued her ever since they fled Lydney. She did not know what to do for the best. The only decision she had reached was to wait until Nell's Season was complete. Maybe that would show her the way forward.

'What is it?' A gentle finger feathered between her tight brows. Leo had finished pulling on his boots whilst she was lost in thought and now stood before her. 'You are troubled. Allow me to help.'

Rosalind swallowed the ache of tears at those gentle words. How she wished...but there was nothing he could do to help.

'I am sorry. It is nothing.' She stretched her lips in a smile. 'We might stay here. I have not decided yet.'

'*You* have not decided? Does your brother not have a say in what you do?'

'It was a figure of speech. I meant *we*.'

'Your brother... He is a man. He has a man's pride.'

Rosalind frowned at him. 'He is *my* brother. You have only just met him.'

Leo regarded her thoughtfully. 'I had no intention of annoying you. I do wonder, however, if—'

'It is not your business to wonder at what my brother and I do or how we live, sir.'

Nerves fluttered within as his brow lowered. That had been rude. Nonetheless, she stifled her urge to apologise. Her family was *her* business and no concern of anyone else.

Particularly someone they had only just met and who could have no idea of what life had thrown at them.

'What happened to your brother's leg?'

The abrupt change in conversation took her by surprise and she answered without any censorship of her words.

'It was a carriage accident. Freddie's leg was crushed and our father was killed. My mother and I were uninjured.'

'I see. And how old was Freddie?'

She did not care for the understanding in those silvery eyes. It made her feel like weeping. 'He was one year old.'

'And you were...what...three? Four?'

'Six. I was six.' Her birthday. She stamped on the memory of that terrible day even as her hand crept, without volition, to the comfort of her locket and the memory of Grandpa, of sitting on his lap as he told her stories.

'Your father was killed, you say. Where is your mother now?'

Rosalind grabbed the poker and stirred viciously at the fire. 'She died when I was nine.'

'And Freddie would have been only four. Do you have other brothers or sisters?'

That deceptively simple question hovered perilously close to matters Rosalind wished to avoid. She dropped the poker on to the stone hearth with a clatter, and marched across the kitchen to haul open the door.

'It was kind of you to retrieve my hat, Mr Boyton. I make no doubt you long to return to your friends at Halsdon.'

Leo raised a brow and scrutinised her from head to toe. Then he smiled.

'We will meet again, Rosalind, before I leave Halsdon. On that you may depend.'

He strolled across the kitchen, taking his hat from the table as he passed. As he neared Rosalind, her breath quickened under the magnetic pull of those extraordinary, omniscient eyes. Might he try to kiss her? Touch her? He did neither. And she was left shaken and bereft as he strode from her sight.

She used her pent-up energy to tidy the kitchen, before taking Freddie his newspaper—ordered daily from London—and the letter she had collected from the village.

'There was a letter from Jack,' she said, on entering the room. 'I could not tell you whilst Mr Boyton was here. Jack writes that Sir Peter visited the school and quizzed him as to Nell's whereabouts.'

Freddie held out his hand. 'May I read it for myself?'

'Of course you may.' Rosalind handed him the letter. 'It is addressed to us both. He suggested to Sir Peter that you had expressed a desire to visit Brighton and that he might enquire for us there.'

She laughed, trying to catch Freddie's attention, but he appeared disinclined to share the joke, managing only the slightest smile in response. Mentally, she shrugged away Freddie's bad mood. He appeared edgier by the day. Being forced out of Lydney must be affecting him more than she realised.

'Jack thinks it a fine jape to hoodwink Sir Peter like that, but I pray it will not rebound upon him. Sir Peter is, like it or not, his guardian. He could, if he chooses, impose sanctions or punishments. I worry—'

'You worry too much.' Freddie's vehemence cut short Rosalind's words.

'Well, yes...but that is, surely, understandable, Freddie. I worry about you all.'

Freddie did not reply, but the mutinous set of his mouth did not imply agreement.

'What is wrong, Freddie? I hate to see you so out of sorts. Do you miss home?'

'Of course I do. Don't you?'

'Well, yes, but I make the best—'

'Do *not*—' Freddie levered himself to his feet '—tell me to make the best of this…this *half*-existence.'

'But…Freddie…we agreed…' Rosalind trailed into silence at Freddie's scathing expression.

'Since we arrived here two and a half weeks ago, I have been stuck in this blasted house and seen no one other than you, Nell and Penny until today. I have been nowhere and now, with the carriage in London, I cannot go anywhere even if my appearance wasn't likely to set people talking and risk bringing Sir Peter post-haste to our door. Can you not realise how that makes me feel?

'And, for all my sacrifices, it seems as soon as you make the acquaintance of some random gentleman, all your strictures about me lying low are forgotten and you bring him home. That is quite apart from your attracting the dubious attention of our new neighbour, Lascelles.'

'*That* was not my fault, Freddie. And, as for Mr Boyton, mayhap you are right to feel aggrieved that I brought him home, but I simply wished to show my gratitude for a favour. Nell is no longer here to be recognised, after all. Sir Peter cannot harm *us*, Freddie, even if he does discover our whereabouts. The danger is past.'

'You *know* that her reputation could still suffer if it became known we had removed her from her guardian's care and brought her here, with only us to chaperon her.' Freddie limped to the door as he spoke. 'You said yourself that nothing must be allowed to taint her if she is to make the marriage she deserves. Why can you never admit to your mistakes? You like to think yourself infallible, Ros, but you are not.'

Knowing he was right made it hard for Rosalind to be angry with him, but still she was loath to admit herself in the wrong.

'There is no reason for Mr Boyton to make the connection between us and Lady Helena Caldicot, even if they do meet in London,' she said. 'She knows not to speak of us or to mention running away from Sir Peter. And *he* will not make a fuss. It can be of no advantage to him to harm Nell's reputation.'

'Let us hope that you are correct, Sister.'

Freddie left the room, snapping the door shut behind him.

Chapter Six

L**eo** waited until he could speak to his cousin in private. After dinner that evening, the other two men disappeared in the direction of the billiards room, Vernon having challenged Stanton to a rematch following his defeat the night before. Leo and Lascelles lingered over their port in the dining room, where the table had already been cleared.

Leo pushed his chair back and stretched his legs out under the table. Lascelles eyed him through a haze of cigar smoke.

'Such a shame you missed most of the chase today,' he said. 'I do hope you contrived to amuse yourself.'

Leo shrugged. 'There is always another hunt, if not this season then next.'

'There should be another opportunity before we leave here.' Lascelles leaned forward to stub out his cigar, then fixed Leo with a narrow stare. 'Something on your mind, Coz?'

Leo raised his brandy glass to his lips and swallowed, savouring the fire of the spirit as it slid down his throat, before answering.

'There is. I understand you did not stay with the hunt the entire day, either.'

A fleeting smirk crossed Lascelles's countenance. 'My

mare was unable to stand the pace. I decided to retire. To save her for another day, don't you know?'

A memory surfaced, of Stanton haranguing Lascelles about his treatment of his horse after their first outing with the hunt. The day they met Rosalind.

'I am pleased to find you have your animal's welfare at heart. Did you spend an enjoyable afternoon?'

Lascelles shrugged. 'It was agreeable enough. I decided to familiarise myself with the neighbourhood and to make the acquaintance of some of my new neighbours.' The smirk returned as Lascelles locked eyes with Leo. His look suggested there was more to his news than one objectionable visit to Frederick Allen. For the first time, Leo wondered if his cousin was aware of his own activities that afternoon.

'I heard you called upon Mr Allen.'

'Allen? Allen? Do I recall…? Oh, yes, indeed. The cripple. His name…somehow…slipped my mind.'

Distaste at his cousin's sneer clawed at Leo. He would not continue to tiptoe around, guest or not.

'You are aware, of course, that Mr Allen is the brother of Mrs Pryce?'

Lascelles's dark eyes widened, mockingly innocent. 'No, is he, Coz? Well, I shall bow to your superior knowledge of the Delectable Dorcas.'

His use of the nickname they had bestowed upon Rosalind—'Dorcas' after Shakespeare's shepherdess in *The Winter's Tale*—irritated Leo, but he held his temper in check. Lascelles was a complex and difficult man, a fact that was becoming more apparent by the day. It behoved Leo to tread carefully around this subject, even though his instinct as head of the family was to lay down the law.

'You are unused to the customs here and of the behaviour expected of a gentleman.' He rose to his feet and paced around the room. 'You do wish to fit in here? You want to be accepted in society?'

Lascelles remained sprawled on his chair, but his eyes were watchful. 'The widow and her crippled brother are hardly prominent members of society. Why, if you came across them in town, my dearest Coz, you would not even deign to notice them, they are so far beneath your touch.'

Again, Leo reined in his temper, distracting himself by examining a model of a Chinese pagoda displayed on a side table. It was exquisite, the ivory carved in intricate detail.

'Ming,' Lascelles said. 'The Prince has one very similar, I am told. Now, *that* is the mark of a gentleman.'

Leo crossed to the fireplace, and settled his left shoulder against the mantelshelf, folding his arms.

'You are mistaken. The mark of a gentleman has nothing to do with money or with fine possessions. Birth is, of course, important but it is manners that mark the true gentleman. Manners and the treatment of others and, in particular, the treatment of those of lower birth. If you do not understand that, Anthony—and *believe* it—you will never earn your place in society.'

Even as he spoke the words, Leo questioned whether Lascelles could ever be a true gentleman. It was not something that could be learned but was, in Leo's opinion, something intrinsic in a man's character. Looking at his cousin, at his insolent sprawl, he doubted Lascelles possessed that trait. Rather, he was more than ever convinced there was something rotten at the man's core…something more than just bitterness over his illegitimacy. Stanton had been right: Uncle Claude—Fourth Duke of Cheriton—*had* been right not to wed Lascelles's mother, and not only because of her profession. She would have made a terrifyingly unsuitable duchess with that temperament of hers. Leo still could not help feeling *some* guilt, however, and it was that guilt that had prompted him to accept Lascelles's invitation to Halsdon Manor, to find out if their relationship could somehow be redeemed.

It seemed not.

He pushed away from the mantel. 'I am going to see how Vernon fares in his revenge on Stan.' He paused by Lascelles's chair, steeling himself against the urge to wipe the mocking sneer from his face. No matter his aversion to Lascelles, he *was* family and he was also, for now, Leo's host. 'Will you accompany me?'

There was a pause. 'Not for the moment, Coz. I shall join you directly.'

As he strode in the direction of the billiard room, his muscles tight with anger, Leo knew he should leave Halsdon and go back to London before he and Lascelles came to blows. It had always been thus between the two men—that constant vying for supremacy. Leo's hope that his cousin had changed—mellowed—had not been realised: Lascelles was merely an older, more confident version of his younger self. He still knew what he wanted and, it appeared, cared even less about the means by which he got it.

Yes. A wise man would leave now before the antagonism lurking beneath the surface erupted.

A memory swirled and coalesced—bringing to his mind not only her image but the smell of her, the feel and the sound of her voice…low and musical, sending quivers of need chasing across his skin.

Rosalind.

No, he would not, could not leave. Not yet.

He was intrigued. He wanted more, wanted to *learn* more. And yet…

He paused outside the billiard room, ostensibly to examine a painting hanging on the wall opposite the door. His eyes were looking inward, however. His mind was filled with her. His blood stirred and his heart beat faster. Her desirability—his desire for her—was without question, and yet, beneath that craving lurked a whisper of disquiet.

Lies. Deceit. Secrets.

Could he trust her? He had already caught her out in one lie and he sensed there was something else. A secret. Something important to her that she withheld, cocooning it deep within.

He abhorred lies and deceit. He'd had his fill of those particular traits with Margaret.

When Leo's father became the Fifth Duke, his health was frail and he had fretted over the continuation of the Beauchamp line. To give his father peace of mind, eighteen-year-old Leo had married Margaret, three years his senior. Looking back, he had been hopelessly naïve. Oh, Margaret had done her duty and presented him with two sons and a daughter, but her only interest from then on was the social whirl. She was a duchess and she wanted to live the life she believed her new station warranted. She lost all interest in both Leo and the children. For most of the year, she had stayed in London, only returning to Cheriton under duress.

And she had lied. Constantly.

And taken lovers. Many lovers.

Leo locked down his memories. The past was done. Long ago he had trained himself not to dwell on what could not be changed. And, after all, what did it matter if Rosalind held secrets? He would soon return to London and there was one thing of which he was certain: never again would he accept an invitation to Halsdon Manor. Once he left, whatever lies she told and secrets she held would have no power to hurt him.

He spun on his heel and walked into the billiard room.

'Leo! Stan is a blasted bandit! I happened to glance out of the window and, whilst my attention was diverted, I swear he moved the balls.'

Stanton grinned and bent to take a shot, his ball hitting first Vernon's cue ball and then the object ball—a cannon.

'With skill like this, I have no need to cheat,' he said. 'That's another two points and I win again. It is time you taught your brother how to lose gracefully, Your Grace.'

Vernon laughed and slapped Stanton on the back. 'Good shot.'

'Seems billiards just isn't your game, Vern.' Stanton shot a look at Leo. 'Where's our esteemed host? You two been locking horns again?'

Leo shrugged. 'That's putting it a bit strong, Stan. I should rather describe it as a robust exchange of views on a certain matter.'

'His Grace—' Lascelles had entered the room unnoticed '—proffered his advice on the behaviour expected of a gentleman and I, in deference to his position as head of our family, have given that advice my due consideration.' He flicked a ball across the billiard table, then settled his dark gaze on Leo. 'I shall call at Stoney End and tender my apologies to the cr—to Mr Allen. And to his entrancing sister.' His eyes gleamed, malice in their depths. 'She *is* entrancing, is she not, Coz? She certainly appeared to mesmerise you when I saw you earlier. Or was it the sun on the water dazzling you?'

Leo's gut tightened. His instinct was right: Lascelles *had* seen him with Rosalind by the river. Quite without volition, the fingers of his right hand curled into a fist.

'Sister?' Vernon nudged Leo. 'Have you found yourself a woman already, you sly dog?'

'Oh, not just any woman,' Lascelles said. 'It was none other than the Delectable Dorcas. I believe my dear cousin is somewhat smitten. Oh, not that I blame you, Coz. She *is* an appetising morsel. I quite fancy a taste myself. Yes, I believe I must pay them a visit, make my apologies and then…let the best man win.'

He smirked. Fiery rage erupted inside Leo and he battled to damp it down. He sensed Vernon's eyes on him, then his brother shifted, moving towards Lascelles. Good old Vernon—ever since boyhood, always ready to intervene when Lascelles pushed Leo close to the brink.

'Dorcas didn't seem too impressed with you the other day, Anthony,' Vernon said, slapping his cousin on the shoulder. 'Now, if I was a betting man, I'd call it a lost cause. It'll take a mountain of grovelling on your part to change her opinion of you and—with the greatest respect, Cousin—you are not the grovelling type.'

Lascelles smirked. 'Is *that* what you think, dear boy? Well, I might take you up on that challenge. I have time on my side.' He caught Leo's eye. 'After all, the lovely Mrs Pryce is going nowhere and neither am I. I am sure I can persuade her to forget our most unfortunate introduction. It was *quite* out of character, isn't that so, Coz?'

Leo held Lascelles's gaze in silent challenge until a muscle bunched in Lascelles's jaw and he looked away. 'Stanton, would you care to try your skills against mine?'

'Certainly.' Stanton set up the table.

Leo wandered over to the window to stare into the dark night. He wondered what Rosalind was doing. How did she pass the evenings? Did she think of him, as he did her?

Vernon's reflection joined his in the window as the click of balls announced that the game had started.

'Is she a decent woman, this Mrs Pryce?'

'She is.'

Vernon drew in a deep breath. 'I do not know what Anthony saw, but—'

'Her hat blew into the river and I retrieved it. Anthony, as usual, is making something of nothing.'

'But I do know what he thinks,' Vernon continued, as though Leo had not spoken. 'If you should happen to see the lady again, do warn her to take care. Anthony always coveted what was yours and he has not changed in that respect. Do you not recall how he tried to ingratiate himself with Margaret?'

He did. He would see Rosalind tomorrow and he would warn her against Lascelles, even though he was convinced she needed no such warning to be cautious.

The next day Rosalind left Stoney End for her daily ride, trying not to hope she might see Leo again. The visitors at Halsdon would not hunt again today and she could not help but wonder how they—Leo—might pass the time. She had already forgiven his criticism over the way she protected Freddie. She should not have risen to his provocation. It had not been deliberate. He could not possibly understand how central her family was to her entire life.

She guided Kamal into the lane that led to Malton and there he was. Leo, astride the same huge bay he had been riding the first time they met, waiting at the edge of a stretch of woodland. Excitement fizzed inside Rosalind. There was no surprise on Leo's face when she came into view—this was no coincidence and he was clearly not about to pretend otherwise. He had been waiting. For her. Her mouth dried and heat erupted through her as her heart thumped against her ribs.

She inclined her head. 'Good morning, Mr Boyton. It is a pleasant day for a ride, is it not?'

His lips twitched. 'It is indeed, Mrs Pryce.' He raised his hat, his black hair gleaming in the light of a stray sunbeam. He manoeuvred his horse alongside Kamal. 'A pleasant day that can only be improved by such agreeable company.'

Presumptuous. Full of confidence. But Rosalind liked that he did not beg permission to ride with her. He accepted it as his right. It was, she decided, refreshing. As long as he did not decide it was his right to criticise her relationship with Freddie again.

She smiled at him. Heavens, but he was attractive. Not just handsome, but...his whole *being*: his appearance, his attitude, his ease in himself. Even though she appreciated his assumption of control, she instinctively reached for the metaphorical reins.

'Would you care to ride with me, Mr Boyton? I am heading for the village. You are very welcome to accompany me, if you wish.'

'You are most gracious, ma'am,' he murmured, a hint of laughter in his voice. 'I should be delighted to ride with you.'

They rode in silence for several minutes.

'I *am* forgiven, am I not?'

Leo's sudden question made Rosalind jump. And then laugh, for it was so close to her earlier thoughts.

'There is nothing to forgive. On my part, at least. *I* should beg *your* pardon for taking offence.'

'Splendid.'

Rosalind reined Kamal to a halt. 'S-Splendid?'

'Indeed. I felt sure you would see the error of your ways if I prompted you.'

'Why, you...you...'

'Speechless, Mrs Pryce?'

Rosalind narrowed her eyes at Leo. 'You are teasing me.'

'I am? Now, can you be absolutely certain of it?'

She could see by the quirk of his lips that she was right. She laughed and shook her head at him. 'It would serve you well if I sent you away for such impertinence.'

'Impertinence? I am not a schoolboy, to be dressed down with a scold.'

'Then kindly do not behave like one.' Rosalind nudged Kamal into a trot, leaving Leo behind, but he soon caught up, his huge bay dwarfing the dainty Arabian.

'And now we have broken the awkward silence, I shall allow you to lead the conversation if you will,' Leo said.

'That way, I shall not get into trouble for straying into territory you consider to be none of my business.'

Rosalind cringed inside as she recalled telling him that Freddie was none of his business.

'I am sorry for saying that. I am protective of my brother. I have cared for him ever since he was a child.'

'But he is a child no longer. His body may be damaged, but he appears to be an intelligent, well-educated man.'

'Oh, he is. I am so proud of him... He has such a thirst for knowledge and to understand what is happening in the world. He is always reading, and he paints and plays the piano exquisitely.'

'A true paragon of virtue,' Leo commented drily. 'If he were female, I might even consider courting him.'

'Oh... *you*! You are teasing again. I merely wished you to understand that he is more than a cripple.'

'You have no need to prove anything to me. I understand that very well.'

Silence reigned once again. As the village came into sight, the sound of crying brought them to a stop. A brick-built store by the side of the road appeared to be the source of the sound and Leo leapt from his horse.

'Mr Boyton,' Rosalind hissed. 'Wait for me.'

'It would be better if I check inside first,' he said, then cocked his head as a shout of laughter erupted from within the building. 'There might be danger. You should—'

'That is a child weeping. Please. You will need me. What do *you* know about comforting a child?'

A fleeting frown crossed his forehead, then was gone. 'Very well.'

He did not wait for her to dismount, but stepped forward and lifted his hands to her waist. She hesitated as heat flared then, with an inner *humph*, she unhooked her leg from around the pommel and placed her hands on his shoulders, ready to dismount.

He took his time, allowing her body to slide—excruciatingly slowly—down the length of his before her feet touched the ground. Liquid warmth pooled at the juncture of Rosalind's thighs and she swallowed hard, drowning in the depths of those mesmeric, silver-grey eyes.

A sudden shriek broke the spell and they sprang apart. Rosalind hooked the loop of her riding habit around her wrist, to manage the draping skirt, and followed Leo into the dark interior of the store. Three boys, possibly ten or eleven years old, clustered in the corner, their attention fixed on something huddled on the ground.

'What are you doing in here?'

The lads turned. 'This is my uncle's store,' the one on the right said. 'We caught *her* thieving.'

A whimper sounded from the crouched shape. Rosalind's vision adjusted to the dimness and she could now make out a small child, with a mass of tangled hair, clutching a half-eaten apple. Blood trickled from her nose, mixing with the snot and the tears that flowed down her face, forging tracks through the grime.

Leo reached into his pocket, then flipped a coin in the direction of the boy. 'Get out of here,' he said. 'That will pay for the fruit. I will deal with the girl.'

The urchin wailed. The three boys fled and, before Rosalind could move, Leo was crouching down before the child, murmuring in his deep voice.

'Hush now. They are gone. Are you hungry?'

The child's wails quieted and then stopped as she hugged the apple to her chest. Leo reached out. 'Come. Where do you live? Let me take you to your mother.'

The child shook her head.

'You cannot stay here. Those boys will come back as soon as we leave.'

The child scrambled to her feet. Leo stood and took her hand. She clung tight to her apple with the other. As they neared Rosalind, and the light from the open door fully illuminated the child, Rosalind could not prevent herself from stepping back. Never had she seen a grubbier, more neglected child and her instinctive reaction was to keep her distance, lest she catch something. For certain the girl was riddled with fleas and lice and all manner of nasty afflictions. Then, almost immediately, compassion arose to drown out her revulsion. The poor child could be no older than six. One look from those huge, sad eyes tugged at her heartstrings.

She fell to her knees in front of the child. 'Tell us where you live. Let us take you home.'

The girl looked up at Leo. He smiled down into her upturned face.

'Do you live in the village?'

She shook her head. Rosalind frowned. If she didn't live in the village, where were her parents?

Rosalind put her fingers to the girl's cheek to turn her face to her. Heavens, the child was thin. 'What is your name?'

'Susie.'

'And where is your mama?'

Those huge eyes filled with tears. 'No mama.'

'Your papa?'

'No papa.'

'Where do you sleep, Susie?'

Her thumb stole into her mouth and she mumbled a reply. Leo crouched next to Rosalind and gently pulled her thumb away from her face. 'Tell us again, sweetie. You will not get into trouble. Did you run away?'

The child had begun to shake and, with a muttered exclamation, Leo scooped her into his arms and rose to his feet.

'I will not leave her here for those lads to terrorise,' he

said, striding out of the store. 'I must find out what has happened.'

By the light of the sun, they could see Susie's true condition: skin and bone and covered with scratches and sores. Not to mention her swollen nose, which still trickled blood.

'Bloody hell!'

Rosalind, behind Leo, saw his back expand as he sucked in a deep breath. 'My apologies for my language, but I cannot...' He faced her. 'I regret cutting our ride short, ma'am, but I must take this little one...' He paused, frowning, an unaccustomed look of indecision in his grey eyes. 'Hmm.'

'Will you take her to your cousin's house? Would he be...amenable, do you think?'

'That is a very good question. But where else—'

'Let us take her to Stoney End,' Rosalind said. Penny would complain, without a doubt, but that was neither here nor there.

'But...' Leo flicked his head in the direction of the village. 'Do you not need to go into the village?'

'I only intended to fetch my brother's newspaper—he orders one daily from London—and to collect any post. I can come again later. We shall take Susie to Stoney End.'

Chapter Seven

Rosalind watched as Leo smiled down at the form huddled against his chest. She wondered at the tenderness in his sometimes hard and often aloof expression.

'Thank you. That is a relief.' He crouched down again and gently persuaded Susie to stand. 'Stay there a moment, Susie, while I help the lady on to her horse. Then you shall come for a ride with me.'

Susie stared up at Leo's bay, terror in her eyes. Before Rosalind could warn Leo to take care, he clasped Rosalind by the waist and swung her on to Kamal's back. There was a flash of movement behind Leo and Susie was haring up the lane away from the village.

'Leo. Be quick. She's running away.'

'Damn it!'

Leo spun round and set off in pursuit. With his longer strides, he soon overtook Susie and scooped her off the ground. She screeched, kicking and wriggling.

Rosalind reached for the bay's reins and led him to Leo. At the sight of the horses, Susie stopped struggling for a moment, her face filled with horror, then she started to struggle again, biting at the arm that Leo had wrapped around her chest.

'You little…' Leo clamped his lips against whatever he

had been about to say. 'Stay still!' His voice commanded
and Susie instantly obeyed, just as Hector had on the day
they first met. Keeping a secure grip of her shoulders, he
crouched before her again. 'What is wrong?'

Susie gulped and shook her head.

'I think she is frightened of the horse,' Rosalind said.
The child's panic had only started after Leo mentioned
riding his bay.

'Is that it? Are you scared of my horse?'

Susie nodded, her mouth quivering, eyes swimming, and
Rosalind's heart melted. She was just a child. She should
not be out here, alone, fending for herself.

'But he will be so sad if you don't like him,' Leo said.
'Come. Stroke his nose and you will see how soft it is.' He
hefted Susie into his arms again and held out his hand to
the horse. 'His name is Conqueror and he is very kind. Especially to children.'

Rosalind could see how tightly Susie clutched at Leo's
jacket with one hand, but she allowed him to guide her
other hand to touch Conqueror's nose. The horse stood like
a statue, as though he sensed Susie's fear.

'See how his whiskers tickle,' Leo then said, moving
Susie's hand to touch the horse's whiskers.

A faint smile tugged at the corners of Susie's mouth and
Leo caught Rosalind's eye and winked. And in that moment…in that split second…she fell in love. And with that
knowledge came a terrible sadness, for she knew this was
but a fleeting interlude in her life. Leo Boyton belonged to
a world in which there was no place for Rosalind, a world
to which she had no wish to belong. He would be gone soon
and they would never meet again.

She swallowed, her throat aching, and smiled at him,
praying her eyes did not reveal her sorrow. She had read
of love at first sight. This might not be first sight, but there
had been an undeniable connection between them from

that first meeting. Physical attraction…but this…*this* was different. Deeper. More. This was about the man himself, not his handsome face.

Whilst Rosalind had been deep in thought, Leo had cajoled and persuaded Susie to allow him to lift her on to Conqueror's saddle. The instant she was up there, he swung up into the saddle behind her and wrapped his arm around her, holding her secure. He nudged Conqueror into a walk, heading towards Stoney End.

Penny's plump cheeks quivered. 'Madam! You cannot expect—'

'I *expect*, Penny…' Rosalind shot a glance at Susie—sitting at the kitchen table chewing on a slice of bread and dripping—and lowered her voice '…that you will do as I ask and bring more water for a bath.'

Penny had been washing a few clothes in the outhouse they used for the laundry when Rosalind had gone to collect a hip bath and to request a pail of warm water.

'But…you cannot just take a child and keep her without so much as a by-your-leave. Even if she is an orphan, someone must have been taking care of her and will miss her.'

'Does it look as though anyone was taking care of her? She is starving.'

'Well, if she is so ungrateful as to run away from them that have responsibility for her, 'tis no surprise, that's all *I* have to say,' Penny muttered as she tipped the bucket of water into the bath that Rosalind had placed before the kitchen fire.

'What is going on?' Freddie stood framed in the kitchen doorway, Hector at his heels. 'Penny, your voice is peculiarly penetrating. I could hear every word from the parlour. What… Oh, g'morning, Boyton, didn't see you there. And who is this? Is this what you are quarrelling about?'

'Good morning, Allen.' Leo pushed away from the door

jamb he had been leaning against and came further into the room. 'Might I introduce you to Susie? Your sister has agreed to house her for a few days until I can make other arrangements.'

'And we are not quarrelling, Freddie.' Rosalind cast a scathing look at Penny. 'It is merely a lively discourse on the best way to proceed with this unexpected addition to our household.'

'Oh, very well articulated,' Leo murmured in an amused voice.

Rosalind shot him a sharp look, which he met with a nonchalant lift of his dark brows, and she felt shame at giving voice to her exasperation.

'I'm sorry, Penny,' she said. 'As Mr Boyton says, it will only be for a few days but, in the meantime, if Susie is to remain here, she needs a bath.'

'Yes, madam.' Penny, too, looked somewhat chastened, and she headed once more for the back door. 'I'll fetch another bucketful.'

Freddie came into the kitchen and sat opposite Susie, propping his crutch against the table. Susie fixed her gaze on it.

'What's that?' she asked around a mouthful of bread.

'That is a crutch,' Freddie said. 'I need it to help me walk.'

'Why?'

'I had an accident when I was young and now my leg doesn't work as it should.'

Susie looked at Leo, eyes beseeching. 'Can I have a crutch?'

'You do not need a—'

'Doggy!'

Rosalind winced at the volume of Susie's shriek. Hector had followed Freddie into the kitchen and had made straight for Susie, who beamed as Hector pushed his nose against her. Before Rosalind could stop her, Susie fed the remainder of her bread and dripping to the dog.

'Susie, you must not feed the dog at the table,' Rosalind said.

'Why?'

'Because it will encourage him to beg. We do not want Hector to think he can pester us for food at mealtimes, do we?'

'Why?'

'This,' said Freddie, 'looks promising. I expect the urchin and the hound to provide me with endless entertainment. Don't be in too much of a hurry to make alternative arrangements for her, will you, Boyton? I am grateful for anything that might alleviate the tedium of this isolation.'

His words squeezed Rosalind's heart. Freddie's growing restlessness fed her guilt, but there was nothing she could do. His withered leg would never allow him to be active like other men. Their only hope was to return to Lydney and take up their old existence. At least there, Freddie had his library and his piano, and his quiet cob he could ride and drive about the estate. Here, he had nothing apart from a few favourite books and his sketch pad and—as he had said more than once—what earthly good was a sketch pad when he could go nowhere worth sketching?

Leo laughed at Freddie's comment. 'I am in no position to arrange anything else for Susie whilst I am staying at Halsdon Manor, but I have connections with an orphan asylum in London so she could go there. I am sure your sister will not want her to stay indefinitely.'

'You leave Ros to me,' Freddie said, with a wink.

Penny returned, carrying another bucket and grumbling under her breath about the bath using up all the water she had heated for the laundry. 'But there—no one else will have the worry of it, so it doesn't signify.'

'The first thing we should do is to make enquiries in the village,' Leo said. 'I cannot be of help in bathing Susie, so I shall go now. I will return later and tell you any news.' He made for the door.

'And I should go and see to Kamal,' Rosalind said, following him. She had done no more than loosen his girth and throw a blanket over his quarters when they arrived back at Stoney End.

'Leave Kamal to me, Mrs Pryce, I shall attend to him.' Leo indicated Susie with a flick of his head. 'I suggest you will be of far more use here.'

Rosalind hesitated in the doorway, dismayed by the flood of disappointment triggered by his words. What had she hoped for? The opportunity to spend a little more time with him...the chance to store away a few precious memories? Her common sense warned her it was pure foolishness for her to be alone with him and risk certain heartache. Why would she wish to play with fire when it would be her who suffered the burns?

'Thank you, Mr Boyton. I appreciate the offer. And, as you are going to the village, would you be so kind as to collect Freddie's paper?'

'Of course. I shall see you later.'

The door clicked shut behind him.

'And I will be in the sitting room if you have need of me,' Freddie said. 'There is nothing I can do to help here.'

He left, but Hector remained, enjoying Susie's attention. Rosalind and Penny set about divesting Susie of her ragged clothes. As her skinny torso came into view, Rosalind clapped her hand to her mouth to stifle her gasp.

'Oh, the poor little mite,' Penny said, her eyes filling with tears.

Tamping down her horror, Rosalind finished stripping

Susie and Penny gathered the discarded clothing. Holding them at arm's length, she headed for the back door.

'These are only fit for burning,' she said. 'Though Heaven knows what the poor mite will wear after her bath.'

Susie sat in the bath, flinching even though Rosalind soaped her back as gently as she could. Every rib could be seen and felt but, more disturbingly, the child's back was striped with welts: some mere silvered stripes, others raised and, in places, scratchy with scabs where the skin had been broken.

'Would you fetch the salve, please, Penny?' Rosalind said when the maid returned.

'I think it's too late for salve, ma'am. These are too old now to benefit from ointments.' She lifted a jug of clean, warm water she had set aside. 'Close your eyes, child. I need to rinse your hair.' Her former brusqueness when speaking to Susie was gone. She raised apologetic eyes to meet Rosalind's. 'You did a good deed, bringing her here.'

'Thank you, Penny.'

Hot tears stung Rosalind's eyes and swelled her throat. The last thing Susie needed was to see Rosalind in tears. What she needed now was calm and quiet, to help her to settle. And Hector—who nuzzled Susie's wet hair, making her giggle as Penny wrapped her in a towel.

'I shall leave you to dry Susie if I may, Penny? I need to speak with Freddie.'

Freddie was sitting in the parlour, forearms propped on his knees, staring into the fire, when Rosalind joined him. He started, then relaxed back into his chair.

'How is she?'

'Beaten and bruised.'

'Where did you find her, Ros? Are you sure you have done the right thing in taking her in?'

'If you saw the state of her back, Freddie, you would not ask such a thing.' She told him how they had found Susie being tormented by village lads and that Susie had told them she had no parents.

'But someone, somewhere, must have been caring for her.'

'Those beatings are not all recent, Freddie. Mr Boyton might discover something about her in Malton, but I suspect she has come from further afield. Although how she has survived, I do not know.'

Freddie resumed his contemplation of the flames. Rosalind studied her beloved brother, hating that he was so unhappy, helpless to know how to make things right.

'What can I do, Freddie?'

'Do? Why, you have already done what you can for her, Ros, and now you can do little other than wait and see what, if anything, Boyton uncovers. Besides, he said he will take her when he goes back to London.'

The knot of sadness that had lodged in her chest wound tighter at the reminder Leo did not belong here, that he would soon resume his life as a society gentleman and Rosalind would never see him again. Without volition, her fingers sought her locket, rubbing over the moulded design of three daisies with seed pearls set in their centres. She was accustomed to loss... Papa, Grandpa, Mama, Step-Papa...and soon Nell would also leave her for good, to live her own life with a new husband and a family of her own.

'That is not what I meant.' She must concentrate on Freddie, not dwell upon her own selfish needs. 'I meant, what can I do for you? How can I help?'

Freddie huffed a laugh. 'You already do more than enough, Ros.'

'But you are unhappy...dissatisfied. Should we go home to Lydney? Now Nell is in London there is nothing to stop us, if you should prefer it. I have no great desire to remain here.'

'We cannot go back while Sir Peter remains. I refuse to expose you to more of his disrespect.'

'I dare say he sees no reason he should treat either of us with respect.' A heartfelt sigh escaped Rosalind before she could stop it. 'And we may have no choice. We shall have to return in a few months anyway, for Jack's sake. I can only pray that Nell does find a husband—he, for certain, will help us to deal with Sir Peter.'

'She had *better* find a husband,' Freddie said, 'or there will be nothing to stop Tadlow marrying her off to Bulbridge after all.' He fixed his gaze on Rosalind. 'How did you come to meet up with Boyton again, Ros?'

She caught her breath. She had hoped Freddie would not question her about that, but she was saved from answering by a loud rap at the front door. She jumped to her feet, knowing Penny was busy with Susie.

Rosalind opened the front door, and her heart plummeted at the sight of Anthony Lascelles on the doorstep. She stepped forward to block the gap, clutching at the edges of both the door and the door frame.

'Good morning, sir.'

Lascelles raised his hat and smiled. A shocked tremor sped through her as she was reminded how much he resembled Leo: the same height and build, the same dark, straight brows and the same black hair.

'Good morning to you, Mrs Pryce. I do not blame you for a frosty welcome, but dare I hope a heartfelt apology for my previous behaviour might melt at the least the outer layer of your icy carapace?'

'Apology?' Rosalind scanned his face, reading nothing but sincerity in his expression.

'Indeed. I fear I was somewhat...*forward* in my dealings with you and I humbly apologise. I can assure you it will not happen again. It was a case of mistaken identity.'

'You thought it acceptable to proposition me because you thought me too insignificant to warrant your respect?'

'No, not all, Mrs Pryce. I am mortified you should believe so badly of me. Might I not persuade you that I was overcome by your beauty and allowed my enthusiasm to override my manners? I have lived overseas for too many years and am consequently unpractised in the exacting standards expected of a gentleman. I beg you will forgive me.'

Rosalind frowned. 'I am certain that ladies in the Americas do not warrant any less in the way of respect and politeness than an Englishwoman.'

'But I did not move in the best circles in America and I admit I need re-educating in the matter of how to treat a lady. I assure you I shall not lapse again. Now…' a charming smile lit his face '…do say you will accept my humble apology.'

Such a blunt request could not be denied. Rosalind inclined her head. 'I accept. I cannot speak for my brother, however. He might not be so willing to forgive.'

She did not know how objectionable Lascelles had been because Freddie had refused to expand upon his earlier visit.

'Ah, your poor brother. I am afraid I allowed my disappointment that you were not at home to sharpen my tongue. I owe him an apology, too, and…' he raised his hand, revealing a bottle he carried '…I have brought a peace offering. There is very little that cannot be settled over a glass or two of brandy, I find. If you will be so gracious as to permit me entry?'

His prompt admittance of fault disarmed Rosalind and now she had no choice but to stand aside and allow him in. As she closed the front door, his very proximity and the strong smell of bay rum that accompanied him sent the hairs on the back of her neck rising and she suppressed a shudder. As much as the thought of Leo's inevitable return to London sent her spirits sliding into a dark pit, Lascelles's departure could not come fast enough. She led the way to the sitting-room door and paused, waiting with her head high for Lascelles to open it for her.

'Freddie,' she said, as she walked in, 'our neighbour, Mr Lascelles, has something he wishes to say to you.'

Freddie pushed himself upright using his crutch, a scowl on his face.

Lascelles walked past Rosalind, striding across the room to Freddie. 'Do not feel obliged to stand on my account, Allen. I am come in peace, to apologise for my rudeness yesterday. And, to demonstrate my regret, I have brought a gift—' he raised the bottle '—in the hope that you will share a glass with me. It is the finest French brandy. Only do not, I beg of you, enquire too closely from whence it came.'

He smiled and, despite her misgivings, Rosalind could detect no hint of deceit in his expression. Freddie raised a brow, but he lowered himself back into his chair and leant his crutch against the wall, within his reach.

'Very well,' he said. 'Although I have since learned that your objectionable attitude extended to my sister when first you met. That, sir, is inexcusable. I shall hear your excuse for that and we shall see. Rosalind, would you fetch two glasses, please?'

Rosalind went to the dining room, where the glasses were stored in the china cabinet. She removed two, then hesitated. If she was to endure a visit from Lascelles, she might have need of a boost to her courage. She reached for a third glass.

Chapter Eight

Leo urged Conqueror into a trot as he left Malton, eager to return to Stoney End and to Rosalind, even though he had no news to impart. His questions had met with blank looks and shaken heads wherever he had enquired. No one had seen Susie. No one knew anything about a lost child, or about a child living a tramp's life. The vicar, however, had promised to make enquiries around the parish, and in the adjoining parishes, and he had also passed on to Leo some clothing suitable for a girl of Susie's age—undergarments and dresses and a warm coat outgrown by his own daughter and destined for the poor of the parish. Leo made a mental note to ask his secretary, Capper, to send a donation to the vicar for the poor fund as soon as he returned to London.

Finding Susie had interrupted his precious time with Rosalind, but he could not regret rescuing the poor child. His heart had gone out to her as she had cowered in the corner of that shed, trapped by those bullies. An orphan. He had seen how his own children suffered when their mother died, but at least they'd still had him and Cecily.

No, he did not regret the interruption. There was always tomorrow. They were due at Foxbourne in the morning, to view the pony pair for Felicity, but he could always slip away from the others in the afternoon, and now he had a perfect excuse to visit Stoney End and spend time with Rosalind. That she was compassionate as well as beautiful added to her appeal. She had shown no hesitation in following him into that store shed, despite the possible danger, spurred into action by the sound of a crying child. He had sensed her hesitation at first sight of the filthy, matted sight that was Susie and yet, very quickly, her concern for a child in need had banished her reluctance.

Stoney End soon came into view and Leo reined Conqueror to a halt with a curse. A striking dappled grey stood tethered to the front gate. He had seen that horse before, in Lascelles's stables. And that could only have one meaning—unless Vernon or Stanton had unaccountably decided to call at Stoney End, his cousin was even now inside the house.

What was he up to? Leo would put nothing past Lascelles and, right now, he was with Rosalind and Freddie. His protective instincts fully roused, Leo dug his heels into Conqueror and cantered him up the path that led to the stable. He leapt to the ground, led Conqueror inside, then strode across the yard to knock on the back door. He did not wait to be admitted, but walked in before the echo of his knock had faded.

Penny stood up when Leo came in. Susie—loosely swathed in a linen towel, the numerous scratches and bruises on her face now even more apparent—sprawled across Hector, who was stretched out by the fire. There was no sign of Rosalind or of Freddie. Leo paused, listening. The remainder of the house was quiet.

Penny gestured at the bundle Leo carried. 'Are those for the child?'

'Yes.' He placed them on the table. 'They are from the vicar. Where is Mrs Pryce?'

'She is in the parlour with Mr Allen. I will take you to them, if you care to follow me.'

Penny led the way from the kitchen, speaking to Leo over her shoulder. 'We had a visitor not long ago, but Mrs Pryce answered the knock as I was occupied with the child. She has not asked for refreshments to be sent in, however, so I doubt whoever it was came inside.'

She opened the parlour door. 'Mr Boyton is here, ma'am. Oh! I did not…that is, shall I bring refreshments?'

Leo strode past the maid, then stopped short at the sight of his cousin, Rosalind and Freddie, all seemingly quite relaxed as they drank from glasses of amber liquid. A scan of the room revealed a half-empty bottle of Lascelles's finest brandy. There was no tension palpable in the room. Apprehension threaded through Leo. His cousin was clearly on a charm mission and that disturbed Leo more than if he had been his usual disagreeable self.

He recalled Vernon's warning about Lascelles always coveting what Leo had, or what Leo wanted. He must caution Rosalind to take care. He should have done so before, but had thought it unnecessary because Rosalind had taken Lascelles in such dislike upon first acquaintance.

'Thank you, Penny,' Rosalind was saying in reply to Penny's question, 'but, as you see…' she raised her glass '…we already have sustenance thanks to Mr Lascelles's generosity. You may fetch another glass for Mr Boyton, however, if he cares to join us?'

Her tawny brows rose in query. Her eyes were clear of any shadows, exhibiting no anxiety at Lascelles's presence in her house. Leo stifled a sigh. Lascelles had given Rosalind and Freddie just cause to dislike and distrust him and yet still he had managed to lure them both into forgiving him. Leo had thought Rosalind more sophisticated than to fall for such superficial charm.

'Thank you, I will.' He remained standing, but moved to the fireplace, to rest one elbow upon the mantelshelf.

'Coz!' Lascelles's black eyes gleamed as he looked from Leo to Rosalind and back again. 'What a surprise, to meet you here.'

'I could say the same.'

Lascelles's eyes widened. 'Why, Coz, surely not when it was you who prompted my visit after our little talk.' He shook his head. 'My cousin is the most perceptive of men, my dear Mrs Pryce. It was he who brought me to the realisation that my behaviour on the day we met might result in a permanent division between neighbours. I decided to make both my apologies and my peace with you and your brother in the hope we will not be strangers, but—and this is the least I can hope for—polite acquaintances. I expect no more than that.'

Leo's gut tightened as Lascelles smiled widely. Never in his life had anyone tempted him to lash out as much as Lascelles.

My own cousin.

The fact he had justification for feeling that way did nothing to improve his self-contempt. He should be able to rise above his emotions.

'I am flattered my advice made such an impression upon you.'

Lascelles smirked in response to Leo's growl.

Penny brought a clean glass, which Leo accepted with a murmured 'thank you,' and Lascelles leaned across to fill it. Leo quaffed a generous mouthful, relishing the ease with which it slid down, his tension beginning to abate.

'Oh, as ever, my dear Coz. And I confess myself relieved that Mrs Pryce and Mr Allen have both found it in their hearts to forgive our poor start.'

'I can assure you, sir, that neither my brother nor I would

wish to be on bad terms with *any* of our neighbours. Would we, Freddie?'

Rosalind smiled at Lascelles, seemingly totally relaxed, but Freddie shifted in his chair, sipping from his glass before replying.

'Indeed not, Sister.'

The hint of reservation in his tone gave Leo heart. Freddie had impressed him with his quick intelligence and it would seem he was not entirely taken in by Lascelles. At least someone at Stoney End would be on their guard against his cousin once Leo left Halsdon Manor.

'Did you discover any information about Susie in the village, Mr Boyton?'

Leo cursed under his breath, his hope that his cousin would not find out about their earlier meeting dashed.

Lascelles's brows rose. 'Are you running errands now, Coz? I confess I did wonder where you sloped off to this morning. You now have my full attention, Mrs Pryce. Who is Susie?'

Rosalind told him the tale of how they rescued Susie from the bullies.

'Most commendable. So, tell us, Coz—what *did* you discover in Malton?'

'There was nothing to discover. Nobody knew anything about a lost child. The vicar, however, promised to make enquiries around the neighbourhood and he also provided some clothing for Susie.'

Rosalind jumped to her feet, beaming. 'Oh, that is splendid. I must go and see them. I have been racking my brain to think how we might clothe her. Her own garments were beyond mending. I had resigned myself to sacrificing one of my own gowns.'

Both Leo and Lascelles rose to their feet when Rosalind stood up and Leo took the opportunity to say, 'We have imposed on your time too long, Mrs Pryce. You are eager to settle Susie into your household and you cannot do that with visitors to entertain. We shall take our leave of you now.'

'Indeed we shall.' Lascelles reached for Rosalind's hand and bowed low over it.

Leo's hands bunched into fists. Lascelles did not go so far as to kiss Rosalind's hand, however, but released it, saying, 'Thank you for your generosity of spirit, Mrs Pryce. I shall look forward to our next meeting. Good morning to you, too, Allen. I am pleased we have settled that little misunderstanding. After you, Coz.'

He gestured with a wide-flung arm towards the door.

'Wait for me at the front of the house,' Leo said. 'My horse is at the rear. I will join you shortly.'

Leo caught Freddie's eye and, with a flick of his brows, indicated that Freddie should see Lascelles out. As he hoped, Rosalind accompanied him to the rear of the house.

'Come with me out to the stable,' he murmured, pausing outside the kitchen door. 'There is something I need to say.'

She held his gaze, her eyes searching his.

God, I want to kiss her.

He brushed the back of his fingers against her cheek, and her lids lowered, lashes lying in a crescent on her skin. She gave a tiny nod.

Penny, wooden spoon in hand, stood at the kitchen table with a large mixing bowl in front of her. Susie knelt on a chair by her side, dressed in the donated clothing. Her long brown hair had been tightly braided, and the green dress donated by the vicar proved an adequate, if somewhat loose, fit.

Leo paused next to the little girl.

'I shall come to see you again tomorrow, Susie. In the meantime, please be a good girl for Mrs Pryce and Penny.'

Susie smiled, revealing a gap in her teeth. Leo cast his mind back to his own children's infancies and concluded the gap was a natural one that would soon be filled again, not the result of violence. Now she was clean and dressed, she was a fetching little thing. If they could not find out where she came from, Leo's eldest son, Dominic, was patron of an orphan asylum where she could be trained as a maid or a seamstress. Her future was much brighter than if she had continued to run wild.

Content they had done the right thing in rescuing her, Leo walked to the door.

'I will see you out,' Rosalind said. 'I must check Kamal has some hay. I will be back in a few minutes, Penny.'

Penny barely acknowledged her mistress's words, too busy showing Susie how to stir the mixture in the bowl.

Leo and Rosalind crossed the yard in silence. As soon as they entered the stable Leo took her hand and tugged her to face him. She tilted her face to his and the pure yearning in her eyes almost undid him. He cradled her face, taking his time, watching her eyes darken. Honey-scented breath feathered his skin, triggering a powerful urge to *take*— swiftly controlled.

He touched his lips to hers, gently tasting her until her mouth softened beneath his and only then did he deepen the kiss. Desire crashed through him, staggering him with its intensity and, again, he brought it under control, lowering his hands to his sides, touching her only with his mouth. She leaned in to him, her lips warm and sweet beneath his, and Leo relished each and every taste of their soft fullness. The instant he sensed her hesitate, he ended the kiss. Her lips were still parted, her lids drowsy, and her full breasts brushed enticingly against his chest with each heaving breath.

Her lids rose, as did her brows, and her gaze sought his. Her lips firmed and twitched into a smile.

'There was something you needed to say to me?'

Was there? He could not concentrate when she stood so close, her scent weaving through his senses. Why had he

succumbed to that impulse to kiss her? All it had achieved
was to leave him craving more. Much more. He stroked her
bottom lip with the pad of his thumb. Her lips parted and
her breath quickened, igniting his blood once more, and
he acted on impulse, covering her luscious lips with his
again. For one glorious second her lips softened beneath
his, but then she wrenched her lips from his, her palms
against his chest, pushing.

'Please. We must not...'

Her beautiful eyes were filled with longing, belying her
words. He tore his wayward thoughts from the image of
Rosalind writhing naked beneath him and forced out the
warning he knew he must voice.

'You should not trust him.'

'Lascelles?' Rosalind folded her arms, her shoulders
hunched. 'I do *not* trust him. Have you forgotten what
happened when we first met? I can assure you I have not,
and nor will I.'

'But...' Leo pictured her again, in the parlour, convers-
ing with Lascelles. 'You are clearly an excellent actress.'

She raised her brows. 'Or an accomplished liar?'

He bit back a smile. 'Tease me if you will—I shall admit
to nothing other than relief that I was mistaken. I am surprised you are quite so undisturbed by his visit, however.'

'It is a matter of practicality.' She huffed a laugh. 'I feel I
have little choice. I cannot see any advantage in my denying
him—a man such as your cousin thrives on confrontation.
Any resistance to our acquaintance on my part will, of a
certainty, encourage more persistence on his. I am hopeful
that he will reciprocate accordingly if I continue to deal
with him in a polite and pleasant, neighbourly manner.'

'I hope you are right.'

Leo's assessment of Lascelles's character was of a more
complex and dangerous individual than Rosalind had de-
scribed, but she did not know him as Leo knew him.

He was conscious he must not give Lascelles further reason to suspect how much he desired Rosalind.

'I must go before my cousin comes searching for me. May I see you again?'

Her expression grew serious. Her chin dropped to her chest as she stared at the ground. She heaved a sigh.

'I am sorry... I must ask you to only call upon me here at the house, where I shall be chaperoned. I *must* have a care for my reputation, particularly with your cousin in the neighbourhood. Heaven forbid he should ever find out...' Her words stuttered into silence and she looked up, meeting his gaze, pink suffusing her cheeks. She hauled in a breath. 'It is shameful enough that I permitted you to kiss me in the first place, without tempting further indiscretions.'

Surprised a widow should be quite so cautious, Leo injected a falsely cheerful note into his voice. 'You admit you might be further tempted? Dare I think there is hope for me yet?'

'Hope?' She shook her head. 'Hope for another stolen kiss? To what purpose, may I ask? We have the most casual of acquaintances, soon to be ended when you go back to London.'

She tilted her head, looking up at him. Light from the half-open door lit her features, and he saw her sadness—an echo of his—but he also recognised her resolve. Without volition, he reached out and tucked a loose strand of hair behind her ear before dropping a brief kiss on her forehead, breathing the scent of her skin, feeling his soul expand.

When he was with Rosalind he felt able to relax, to be himself. Was that part of her appeal—that she reacted to him as a man and not a duke? Although he longed to bed her, he also craved her company and if he could not have the former then he would enjoy the latter whilst he might.

'In that case, I shall call upon you here, tomorrow afternoon, to see how Susie is settling in.'

Chapter Nine

'Well, here's a pretty sight to brighten an old man's day.'

'Good morning, Sir William.'

Rosalind crossed the spacious hall to take the baronet's proffered hands in hers. It was the day after Susie had come into their lives and Rosalind, Penny and Hector had taken a brisk walk over to Foxbourne Manor, braving the chill February wind and the threat of rain, or even snow. Rosalind had come to welcome home her stepfather's oldest friend and Penny to call upon Sir William's cook with the gift of a cake, to thank her for the herbs and pickles. They had left Freddie and Susie at Stoney End, playing endless games of hunt the slipper.

'I trust your journey home was uneventful?'

Sir William's face sagged, worry creasing his brow.

'What is wrong? Is your daughter well? And your grandsons?'

'Oh, yes, yes.' Sir William ushered Rosalind into the morning parlour where a very welcome fire blazed in the hearth. 'They are all well, thank you. That is, as far as Jane's physical health is concerned.'

They sat side by side on a sofa in front of the fire. Rosalind shifted so she was half-facing Sir William and again took his hand. She waited for him to continue.

'It is her mood that is so very low.' His bushy brows beetled over his eyes. 'She tries her best to conceal her unhappiness from the children but, when they are not around, she appears to have neither the energy nor the will to do anything but weep.'

'It is to be expected she will mourn her husband,' Rosalind said.

'Of course it is, but I cannot help being anxious. She appears to be spiralling lower and lower in her spirits.' He patted Rosalind's hand. 'You will understand, I am certain, when I tell you I have decided to leave Foxbourne and move north to live with Jane and the boys.'

'Leave? But…you have lived here your entire life, sir. Is it wise to leave your family home and all of your memories?'

'But that is it, do you not see? They are merely memories. Jane and the boys…they are real. And they are suffering.' He heaved a sigh. 'To tell the truth, my dear, it is nice to feel I am needed at my age, although I do realise my decision will affect you and Frederick, for which I am sorry.'

'You must not trouble yourself about us, sir. When do you plan to leave?'

'Very soon, I am afraid. There is no necessity for me to remain here until the old place is sold and it will be less painful not to see strangers taking it over. I have instructed my agent to find a buyer. Foxbourne is not entailed and I have no son so there is nothing to prevent me selling up.'

'Your younger grandson might appreciate a property such as Foxbourne when he is older.'

Sir William had two grandsons. The eldest, still only four years old, had inherited his father's title and estates the previous year.

'Do not think I have not considered young Henry's needs. He is only a year old, however, and the thought of running this place from a distance for that length of time…

well, the burden would fall upon Jane were anything to happen to me. I am not a young man and I do not wish to add to her liabilities.

'No, I have made up my mind. I shall not be easy until I have moved in with Jane and can take care of her. I shall invest the proceeds in land in Cheshire and that shall be Henry's inheritance.'

'What about your horses?' Breeding and training quality horses had been the old man's passion for years. 'Will you take them with you?'

'No. It is a wrench but, as I said, I am getting no younger. I am hopeful that whoever buys Foxbourne might take on the stock, as well. I should like to think my work will be continued.'

A maid came in with a tea tray and, as Rosalind poured, Sir William said, 'I am sorry my moving will force you and Frederick to leave Stoney End sooner than perhaps anticipated, but you should be able to remain for the foreseeable future. There will be no need to leave until a buyer wishes to take possession.'

Rosalind sipped her hot tea, thinking about her options. 'In a strange way, your plans have made it easier for me to reach a decision.'

'How so?'

'Well, for a number of reasons, I have been thinking Freddie and I should move on.'

'But where will you go? Back to Lydney?'

'Probably.' Rosalind caught her bottom lip between her teeth, thoughts tumbling through her brain. 'We left for Nell's sake and, now she is in London with her Aunt Glenlochrie, she will be safe from Sir Peter's bullying. There is nothing to stop Freddie and me returning to Lydney Hall.'

'What does Frederick think?'

'It is too isolated here for Freddie. I am convinced he will be more content back at Lydney.'

'From what you told me of Sir Peter when you first arrived, I cannot believe you would willingly go back to live with him.'

It was Rosalind's turn to sigh. 'Neither of us relishes the idea of living in the same household as him, but I cannot help fretting over what will become of Jack if we do not try and curtail some of Sir Peter's excesses.'

'What of your Step-Papa's solicitor? Surely he will look out for Jack's interests?'

'I did consult him, but it seems he and Sir Peter are old acquaintances and he is reluctant to intervene. Or, as Freddie says, he is being paid to turn a blind eye.' She shook her head, frustrated by their sheer impotence to stop Sir Peter. 'I worry, too, that Nell may not secure a husband this Season and then what might become of her? Even if Lord Bulbridge withdraws his suit, I cannot believe Sir Peter will pass by the opportunity to marry her off in such a way that will benefit him rather than her.'

'It is a quandary, I see that,' Sir William said. 'Let me have a think and see if I can come up with a solution. I could always consult my own solicitor for advice. Now...' he pulled a pocket watch from his waistcoat pocket and consulted it '...I apologise for cutting short your visit, my dear, but I have an appointment with a new neighbour of mine in five minutes' time—a Mr Lascelles.'

Just hearing his name spoken left a nasty taste in Rosalind's mouth. At least she no longer feared the man, but she could neither like nor trust him.

'Mr Lascelles has recently taken occupation of Halsdon Manor—although I make no doubt you have neither heard of nor seen the place. I keep forgetting you have been here such a short time. It transpires he has guests from London staying at the Manor and one of them is seeking a safe driving pair for his young wife.'

'I may have never been to Halsdon Manor, but I have heard of it and I *have* met Mr Lascelles. And his guests.'

Rosalind gave Sir William a brief, censored account of her acquaintanceship with the men, including Leo Boyton, a blush warming her skin as she spoke his name.

'You have the advantage of me. What sort of a man is Lascelles?'

What could she say? She could hardly tell Sir William that Lascelles was the reason she was happy to quit Stoney End earlier than planned.

As she hesitated over her reply, Sir William said, 'No, no—that was unfair of me. I shall find out for myself what sort of man he is soon enough.' He struggled to his feet and slowly straightened. 'My bones are aching after being rattled around in that carriage for the past three days,' he grumbled. 'Not to mention the lumpy beds in the inns. That in itself is a good reason to move north. I am far too old to contemplate such a journey on a regular basis.'

He headed for the door. 'I shall ring for Sally. She will let your Penny know you are ready to leave.'

Rosalind followed him. 'Do not bother Sally, sir. You go on down to the stables or you will be late for your appointment, but please do not forget that Mr Lascelles and his visitors know me as Mrs Pryce. I shall find my way to the kitchen and collect Penny and Hector.'

'Very well.' Sir William pointed along the hall. 'It is the door at the far end.' He smiled at her and patted her cheek. 'You're a good girl, Rosalind. You worry about everyone rather than yourself. I only wish I could do something to help with that rascal Tadlow, but I have no influence in the places that matter, even if it were possible to challenge his guardianship.'

'Do not worry, sir. You provided us with a safe haven when we needed it and I am grateful for that. Freddie and I will manage, whatever happens. Step-Papa left us provided for, so we have no concerns on the financial front. It is Nell and Jack who are vulnerable. I can only hope and pray Nell will find an influential husband in London—that will surely be the best solution to protect Jack.'

On impulse, she kissed Sir William on the cheek. 'Thank you for everything, sir. I am convinced you will be happier when you are living with Jane and the boys and can be reassured of their welfare. Indeed, you look much happier than when I first arrived.'

She, on the other hand, felt worse. Options and solutions crowded her thoughts now that she could no longer procrastinate over whether or not to move on from Stoney End. *That* decision was made, but many more awaited her and filled her with anxiety.

'I confess I feel easier in my mind knowing my decision will not create too many problems for you and Freddie,' Sir William said. 'Speaking of whom, please tell Freddie he is more than welcome to make use of my library whilst I am still here and my carriage is at his disposal. I know he must miss the library at Lydney. Your Step-Papa used to write to me and tell me how Freddie lived for his books.' He sighed and shook his head, his eyes moist. 'Such a shock, my oldest friend dying so suddenly...it forces one to think and to reassess one's priorities.' He straightened then, reddening. 'My apologies, my dear. You do not wish to hear my maudlin thoughts.'

'That is most thoughtful, sir. Thank you, Freddie will be delighted when I tell him.'

Sir William made for the front door, leaving Rosalind to make her way to the kitchen, wondering, with a frisson of anticipation, whether Leo was even now at the stables and if she would see him as she passed by on her way home.

Leo examined the man crossing the stable yard with interest. He had never met Sir William Rockbeare before, but was aware of his reputation: the man's skill in breeding and schooling the highest quality carriage and riding horses was legendary. Stanton was the only one of the four of them who had prior acquaintance with the baronet and it fell to him to make the introductions.

'Good morning, Rockbeare.' Stanton stepped forward to shake hands. 'Might I introduce your new neighbour, Anthony Lascelles, from Halsdon Manor?'

The two men exchanged greetings.

Stanton indicated Leo and Vernon. 'Mr Boyton and his brother, Vernon.'

Before Leo could respond, Rockbeare threw back his head and guffawed.

'Boyton? Poppycock! Can't fool me, m'boy. I'd know those features anywhere. Knew your father well—yours, too, Lascelles. Fine men, the pair of them. Not but what I don't blame you lads for keeping a low profile. If the ambitious mamas hereabouts get wind of a duke in the area, you'll get no peace at all, m'boys, none at all.' He tapped the side of his nose. 'Your secret's safe with me.' He shook hands with both Leo and Vernon. 'Now, let us get down to business. Why don't you gents take a look around—everything is for sale—whilst we get the ponies ready for his lordship.'

'Everything?' Stanton's brows rose in surprise. 'Not… Do you mean the breeding stock, too?'

Rockbeare sobered. 'I do. My mind is made up, I am selling up. Lock, stock and barrel, as they say. You are the first to know.' His cheeks, already ruddy, deepened in colour. 'I shall be sorry to leave the place, but m'daughter needs me.' He harrumphed noisily and waved his arm. 'Go on. Go on. I've got a pair of ponies to sell to his lordship.'

Leo and Vernon exchanged an amused glance, then wandered off to look over the animals in the stalls whilst Stanton and Lascelles remained, watching as Rockbeare busied himself interfering with the harnessing of a pair of smart chestnut ponies with flaxen manes and tails.

'Useful set-up here,' Vernon commented when they were out of earshot.

'It is. Are you thinking what I'm thinking?'

'It would be a useful addition to our racing stud.'

'It would mean Anthony as a neighbour.'

Vernon grimaced. 'If that proved a problem we could always move the breeding stock elsewhere and sell again.'

'True. I shall have a word with Rockbeare later,' Leo said. 'I don't want Anthony to know I'm interested.'

Vernon snorted as he tried to hold back a laugh. 'Indeed not,' he said when he was able to speak. 'He'd move heaven and earth to scupper your plans.'

'Come, we shall say no more for now. The harnessing is complete—let us see those ponies put through their paces.'

They wandered out into the yard to join the others as a groom leapt into the phaeton. He drove the ponies along the carriageway at a spanking trot.

'What do you think?' Leo asked Stanton.

Stanton beamed. 'I think they'll suit Felicity perfectly. Nutmeg and Spice, they are called. They look sound, with straight paces,' he added as the ponies trotted back towards them, 'and if they drive as well as they look, I'll have them.'

As Stanton swapped places with the groom and Vernon climbed in beside him, Leo's attention was caught by two figures approaching from the direction of the house. Rosalind. He would know her anywhere. As he watched, Hector bounded up to Rosalind, who attached a leash to his collar and then looked across to the stable yard. She waved, her smile radiating forth, and Leo pressed his lips together to disguise the pure pleasure that engulfed him.

'Ah, the charming Mrs Pryce, if I am not mistaken,' Lascelles murmured, moving so that he obscured Leo's view.

'What? What?' Rockbeare dragged his attention from

the phaeton and pair. 'Oh, indeed. Mrs Pryce. Of course. My new tenant… She lives at Stoney End, you know. Have you met? Yes, yes, of course you have. She did tell me. If you will excuse me a moment, gentlemen, I have thought of something…that is, I must have a quick word with her before she leaves.'

He set off towards Rosalind, his voice carrying clearly. 'Rosalind, my dear. There is something I forgot to tell you.'

His informality piqued Leo's interest. He sidestepped around his cousin in time to see Rockbeare take Rosalind's hand between both of his. He looked away, quashing his absurd surge of irritation towards the old man.

'Most interesting,' Lascelles said.

Leo felt his cousin's gaze on him and blanked his expression. 'Interesting?'

'An overly familiar way for a landlord to greet a tenant, would you not agree, Cousin?'

Leo did agree. 'No.'

Rockbeare spoke rapidly into Rosalind's ear and her gaze drifted more than once in Leo's direction as she listened. What on earth was the old man saying? Without volition Leo's feet started to move towards the pair. As he drew nearer, Rockbeare stopped speaking.

Leo raised his hat. 'Good morning, Mrs Pryce. How is Susie today?'

'We left her happily playing games with Freddie, sir. She appears none the worse for her ordeal, I am pleased to say.'

'I wonder if the vicar's enquiries have met with any success.'

'He called at Stoney End earlier,' Rosalind replied, 'but he had no news. He was most shocked at the extent of her injuries, however.'

Lascelles joined them in time to hear her words. 'Poor child,' he murmured. He raised his hat and smiled. 'Good morning, Mrs Pryce. It is a pleasure to see you again.'

Leo noticed that Lascelles maintained a cautious distance between himself and Hector, whose gaze fixed upon Lascelles, a low growl rumbling in his chest. Leo bit back a grin. Rosalind would be safe from Lascelles whilst she had Hector by her side.

'I am sure we shall meet from time to time, Mr Lascelles,' Rosalind said. 'We really must attempt to correct Hector's opinion of you, but I fear that might prove a challenge. Once his mind is made up about a person, you see...' She smiled and that adorable dimple appeared. 'I shall take care to attach his leash whenever you appear, however, so you need not fear an attack.'

Leo bit back another grin at Lascelles's expression.

'And now, gentlemen, I must take my leave of you. Good morning.' She encompassed all three of them in her smile and walked on.

'Do not forget to tell Freddie I shall collect him at two o'clock,' Rockbeare called after her.

'You can be sure I will not,' Rosalind called over her shoulder. 'And thank you.'

Later, after Stanton and Rockbeare had sealed the deal on the ponies, Rockbeare said, 'Forgive my presumption, Your Grace, but I wonder if I might impose on your goodwill? I have a matter I wish to discuss with you. I find myself in need of advice and, possibly, some help.'

'By all means,' Leo said, intrigued. He looked at the other three men. 'I'll see you later, back at Halsdon.'

'Let us go up to the house,' Rockbeare said. 'I have a bottle of very fine Madeira we can sample whilst we talk.'

Chapter Ten

Rockbeare maintained a stream of inconsequential chatter until the two of them were comfortably ensconced in two chairs either side of the fire in his library: a dark, masculine room lined with tightly crammed bookshelves.

'Well, now, Your Grace,' Rockbeare said, leaning forward, his elbows on his knees. 'I make no doubt you are wondering what is of such importance that I needs must steal you away from the company of your friends.'

Leo murmured a non-committal response.

'Did you ever make the acquaintance of the late Earl of Lydney?'

Leo frowned, searching his memory as he sipped his glass of Madeira, which was, indeed, excellent.

'Lydney?' In his mind's eye he saw the man: fair-haired and slightly stooping with a penchant for making impassioned speeches in the House of Lords on the few occasions he attended. 'I knew him by sight, but only to exchange pleasantries. Our paths crossed very occasionally, in the House and around the clubs. He died recently, did he not?'

'He did—about a year ago. I shall come straight to the point, sir. Lydney died quite unexpectedly. He left a will, naming his younger brother as guardian to his children. Unfortunately, however, his brother predeceased Lydney by three months. I dare say he thought he had time enough to amend his will, but events overtook him.' His gaze rested on Leo as he added, 'We all think we have enough time, do we not? One day, we will be wrong.

'But…I digress. Lydney's daughter, Lady Helena, is eighteen years of age and his son, Jack—the new Earl—is but fourteen years old. A schoolboy still. The Court of Chancery appointed their maternal uncle, Sir Peter Tadlow, as their guardian and trustee of the estate.'

'Tadlow?' Again, Leo dredged his memory. 'Yes, I know the man by sight, but know nothing about him. Am I to presume there is a problem with his appointment?'

'I doubt he moves in your circles, Your Grace, but it transpires the man is a gambler, and is deep in debt. Now, Lydney and I went back a long way. We were friends at school and we did the Grand Tour together. Although we saw one another infrequently in more recent years, we were avid correspondents and I have concerns about the welfare of his children. Tadlow has already established himself at Lydney, living it high at Jack's expense and inviting all manner of ne'er-do-wells to stay. Helena has a generous dowry and I hear Tadlow has already tried to force her to wed Bulbridge, to whom he is in debt.'

'*Bulbridge?* I wouldn't let that scoundrel anywhere near my daughter.'

'Quite. Well, Helena was forced to flee—her own home!—and she is safe enough for now in the care of her father's sister, Lady Glenlochrie. It was always intended her aunt would present her to society, so Tadlow cannot do much about *that*, but he is still living at Lydney with no one to prevent his plunders.'

Leo tapped his fingers against his glass, frowning. 'How do you imagine I might advise you, Rockbeare? It sounds as though Lady Helena is safe for now and I must assume Jack is out of harm's way at school?'

'Yes.' Rockbeare paused, frowning. 'The truth is that I am uncertain how they may be helped, but…I had hoped… Maybe I should not…but…'

Rockbeare paused again and Leo waited. He thought he knew what the old man was angling for, but he wanted the suggestion to come from him. Rockbeare drained his wine glass, set it decisively on a side table and dragged in a deep breath.

'I dread to think what will happen to Helena if she fails to secure a husband this Season. Tadlow will be within his rights to demand she return to Lydney and I fear she will be unable to withstand his demands. As for Jack's inheritance, I understand Tadlow has a past acquaintance with the solicitor handling the trust. Who is there, then, to ensure the estate is not bled dry before Jack comes of age?

'I am a simple man. I have lived in the country most of my life and, as I said, I am moving north very soon. Who is there to look after their interests? They have need of someone who will champion their cause.'

'And you thought I might be able to help?'

'Your influence is considerable, Your Grace, where I have none. If you were to write to Tadlow and that rogue of a solicitor…if they know you are watching their conduct… it is a lot to ask but, when you return to town, would you at least call upon Lady Glenlochrie and speak to Helena? Or, if you cannot bring yourself to intervene, at least tell me what steps…legal steps…might be open to me to help protect those children.'

Leo would not refuse. Young Lydney was a peer of the realm and, as such, warranted his protection. He would set Medland—his man of business—on to it when he went to London.

'You did right to consult me, Rockbeare. I will do what I can.'

Rockbeare passed a shaky hand over his forehead as

his breath escaped in an audible rush. Gone was the bluff, hearty countryman of that morning. He suddenly looked his age.

'I didn't realise,' he said in a shaken voice, 'quite how heavily the responsibility weighed upon me until now, Your Grace. I am most grateful.'

'You can safely leave matters with me. Now,' Leo continued, 'before I leave, there is a matter of business I should like to discuss with you.'

An hour later, the purchase of Foxbourne Manor having been concluded to both parties' satisfaction, Leo took his leave of Sir William.

Freddie and Susie were in the sitting room when Rosalind arrived home and she sent Susie to help Penny in the kitchen. She and Freddie had matters to discuss but, first, she relayed Sir William's offer to collect him at two, to take him to the library at Foxbourne. Freddie's face brightened at the prospect of spending the afternoon amongst his beloved books.

'Sir William had other news, as well,' Rosalind said, taking a seat on the sofa. 'News that was not as welcome. He intends to move north to live with his daughter and her family, and he is selling Foxbourne Manor.'

'And, by definition, this place. How soon must we leave?'

'He has to find a buyer first,' Rosalind said. 'I should think we have a few weeks to make our plans. Even if he does sell, I should hope the buyer would not eject us immediately, but we cannot rely upon that.'

Rosalind was now convinced their duty was to return to Lydney Hall, but Leo's comments about her overprotectiveness had stirred her conscience and she was determined this would be a joint decision.

'It is time we decided on where we shall go when we do leave.'

'You mean you have not already decided?'

'Freddie!' Rosalind's protest was half-hearted. Mayhap she deserved that taunt. 'We must find a solution that suits us both. Do we go back to Lydney and Sir Peter, or do we look elsewhere?'

'I did hope we could leave that choice until after Nell's Season,' Freddie said. 'We would better understand our options.'

'That is true, but we no longer have that luxury. I shall not, however, regret losing Mr Lascelles as our neighbour. He was polite enough this morning at the Manor, but I cannot find it in myself to trust the man.'

'Neither can I. I must confess, I found the charming Lascelles even scarier than the offensive version,' Freddie said, with a grin. 'Was he at the Manor when you arrived?'

'No. I saw him as I left. Mr Lascelles and his guests had an appointment to view the horses for sale. Sir William is selling them all, Freddie.'

'I suppose he must, if he is to move.' Freddie spoke absently, his eyes on Rosalind but it seemed as though he barely saw her. His brows twitched into a frown as he then said, 'Was Boyton there?'

Rosalind felt her cheeks glow. 'Yes. He enquired after Susie.'

'So he will now have no need to call this afternoon.' The satisfaction—or was it relief?—in Freddie's words set Rosalind's hackles to rise.

'Why should he not call? He will wish to see Susie for himself, I should imagine.'

'But you should not receive him, Ros. It would be improper without me here. You must take care where your Mr Boyton is concerned.'

'My...? He is not my Mr Boyton, Freddie.' Rosalind

forced a light laugh. 'The man is a virtual stranger. He is merely concerned for Susie's welfare.'

A muscle bunched in Freddie's jaw. 'Do not try to hood-wink me, Ros. I have seen the way you look at him and I make no doubt he sees it, too, and recognises it for what it is.'

Rosalind shot to her feet and marched across the room to the window, battling to control her anger and humiliation.

How dare he criticise me after all I have given up?

No sooner did that thought fly into her thoughts than she shot it down. Yes, she had sacrificed her future for her family, but she had done it willingly. With love.

'You may be older than me, Ros, but you are naïve in the ways of men,' Freddie continued. 'Sir Peter's methods were more direct and disrespectful, but sweet words and come-hither glances are simply a more subtle and socially acceptable way to achieve the same end.'

Rosalind faced her brother again. 'I am not a green girl to be duped by such tactics, Freddie. Besides, Mr Boyton is a gentleman and, if he does happen to call later, do not forget that both Penny and Susie are here. There is nothing for you to worry about.'

Freddie snatched up his crutch and limped across to Rosalind. He took her hands in his.

'You may not be so young, but you *are* inexperienced, Ros. Please take care not to be alone with him. Do not forget he believes you to be a widow. A man such as he—no matter how much the gentleman—is interested in a widow for one reason. It is up to you to set the correct standards of behaviour. He will be gone all too soon, after which I doubt he will give you another thought. As for his cousin, well! There is your proof of the sort of *gentleman* Mr Boyton is.'

Rosalind set her teeth and forced her lips into a stiff curve.

'I promise I shall take care, Freddie.'

He nodded, and returned to his chair, but his cautions had stirred a cauldron of resentment deep inside Rosalind, swamping yesterday's vow not to risk being alone with Leo again.

Why should I not have a gentleman admirer?

Freddie was wrong about Leo—he was indeed a gentleman. A gentleman, moreover, who kissed like a dream and made her, for once, feel like an attractive female and not just someone's sister or an over-the-hill spinster.

That kiss!

Never before had she felt like this about a man, but it was not only his kiss that had seduced her—all it had taken was one look from those silver-grey eyes of his, the first day they met, and she had known. Deep down.

Deep in the core of her body and the centre of her soul, what she had felt was pure, instinctual recognition. Of him.

Leo was gentleman enough to accept any limits she set—he had already proved that to her—so, if she wished to experience again that intoxicating rush of desire, aroused by the brush of his lips against hers, why shouldn't she? Why should Freddie dictate what she might or might not do? A kiss was not the same as relinquishing one's virtue. If she wished to snatch a few more minutes, or hours, with the man who had captured her imagination and her heart, then why should she not?

She did not fool herself there would be any future for her and Leo—she might be naïve, but not *that* naïve—but why should she not create some wonderful memories to sustain her through the lonely years ahead?

Quarter past two that afternoon found Rosalind pacing the parlour at Stoney End, kneading her handkerchief between her hands.

*I should have listened to Freddie. Why didn't I send
a message to Leo, telling him not to call this afternoon?*

Any sane woman would protect herself from temptation
and scandal, but she had allowed her anger with Freddie
to colour her good judgement and fuel her defiance. Now,
with Freddie gone—Sir William had arrived on the stroke
of two, as promised—Rosalind's nerves had resurfaced.
After another circuit of the room, common sense reasserted
itself. She would not wait here for Leo to arrive. Kamal
needed exercise. When Leo came to see Susie, Rosalind
would not be at home.

She picked up her skirts and ran up the stairs to change
into her riding habit. She bundled her hair up, pinning it
haphazardly, and secured her hat in place, memories of Leo
and that kiss playing havoc with her nerves. She *knew* she
could not resist the urge to kiss him again. She tugged on
her leather riding gloves, threw her fur-lined cloak around
her shoulders and hurried down the stairs and down the
hall to the kitchen.

'Penny, I am going out. I am in the mood for a long ride,
so do not be concerned if I am gone for a while.'

'But it is so cold, ma'am. You'll catch your death.'

'I will soon warm up with a vigorous gallop.'

'But…it is not safe. Nor is it proper for you to ride out
alone.'

Rosalind curbed her irritation. 'I ride down to the village on my own most days, Penny. I did not hear you raise
objections.' She lifted the latch on the back door. 'And I
have no choice but to ride alone. I shall take Hector and I
shall stay on Sir William's land. Do not worry.'

'But…I thought Mr Boyton was to call?'

'*If* Mr Boyton visits, it will be to see how Susie is. He
is unlikely to call after we saw him this morning but, if he
should, I make no doubt he will be relieved not to have to

sit and make polite conversation with me.' She opened the door, conscious of the minutes ticking past. 'Give him my apologies, and tell him…no. There is no need to tell him anything. Merely apologise I am not at home to receive him.' She craned her neck to peer over Penny's shoulder. 'Be a good girl for Penny, Susie. I shall see you later. Hector! Come, boy.'

With one bound, Hector was at Rosalind's heels. She closed the door and hurried across the yard.

Behind her, she heard the back door open and she was forced to bite back a caustic rejoinder as Penny called out, 'It looks like rain, ma'am. Please, do not go too far.'

Rosalind was forced to retrace her steps to reply, her insides a mass of collywobbles in case Leo appeared.

'If it does rain, I shall take shelter. Please, Penny, stop fussing. My mind is made up. I need the exercise and the fresh air. I shall be quite safe with Hector. Go in and shut the door. You are letting the cold air in.'

She saddled and bridled Kamal with more speed than ever before, and led him from the barn. If Leo arrived now, all this rush and hurry would be for nothing. She needed to get away: away from the temptation in those sinful silver eyes and those sensual, persuasive lips. She led the horse outside to the mounting stone and settled herself on to his back, arranging the folds of her cloak around her. She picked up the reins and hesitated, her brain racing. Rather than venture out on to the lane and risk meeting Leo, she decided to ride up the path that led behind the barn and in the direction of Foxbourne Wood.

She was barely out of sight of Stoney End when she brought Kamal to an abrupt halt, an unladylike curse escaping her lips. Ahead of her was a familiar figure on a large bay horse. Rosalind's heart hammered in her chest as Leo, a slow smile stretching his lips, nudged Conqueror forward to close the gap between them.

His eyes were dancing with suppressed laughter.
Despicable wretch.

'What are you doing here?'

'Waiting for you.'

Chapter Eleven

Rosalind stared at Leo. How could he possibly have known? He held her gaze as he sat his horse, reins loosely held in one hand, the other resting on his thigh. Powerful. At ease. Confident. Freddie's warning whispered through her thoughts, but she shook it away, as a horse might shake its head to rid itself of pestering, buzzing flies. This man—she felt it deep in her soul—posed no danger to her. Whatever transpired between them today, she knew instinctively that she held the power to stop wherever and whenever she wished. She would be in control.

She drank in the lean, hard planes of his face, his dark-shadowed jaw and the teasing light in his silver-grey eyes and her doubts dissolved like early-morning mist under the onslaught of the rising sun. She sucked in a deep breath and smiled. Leo had anticipated her attempted flight and she was happy. Laughter bubbled and her smile widened. He would leave soon and their paths would never cross again. She baulked at looking that far into her future.

Pain was inevitable, whether she spent this afternoon with him or not. She was a thirty-year-old spinster with the chance to experience something of the passion and the joy she had relinquished for the sake of her beloved family. She would take this chance to create memories and to discover something of her own femininity and desirability.

Boldness rose to take control, to shrug aside her conscience. This afternoon, she had the chance to learn and explore. A delicious shiver caressed her skin at the thought. She had no need to guard her reputation in the same way a society lady must. Whatever happened, no one would ever know apart from her and Leo, and she trusted him instinctively not to gossip.

She rode towards the trees, the mantle of responsibility slipping from her shoulders leaving her weightless and worry-free as she led the way into Foxbourne Wood, following a broad track forged by the wheels of timber carts. The heat of Leo's gaze was upon her, the air between them heavy with words unspoken and all too soon those doubts she had so successfully crushed mere moments ago resurfaced to peck at her resolve. She fidgeted in her saddle. She could not change her mind now. Leo would think her an irresolute fool and she... With a thump of her heart she knew she would regret her lack of courage.

She cast a sideways glance at Leo. His strong profile, the set of his jaw and those all-seeing eyes—now fixed unwaveringly on the path ahead—made him seem remote and unapproachable. Severe, even. Rosalind shifted again in her saddle and Kamal flicked an ear back in response.

'How did you know?'

'I guessed you might panic, given too much time to think, and that you would head away from the lane. We rode along this path with the hunt the other day...the day we met.' He reached for Kamal's rein and brought both horses to a halt. 'Freddie's absence would have made no difference. I would quite happily have sat in the kitchen and talked, and Penny would have been an adequate chaperon.'

Heat rose to burn her cheeks.

'However...I cannot be sorry you ran away.'

'I did *not* run away. I merely…merely…'

'Yes? You merely…?'

'I acted, as I thought, with discretion.'

'Discretion. Ah, yes.' He looked around, then brought his unsettling gaze back to her face. 'I can see that.'

Indignation battled for supremacy over an irresistible desire to giggle. The giggle won. Leo laughed and relinquished his hold on Kamal's rein.

'I suggest we keep moving.' He peered up through the bare branches laced over their heads. 'I wonder if it's cold enough to snow.'

Rosalind shivered—stopping for those few minutes had allowed the chill to penetrate her warm cloak. Leo wore a caped greatcoat, its collar pulled up against the cold. She urged Kamal into a canter and Leo followed suit.

Hector had been busily ranging far and wide amongst the trees, lost to sight for minutes at a time but now, with the increase in pace, he bounced on to the track in front of the horses and loped ahead of them.

Several minutes later the trees grew denser and the track narrowed. Leo held Conqueror back and allowed Rosalind to ride ahead. She steadied the pace, giving them both time to duck under the occasional low-growing branch. After a few minutes, even a trot was too fast, the low branches becoming more frequent. Rosalind slowed Kamal to a walk and, as she did, she heard a muttered curse from behind her. She twisted round and reined in Kamal with a gasp of horror. Leo had a nasty gash on his head.

'You're bleeding!' She unhooked her leg from the pommel and slid to the ground. She barely noticed the mud that sucked at her half-boots. She was by Conqueror's side in an instant, fumbling through the slit in her skirt for the handkerchief inside the pocket tied at her waist. 'Here.' She handed it up to him.

He took it, glanced at it and handed it back with a laugh.

'I am far too badly injured for *that* scrap of lace to help.' He brought out his own handkerchief. 'In the absence of a bedsheet to staunch such a flow of blood, however, I shall have to make do with this.'

Rosalind laughed up at him, relieved he wasn't badly injured, although the cut on his forehead bled freely, leaving a red trail down the side of his face. Whilst Leo staunched the flow, Rosalind trudged back along the path to collect his hat, which had been knocked from his head.

As she handed it back to him, she said, 'I can tell the hunt has been this way. This path was not this badly churned when I walked here last week. I'm surprised it is not firmer underfoot with this cold weather.'

Leo scanned their surroundings. 'The tree cover helps protect the ground from freezing.'

As Rosalind turned to head back to Kamal, the mud clung to her boot and she overbalanced. She flung her hands out and managed to stop herself falling flat on her face, but her gloves and the cuffs of her jacket were now covered in thick, sticky mud. Leo appeared by her side, supporting her elbow as she wriggled her foot to free it.

'Ugh. Thank you.' She trudged over to Kamal. 'Sorry, lad.' She wiped her gloved hands over the horse's rump, leaving brown smears on his light grey coat. 'I'll clean it off when we get home, I promise.'

She gathered his reins and two large hands settled at her waist. Cool lips feathered a kiss beneath her ear, setting her pulse pounding and sparks of pure pleasure racing through her veins.

'You need me.' His breath whispered over her skin, raising a shiver.

Rosalind turned. He was so close. She tilted her head to look at him and he captured her lips as he snaked one arm beneath her cloak and around her waist, hauling her against the hard length of his body. She melted against him, his musky scent surrounding her as she wound her arms around his neck, reaching up on to her tiptoes as she clung to him, parting her lips in response to his demands.

This... Her heart swelled and she poured everything into her kiss, tasting him, revelling in the sensations that tugged deep inside—hot and exciting—committing them to memory. This was her chance to discover...she might never again be alone with him. She tugged her gloves off, heedless of where they fell, and spread her fingers through his thick, soft hair, mirroring the play of his tongue as he explored her mouth.

He cupped her bottom, pulling her hard against him, and she felt a solid ridge against her belly. A strange, aching pleasure gathered at the juncture of her thighs. She pressed closer still. Leo tore his lips from hers. Rosalind searched his face, spine-tinglingly aware of every inch where their bodies touched. His hat had fallen from his head again, but at least his wound now only trickled blood. She touched the wound with her forefinger.

'That cut needs bathing. There is a stream at the end of this path.'

His eyes gleamed. 'I remember.' His voice deepened. 'There is a shepherd's hut nearby.'

Her insides tumbled crazily and her breath caught in her throat. She knew the place he meant: a single-roomed building at the edge of the wood, overlooking pasture. She had discovered it on one of her walks. Old Tom, Sir William's shepherd, used it when he needed to stay close to the sheep at lambing time. She covered her reaction by stooping to pick up her discarded gloves. When she straightened, Leo settled his hands on her waist and swung her on to Kamal. Even through the thickness of her cloak each one of his fingers seemed to brand her flesh. Her throat constricted as a mixture of nerves, anticipation and yearning assaulted her—a flood of pure desire.

As the end of the path drew nearer, Freddie's words whispered through her head, struggling to be heard above the headlong rush of blood through her veins.

'Do not forget he believes you to be a widow.'

But the bit was tight between her teeth… She wanted more… She wanted this…wanted *him*. She was thirty years old and, until yesterday, had never even been kissed. And Leo's kiss had awoken within her such longing…such need… How could she go to her grave without ever knowing what love…passion…felt like?

They reached the hut and Leo tethered the horses in a lean-to at the side whilst Rosalind hurried to the stream to dip her handkerchief in the water. When she returned, Leo was nowhere in sight. The horses stood quietly, side by side, mouthing at a few wisps of hay that littered the floor. Hector cast her a baleful look, but did not move from where he was curled in the corner. She walked around the hut to the door and went inside.

The hut was small and windowless, with a floor of beaten earth. The lime-washed stone walls reflected the light admitted by the open door, allowing Rosalind to discern a dark shape crouched by a hearth. A flame flickered, casting an orange glow over Leo's face as a bundle of twigs caught fire. The spicy tang of wood smoke drifted across to tickle Rosalind's nose, masking the not-unpleasant earthy smell inside the hut. As the fire flared, the smoke began to draw up the chimney.

'Close the door, sweetheart, and come to the fire. The room will soon warm up.'

He spoke without looking at her, reaching to one side of the hearth to select a few larger sticks to add to the fire. Then he regained his feet and faced her. He radiated raw masculinity, his sheer presence dominating the hut, filling her vision, causing all her senses to come alive. Her stomach clenched and she clutched at her cloak, drawing it closer around her as the wood flared and crackled.

He tilted his head to one side. 'Shall we leave? Do you not want to be here?'

If we leave, I shall never...

'No. I do not want to go.'

She shut the door and skirted around the table in the middle of the hut, halting in front of Leo. She was close enough that he could scoop her into his embrace if he chose to do so, but he made no move to touch her. He held her in place with that mesmeric gaze of his and smiled. She took off her gloves, then reached up to remove his hat, putting them all on the table. In the light of the flames, she cleaned the blood from around his wound.

This was her choice. He had made that clear.

Rosalind cast her soiled handkerchief on to the table and then she took his hands.

'You are sure?'

His deep voice was soothing. He stroked the backs of her hands with his thumbs. Reassuring. He released her hands and he, in his turn, removed Rosalind's hat. Her lids drifted shut as he cradled her head and feathered tiny kisses, gentle as the brush of a moth's wing, over her upturned face.

Slowly...excruciatingly slowly...his lips travelled across her skin until his mouth covered hers. Long fingers pushed through her hair, and she felt her hastily applied hairpins relinquish their grip and scatter. Her lips parted and he accepted the invitation, plundering relentlessly as his fingers teased her hair until it fell down her back in a heavy mass. He hefted it in his hands, a low growl vibrating through his chest, then combed his fingers through her tresses, spreading them around her shoulders.

'Exquisite,' he murmured. 'You have no idea how I have dreamt about this: your hair unrestrained, slipping like silk through my fingers.'

He shrugged out of his greatcoat, dropping it on the floor, and then he undid the clasp of her cloak and cast it, too, aside. Rosalind pushed her hands beneath Leo's jacket, slipped her arms around his waist and pressed herself to his firm body. His heat radiated through her, relaxing every muscle in her body and seemingly dissolving every bone, until her legs felt as though they could no longer support her. His scent enveloped her—musky and inherently male—and his hands slid between them, working the buttons of her jacket undone as his lips slid across hers, their tongues tangling. He cupped her breast then, with a muttered exclamation, he pushed her jacket from her shoulders and down her arms.

'May I?'

The heat in his eyes captivated her. 'Yes,' she breathed.

He untied the drawstring of her chemisette and slipped the straps of her riding skirt from her shoulders. Rosalind kicked it aside as it pooled to the floor. She removed her chemisette and he paused to stroke the swell of her breasts above her corset with a moan of appreciation that fired her blood. He gently turned her and nibbled the side of her neck as he loosened her laces, reaching around to knead her breasts as her corset fell away. Rosalind leaned back against him, closing her eyes, pleasure darting through her with each tweak of her nipples. She tugged her shift off and, naked, she faced him, his jacket brushing against her sensitised breasts.

She reached for his waistcoat buttons.

'I need to feel you against me.'

He smiled at her words—a tantalising smile that ignited an urgent fire deep inside her. He shrugged out of his jacket and waistcoat, tore his neckcloth from around his neck and tugged his shirt from his breeches and over his head. She touched his hair-roughened chest, spreading her fingers, caressing the defined muscles and then tracking the hair as it arrowed temptingly downwards. Below his waistband a thick bulge strained at the buckskin and her pulse leapt as he reached for the fastenings.

She wound her arms around his neck, threading her fingers through the soft hair at his nape, and pulled his head down, kissing him ravenously, rubbing her breasts against his chest as desire burgeoned. He groaned, low and heartfelt, and urgency sparked in her blood, sending wild streaks of desire to the tender, swelling folds between her thighs.

He tore his lips from hers and dipped his head, sucking her nipple deep into his mouth. She whimpered, arching back, her fingers tangled in his hair as he suckled first one breast then the other. Then he lifted his head and studied her with a smile of pure masculine appreciation.

'You are so beautiful.'

And he was so strong, so powerful next to her—innately male with his wide shoulders, broad chest and muscular arms, but the hot desire and the pure need in his eyes made her feel as though she were the one in control. The one with the power.

He straightened, lifting her, and took her lips in a slow, soothing kiss, sucking gently on her lower lip before crouching to spread his greatcoat and her cloak in front of the hearth. She delighted in the slide of smooth skin over muscle in the firelight and, when he looked up at her, in silent invitation, she went to him willingly, sinking to her knees beside him. Together they lay down, the fur lining of the cloak warm and sensual under her skin.

After that, she was sure of nothing. Fleeting moments of awareness were etched on her brain as Leo kissed and stroked every inch of her until his fingers slipped between her thighs. She tensed at the shocking intimacy of that touch.

'Don't…' she breathed. 'I can't…'

He raised his head, his eyes dark, almost black.

He touched his forehead to hers. 'Hush, now. Hush, my Rosie.'

His breath was warm on her cheek. He eased his body away from hers, but did not remove his hand. He remained still. Waiting. Watching.

A storm was gathering: intense, irresistible, inexorable. Forces deep within her were amassing, rolling over any resistance, smothering any doubt. She willed herself not to move, but the compulsion to do so swept over her and through her. Her lids drifted shut, her thighs parted and her hips tilted. His fingers moved once more, stroking, circling, pressing, his touch gentle but at the same time insistent. Wonderful, intensely intoxicating sensations swirled again, deep inside, overwhelming her. She moaned his name, pulling him over her, arching towards him. She wanted… She didn't quite know what she wanted. She felt him move between her legs, pressing them wide with his weight as his hands scooped beneath her buttocks, lifting her as he drove into her with one deep powerful thrust.

Sharp pain sliced through her and her scream echoed around the hut as she raked at his shoulders, her eyes squeezed tight against the sudden scalding tears.

'My God!'

Chapter Twelve

The words were torn from Leo's throat, leaving it raw. He flung his head back, screwing his eyes shut, the tendons in his neck extended to near breaking point, unable at first to process what had happened.

Slowly, inescapably, the truth asserted itself.

A virgin!

The word shocked him into crystal clarity. How had he fallen for this trap? *Was* it a trap? Did she *know* who he was?

Would Frederick Allen appear, demanding he make an honest woman of her?

That hasty, whispered conversation between her and Rockbeare—punctuated by guilty glances in his direction—loomed large in his memory. Had Rockbeare told her the truth? He had called her Rosalind. They were obviously close...

He had come to her as Leo Boyton, not a bloody duke. Yesterday, she had told him they must always be chaperoned. She was worried about her reputation, insisted they must not tempt further indiscretions. Yet now, a mere day later, she had given herself to him. Sacrificed her virtue, for the chance to be a duchess.

It was not the first time a woman had tried to trap him

into marriage, but it was the most brazen to date. Even Lady Deborah Wootton's effort—when she had crept into his bedchamber at a house party and locked them both inside, throwing the key from the window—came nowhere near the desperation of *this* attempt.

And then sorrow seeped into his bones, dampening his rage. He had thought better of her, yet here was another woman who thought nothing of lies and manipulation to suit her own purposes.

Just like Margaret. Disillusionment crashed through him and he hauled in a ragged breath, thrusting aside all thought of his late wife.

'You are—were—a virgin?'

His voice emerged as a hoarse whisper. He was still buried to the hilt inside her and the urge to finish what he had started battled with his immediate impulse to leave. To banish this, and her, from his life and his memory.

He clung to the tenuous hold he had on his own control as he waited for her to respond. Her face was averted, her lids closed. He did, however, see the convulsive movement of her slender throat as she swallowed and he forced down his rage. And his pain.

'Rosalind?'

She shook her head—a negligible movement—and he caught the glint of tears on her lashes. He had two choices: he could withdraw and leave them both unsatisfied, or he could finish what they had started and then establish the truth. Whatever her motive for changing her mind, she *had* been a virgin and he had hurt her. And she must live with what she had done. He should at least demonstrate that pain was no normal part of lovemaking. He withdrew—an inch, no more—and pressed home again, savouring the tight, moist heat that gripped him.

Her eyes widened and, when he repeated the movement, she looked up at him. Her lips, swollen from his kisses, were parted and Leo wanted nothing more than to take her mouth as he took her body—plunder her mouth as he pounded out his own pleasure. It had been so long and she was so lush and tempting, lying beneath him where he had imagined her since the day they met by the river.

But…he reined in the impulse. He would give her pleasure and he would, without doubt, enjoy the ride in a physical sense. But he would not lose himself in her. He would not forget she had deceived him.

Leo let instinct take over. Hands and mouth moved without conscious thought over her petal-soft skin, gauging her spiralling tension and the increasingly urgent movement of her hips. He neither looked at her nor kissed her, although it was a constant battle not to do so as her sweet scent and breathy moans surrounded him and his own orgasm drew near. He reached to the place where they were joined and she arched beneath him, cried out and then shuddered beneath him, driving him so close to the edge he only just withdrew before spilling his seed. He collapsed on to her, then immediately rolled aside, retaining enough conscious thought to stop himself from gathering her into his arms.

She was already under his skin. Any tenderness now would make it harder to forget.

Moments later, a noise at the hut door sent his pulse hammering again. With a muttered curse, he leapt to his feet. Pausing only to throw the edge of her cloak over Rosalind to cover her nakedness, he strode across the hut. He cracked open the door to see Hector standing there, head cocked to one side.

'It's your dog.' He shut the door, leaving Hector outside. 'He must have heard you scream.'

He fastened his breeches before returning to stand over Rosalind, now sitting up, her hair tangled around her face, her cloak clutched to her chest. She looked gorgeous and wanton, and yet bewildered and vulnerable. He hardened his heart. The warmth from the flames licked at his face and the bare skin of chest and arms, but did nothing to warm the chill inside.

'You claimed to be a widow.'

Rosalind looked up sharply. 'I am a widow.'

'Your husband…?'

Her lips parted, but no sound emerged.

'He could not perform?'

She hung her head. 'No.' Then she raised her chin and met his gaze. 'He was not a young man.'

Yesterday's exchange echoed through his head.

'You are clearly an excellent actress.'

'Or an accomplished liar?'

He did not know which. Or were they one and the same? A sound of exasperation erupted from him, at which Rosalind closed her eyes and averted her face, foiling any attempt to read her thoughts. Yet even though he distrusted her, he felt the urge to reassure her. There was no denying she had been a virgin. Her scream of pain as he had driven into her had been genuine. He crouched beside her and pushed her hair from her face.

'I am sorry I hurt you. You do know that pain only happens the first time?'

Her gaze flicked to his and then away. 'Yes. I knew.'

She was lying. Why lie about that, of all things?

'Why did you not tell me? I could have made it easier.'

She scrambled up on to her knees… She was close—*too* close—and so very tempting as her cloak slipped, exposing the generous curves of her bosom. She clutched his hand.

'I am sorry, but I was afraid you would not…' Her words faltered. She inhaled and continued, 'You are angry, but… please…let me explain to you. I am thirty years of age. If I had told you… If you did not… I might never again have this chance—'

With a vicious curse, Leo shot to his feet, wrenching his

hand from hers. Her forehead puckered as he grabbed his shirt and pulled it over his head, shoving it haphazardly into his breeches. He knew only too well what she was about to say… She was about to tell him he must wed her.

Make an honest woman of her.

Honest! Humph! Over my dead body!

Rosalind wriggled into her shift before scrambling to her feet. She snatched up her corset and, reluctantly, he went to help her—loosely re-lacing the garment—before dealing with the fire, throwing earth on to the flames, taking his time. When he faced her again, she was fully clothed. She pulled her hair back and roughly braided it before looping it on her head and cramming her hat on top.

'I am ready to go.' She swung her cloak around her shoulders and marched to the door, then hesitated. She did not look at him. 'You are angry now but, when you have had time to think, I hope you will understand why I did not admit the truth.' Her voice was cold and matter of fact. She opened the door and was almost bowled over by an enthusiastic Hector.

'Rosalind?'

She paused, silhouetted in the doorway, her hand on Hector's collar. He understood too well her wish to climb the social ladder, but that did not mean he welcomed her attempt to better herself at his expense.

'I know precisely why you did not tell me and I am angry because I resent being manipulated in such a way. I'm also disappointed in my poor judgement of your character. I never believed you would behave in such an unladylike way.'

She stiffened, a gasp escaping her lips, and then she pivoted on her heel and disappeared from view. Leo scooped up his greatcoat and shrugged into it as he walked to the door. Rosalind had already fetched Kamal from the lean-to and she waited with a stony expression for Leo to lift her to the saddle. As soon as she was mounted, she kicked the Arabian into a trot along the track at the edge of the wood that led, from memory, down into Malton village.

Leo hastened to untie and mount Conqueror who, with his bigger stride, soon caught up with Kamal.

Leo glanced across at Rosalind as they came alongside. 'I shall escort you home.'

'There is no need. I am quite accustomed to riding alone.'

'You should not ride unaccompanied. I will escort you.'

They rode in silence, neither, seemingly, with any appetite for conversation. Instead, Leo pondered the events of that afternoon and concluded there was no longer any reason to prolong the unpleasantness of this visit to Halsdon Manor. It was time to go back to town.

The village eventually came into view and Leo recognised the turning to Stoney End up ahead.

'I shall be perfectly safe from here,' Rosalind said, tight-lipped.

'You should not ride unaccom—'

'Yes!' Her curt response cut him short. 'So you said. I—'

Her mouth snapped shut and a look of dismay crossed her face before it bloomed fiery red. He followed her gaze to a horseman, riding along the road leading from the village, and he cursed silently. Even at this distance, Leo could recognise the vicar, the Reverend Phillips.

'Hurry,' Rosalind hissed. 'Please. I cannot face…'

She did not finish, for the vicar had seen them. He waved a greeting and spurred his horse into a trot.

'Good afternoon, Mrs Pryce, Mr Boyton,' he called as soon as he was within hailing distance. 'This is a fortunate meeting indeed. You have saved me the journey to Stoney End. I have news of the child.'

Leo nudged Conqueror in front of Kamal, half-shielding Rosalind from the vicar's sight. Susie! He had forgotten all about Susie and he realised with a surge of dismay he would have no choice but to see Rosalind again.

'You have found out where she came from, Reverend?'

'I believe so,' the vicar said. 'I have received news of a child who is missing from her home in Cucklow. I intend to drive over there tomorrow to discover more. I confess that, should the missing child prove to be Susie, it will place me in a quandary. I can only trust in God that I can educate her parents against quite such severe beatings as the child appears to have suffered.'

Leo heard a stifled gasp behind him, then Rosalind urged Kamal past Conqueror to stare at the vicar, the light of battle in her eyes. 'You *cannot* think to send Susie back to such people,' she declared. 'How *anyone* can justify beating a child so badly I cannot begin to understand. Besides, Susie told us she has no mama or papa and I believe her.'

'Quite, quite.' The vicar turned his attention to Leo, clearly uncomfortable with the passion of Rosalind's speech. 'You may rest assured I shall carry out a very thorough investigation, sir. In fact, if you care to accompany me on the morrow, you would be most welcome.'

Leo caught the silent plea Rosalind sent him. His jaw tightened. He would do this for Susie. Not for Rosalind. She did not deserve his help after that cynical attempt to entrap him. He must count himself lucky there were no witnesses. He concentrated his attention on the vicar.

'I shall be delighted to accompany you, sir. I also have reservations about returning a child to people who have ill-treated her in such a way. If we are not satisfied with their story, I do have connections with an orphan asylum in London where she could receive some education and be trained in service for when she is older.'

'Splendid!' The vicar raised his hat. 'I shall leave at ten, if you care to come to the parsonage for that time. Good day to you both.'

He reined his horse around and headed back up the lane to Malton.

'Thank you,' Rosalind said.

Leo nudged Conqueror into a walk. 'There is no need to thank me. I am as eager as you to ensure Susie will be safe in the future.'

A weighty silence fell again between them, the only sound the occasional clink of horseshoe on stone as they rode around the corner and up the lane towards Stoney End. The lane ended at the junction where they would part company: the chimneys of Stoney End visible through the trees to their right and the lane that would take Leo to Halsdon Manor stretching to their left.

He heard Rosalind take a deep breath. 'Leo. We must talk about…'

He raised his hand, palm facing her, and her words faded. If she spoke one word of marriage, the fragile threads holding his temper would surely snap.

'Not now, Mrs Pryce. This is neither the time nor the place for this discussion.'

'Mrs Pryce?' She looked at him, her eyes wounded, and then looked away. 'Then when will be the right time and place? I want to explain…to make you understand, from my point of view—'

'I said not now.' He bit the words out through clenched lips. 'I shall call upon you tomorrow, following my return from Cucklow. Our discussion can wait until after we know what is to happen to Susie.'

Maybe by tomorrow the cut of her betrayal would sting less. Maybe his bitter anger at being once again deceived by a woman he trusted would have cooled to a simmer. Maybe he could speak to her without revealing his contempt for her character and her morals.

He shut his mind against the plea shimmering in her

golden-brown eyes. Pleas would not change his mind. He would make no offer of marriage.

'Until tomorrow.'

Cucklow was a mere five miles from Malton. If Leo and the vicar left Malton at ten, even if they stayed at Cucklow for a whole hour—which seemed unlikely—they should have returned an hour since. Leo had promised to call. He must know she would be waiting and not only to find out about Susie.

She had gone over and over what happened. His fury still mystified her—was her failure to tell him it was her first time really so terrible? Or was his anger a ruse, an underhand ploy to allow him to slip out of her life as easily as he had slipped into it?

Rosalind looked again at the mantel clock, huffed a sigh and shifted into a more comfortable position in her seat by the window. She picked up her mending and peered at the stitches. If she had set two in the past half an hour, that was as much as she had achieved. With another sigh, she packed Freddie's shirt into her sewing basket and tucked it out of sight beneath the table next to her chair.

She sensed a gaze upon her and her head snapped round to the door.

'Do you intend to enlighten me as to what ails you, Sister?' Freddie limped into the room. 'You've been as fidgety as a dog with fleas ever since noon. Even Penny has remarked upon it.'

'Fidgety as… Freddie! That is a dreadful saying.'

Freddie shrugged, throwing a charming smile in her direction. 'But it *is* accurate. What is wrong, Ros? You've been very quiet ever since I got back from Foxbourne yesterday. Lascelles hasn't been bothering you, has he?'

'No. If you must know why I am restless, it is that I am

wondering what the vicar might have discovered about Susie. I hoped he might call in on his way back to Malton.'

No sooner had the words left her mouth than there was a knock at the front door. She leapt to her feet, heart in mouth, and hurried to the front door, throwing it wide with a mixture of anticipation and trepidation agitating her nerves. She need not have worried. The vicar stood alone upon the step. Leo was nowhere to be seen. Her heart plummeted back to its rightful place. Had Leo decided to wait until after the vicar's visit in order to avoid any awkwardness?

'Good afternoon, Reverend Phillips. Please, come in.'

The vicar removed his hat. 'Good afternoon, Mrs Pryce. Thank you.'

As she showed him to the sitting room, she said, 'I quite expected Mr Boyton to be with you, sir.'

'Ah, yes…it is the strangest thing… Oh, good afternoon to you, Mr Allen. I hope I find you well today? No,' he continued to Rosalind, 'it is the reason I am somewhat later than I anticipated. I waited until a quarter to eleven for Mr Boyton, but he did not come. As I received no message in explanation, I rather thought you might have had word from him.'

'No. I have heard nothing.'

That nervous roil of Rosalind's insides stilled, leaving a leaden lump of misery weighing her down.

'I shall go and order the tea tray, if you would care to take a seat, Mr Phillips. I cannot wait to hear what you have discovered about Susie.'

As she went to the kitchen and gave Penny her instructions, Rosalind's mind raced, plucking at any likely reason she could think of for Leo's absence and then discarding it. The only reason that made sense was that he'd never intended to call upon her as promised and her own fury— kept at bay by the hope that his anger might fade overnight—boiled up. How dare he place all the blame…all the responsibility…on to her?

Rosalind returned to the parlour, battening down her pain and caging her snarling rage. She painted a smile upon her face as the vicar told her of his discoveries.

'The parson of Cucklow knew of a child named Susie, fostered from birth with a farming family called Wilton. It seems…' he lowered his voice '…her mother was a gentleman's daughter, seduced by the eldest son of a viscount who had no intention of wedding her. The girl was sent down here to give birth and the Wiltons were paid a sum of money to bring the child up as their own.'

Rosalind near choked with fury. 'As their own? Well, they have signally failed in that regard, have they not? She has been half-starved and badly beaten. What have they to say about that?'

'They are rough, poorly educated people, Mrs Pryce. They work hard to scrape a living from the land but, good harvest or poor, they must still pay their rent and their tithes. I suspect the money they were paid for Susie has long since been spent.'

'But—'

He held up his hand to silence her. 'I am not saying I condone their treatment of Susie, but at the same time I cannot help but have some sympathy for the family. They have five other children—all their natural offspring, so they tell me—and they did not look in much better condition than Susie.'

'If what you have told us is true, Susie is not to be returned to these people,' Freddie said. 'Mr Boyton has a connection with an orphan school in London. He will find her a place there.'

'But it is a school to train children to have a useful trade, Freddie,' Rosalind said. 'You heard what Reverend Phillips said: Susie's father is the heir of a viscount and her mother is a gentleman's daughter. She deserves better than to end up in domestic service.'

'Your sentiments do you credit, madam, but you must see that Susie's prospects are poor. She is, when all else is said and done, illegitimate. An education such as Mr Boyton suggested, and the prospect of decent employment, is as much as she can expect given her start in life.'

Rosalind compressed her lips. She would not argue with the vicar, but she did not agree. She vowed to do as much as she could to give Susie the chance of a better life.

'You are right, sir,' Freddie said, 'and I know my sister will see the sense in what you say when she has had time to think about it.'

Mr Phillips rose. 'The sentiments expressed by Mrs Pryce can only be admired as quite proper in a member of the gentler sex, my good sir. I do not decry them but, equally, sentiment cannot be allowed to rule our decisions.'

He smiled condescendingly at Rosalind, who gritted her teeth.

'Oh, quite, sir.' Freddie's clear amusement made Rosalind's hand itch to slap him.

'Well, I have brought you my news,' Mr Phillips said. 'The Wiltons are not expecting Susie back, so when you see Mr Boyton you may tell him to go ahead and arrange a place for her at the orphan school.'

Chapter Thirteen

As soon as the vicar left, Rosalind rounded on Freddie. 'I do not need time to think about it, Freddie. Susie is not going to some horrid school to be trained as a maid or a milliner. She will stay here with us.'

She was conscious of Freddie eyeing her with raised brows and she felt her cheeks heat. She sat down, folding her hands in her lap.

'*You* have decided, have you?'

'It is what I want.'

'And do I have any say in the matter? And what about Boyton? He may not be happy to leave Susie in your care.'

Rosalind hunched a shoulder, suspecting Freddie was right, albeit for the wrong reasons. Leo might not willingly allow Susie to remain with a woman such as he clearly believed her to be, but surely he had relinquished any rights to a say over Susie's future by failing to keep his appointment with the vicar.

But why did he fail to send an apology? That small, doubting voice would not be silenced, offering a fragile straw of hope to which she clung. It seemed so very out of character.

Could he be ill? Her heart skipped a beat. *What if he has met with an accident?*

She leapt to her feet.

'Ros?'

Freddie's voice penetrated Rosalind's surge of panic, which had been foolishly laced with hope. Foolishly because, she realised—her heart sinking in tandem with that irresistible burst of energy that had assailed her—Leo's non-appearance did not alter what had happened yesterday, or his coldness afterwards.

'Ros? What is it? You are as pale as can be. Are you ill?'

Freddie was by her side, loosely grasping her arm. She'd been so caught up in her thoughts she had not even noticed him move. She shook all thought of Leo from her head and smiled at her brother, quick to soothe his concern.

'I am well, Freddie.' She patted his hand. 'Mayhap you are right about Susie. We need not make a decision yet. Let us see what tomorrow might bring. Now, if you have no need of me, I shall go for a short ride. Kamal needs exercise and I am in need of some fresh air.'

She was not so bound up in her own concerns that she did not notice Freddie's eyes dim at her words and her heart went out to him. He did not have the choice to ride out and she knew how frustrated he felt at being so confined. She lifted one hand to the side of his face and wished—futilely, as she had so many times before—that she could make his life easier.

'When I return, we will discuss our plans again. There is no need for us to stay here until Foxbourne is sold, if we choose not to. We can either go home to Lydney or, if you prefer, we could lease a house in a town somewhere, until Jack finishes school for the summer.'

Once mounted on Kamal, Rosalind hesitated. It was madness, surely, to hope to meet Leo but...her thoughts stuttered as she tried to analyse the feelings that had driven her out of doors. The awful fear she had successfully suppressed fought its way to the surface. It was not that he had not called upon her as promised. It was the fact that he had sent no word to the vicar. She had thought him, at the least, an honourable man. To have sent no apology...to have simply failed to keep an appointment...had she been so very wrong about his character? Mayhap he thought a country parson did not warrant any degree of attention from a fine London gentleman such as himself, but she was loath to believe her gut feeling about him had been so very wrong.

Which left an accident or illness and, if it were the latter, surely he would have sent *someone* with excuses? If, however, he had suffered an accident on his way to the parsonage...

With a muttered oath, she headed for the village. Her ride could take her past the parsonage and in the direction of Halsdon Manor. She could at least make sure he was not lying insensible in a ditch somewhere. If she saw no sign of him on her travels, then she must accept she had been completely mistaken about his character and maybe, in time, she might forgive herself for the momentous mistake she had made. She would have a lifetime to regret her actions of yesterday.

As she rode, she discovered it was one thing to decide— quite dispassionately—on a course of action and how one should feel. Emotions, it seemed, had an agenda of their own, her insides churning, squeezing and bubbling until she felt quite ill.

Some time later she reined Kamal to a halt next to the stone pillars that marked the entrance to Halsdon Manor. Well. That was it. No sign of Leo on the road. She could hardly ride up to the front door of the Manor and demand to see him. She urged Kamal into a trot, straight past the pillars and in the direction of Stoney End. The afternoon light was fading and it was time she went home.

She must accept she had been mistaken in Leo. She dashed at a tear that dared to spill over and trickle down her cheek. It was the knife-edge breeze that made her eyes water. He was unworthy of regret, let alone tears. Better to concentrate on her anger than her sorrow. Anger at herself, for being taken in by a...by a...

'Oh, no!'

She halted Kamal and frantically looked for an escape, but there was none to be had. She looked beyond the solitary horseman who approached, but no further riders hove into view. Ironically, she was almost level with the gate through which she had driven those straying sheep that first day they met. Instinct took over and she nudged Kamal into motion again. She straightened her back and squared her shoulders, forcing eye contact with Anthony Lascelles as he drew his horse to a halt and raised his hat. Rosalind stopped Kamal a good six feet away, conscious Lascelles was now between her and home.

'Good afternoon, Mrs Pryce. How propitious, our meeting in this way.'

Rosalind inclined her head. Why, oh, why hadn't she brought Hector with her?

'Good afternoon, sir. May I enquire in what way our meeting is propitious?'

'Why, I had it in my mind to call upon you at Stoney End as I was in the vicinity, but I hesitated to disturb you so late in the day. I thought you might already be dining.' He smiled charmingly, but his eyes remained cold. Calculating. 'Country hours and so forth.'

'As you mention the subject, sir, the hour is rather late. I have stayed out longer than intended. I should make haste... my brother will be looking out for me, I am sure.'

'Your brother...yes...' Lascelles shook his head, sympathy writ large on his face. 'How the poor fellow must suffer with the knowledge that, should anything happen, he would find himself quite unable to take action. It is the first instinct of family, is it not, to protect one another?'

What does he mean? Is it a threat?

'You are mistaken, sir, if you think my brother incapable of protecting those he loves.'

Rosalind nudged Kamal into motion. Lascelles reined his horse to the side of the lane, opening up a gap for her to ride through.

'I was making reference to my dear cousin. He has been much in my thoughts today,' Lascelles said as she drew alongside him.

His words grabbed Rosalind's attention. 'Your cousin?'

Lascelles lounged in his saddle, smiling. 'Why, yes.' He shook his head again, his lips pursed. 'Poor Cousin Leo... Young Alex is such a scamp, always getting into scrapes. What can a father do but drop everything and rush to the rescue when a family crisis summons him home?'

His words fell like blows on Rosalind's heart. The one eventuality she had not foreseen...that Leo might be married, with a family. He had mentioned nothing of a son in all their conversations, not even when they had discussed Susie and her family. She gathered her pride, willing her voice to remain light and uninterested.

'I did not know he had a son. Now, pray, excuse me, for I must be on my way.'

'He has two sons,' Lascelles continued, as though Rosalind had not spoken. 'And a daughter. I am surprised he did not mention them; his family is his pride and joy. He would do anything for them.'

'As a father should,' she snapped. A thought struck her. 'Did he mention Susie before he left?'

Lascelles frowned, appearing to search his memory. 'No,' he said, after a pause. 'I do not believe he did. I fear the news about Alex quite blocked *everything* else from his mind. Shall I enquire on your behalf, when I go to London? He has no plans to return to Halsdon Manor, so you will be unable to ask him yourself.'

'I thank you, but, no. I shall make alternative arrangements for Susie. There is no need to involve your cousin further—I am loath to abandon her to an orphan asylum such as he suggested.'

'You have confirmed she is indeed an orphan, then, ma'am?'

'I… No, she is not an orphan. Not precisely.' Her cheeks burned at the thought of discussing such matters with Lascelles. 'The vicar made enquiries. It seems her mother fostered her out with a farmer's family.'

'Ah. I understand, dear lady. No need to elaborate. She and I have much in common, then.' He bowed. 'Pray, allow me to place myself at your service, should you need any help or advice for the little one.'

'I… Thank you.'

'You look puzzled, my dear lady. My cousin refrained from discussing my personal circumstances with you, I take it?'

Rosalind frowned. 'Your cousin barely spoke of you, sir. I do not understand your meaning.'

Lascelles shook his head. 'It is the shame,' he said, with a sigh, 'and yet the guilt will not allow him to disown me entirely. *That* is the reason we have a somewhat…shall we say, testy…relationship.' He smiled. 'I have no wish to shock you, Mrs Pryce, but my father and my mother were unmarried. Had they been, of course, then our lives would be very different. But it is of no use to dwell upon what might have been. I am inured to my lot and I must count myself fortunate that I am not entirely disowned by my cousins.

'That is why I am uniquely placed to offer any help or advice you might need for young Susie.' He smiled again and tipped his hat. 'I, like you, am conscious of the passing minutes, my dear lady, so I shall bid you farewell. My other cousin and Stanton remain as my guests until Sunday, when we shall all leave together, so I must hasten home to take up my duties as host.

'Until next time we meet.'

He dug his heels into his horse and cantered off down the lane, leaving Rosalind shaken and even less certain of her own judgement of character.

Leo, the man she had trusted and thought of as honourable—the man with whom she had thought herself in love—had ignored the existence of his family and befriended her, seemingly with the sole intention of seduction. He had then cruelly left without a word, even though he must know how confused and upset she would be. His fury at her had been contrived. *Her* omission of the truth was surely as nothing compared to *his*. Quite why she continued to be surprised by such immoral and selfish behaviour by a gentleman of his ilk, she did not know.

And then, to add to her confusion, Anthony Lascelles—who she had so feared and whose appearance just now in the dimming twilight had sent panic soaring—had behaved as a gentleman.

She rode the rest of the way to Stoney End with the heaviest of hearts, the harshest condemnation of her own behaviour pounding her thoughts.

The decision was made.

Rosalind and Freddie would return to Lydney Hall. Sir William had found a buyer for Foxbourne Manor and preparations for him to remove to his daughter's property in the north were well under way. Sir William's buyer—who had bound Sir William to secrecy as to his identity—had agreed Rosalind and Freddie could remain at Stoney End for as long as they might wish, but they had decided to go home immediately and face Sir Peter. Rosalind had written to Nell to apprise her of their plans and to the housekeeper at Lydney to give the staff time to prepare for their arrival.

The date of travel was set for two weeks hence. Rosalind had persuaded Freddie that Susie should remain with them and caring for the little girl helped distract Rosalind from her constantly circling thoughts of Leo: where he was, what he was doing, whether he ever thought of her or had wiped her from his mind as casually as he appeared to have done. Her heartache was not eased by telling herself he would soon have gone in any case. It was the manner of his leaving—his casual, cruel dismissal of her and the confusion he must know she was suffering that ripped at her heart and battered her pride.

She buried her pain beneath busyness and a determined cheeriness that only slipped once she was alone in her bed at night. Then that tangle of raw emotion fought its way to the surface and wrapped around her, squeezing until she felt she could no longer breathe. Anger mixed with hurt and she held imagined conversations with him during which her scathing eloquence would awaken his conscience and he would have a change of heart…but then she would remember.

He was married. He had a family. She meant nothing to him, even though meeting him had proved to be the most significant event in her life.

I am nothing more than a stupid, naïve fool. I knew he would leave and I would never see him again, but I still chose to give myself to him. I only have myself to blame.

And each morning she awoke with her throat tight and aching and her eyes red and sore. And she arose and went about her day with yet another determined smile upon her face. She could not wait to go home and for her life to return to some semblance of normality.

They saw nothing more of Anthony Lascelles and his guests, but they knew through Sir William that the men departed for London three days after Leo failed to honour his appointment with the vicar.

The day before their scheduled departure, Rosalind was in the parlour with Susie, teaching her how to embroider, when Freddie came in, an opened letter in his hand.

'This—' he waved the letter '—is from Lady Glenlochrie. It has just been delivered by one of her footmen.'

Rosalind shot to her feet, stomach clenched with fear as she tried to imagine what had happened to prompt Nell's aunt to write with such urgency. 'Nell is not ill, is she? Oh, Freddie...please tell me what is amiss... I cannot bear the suspense.'

Freddie flicked a meaningful look at Susie and Rosalind said, 'Go to the kitchen, Susie, my dear. Ask Penny to give you an apple.' As Susie left the room, Rosalind said, 'Is the footman still here? Does he await a reply?'

'He is still here, yes. But he made no mention of a reply.'

Rosalind waited in a fever of impatience whilst Freddie settled into his chair and wordlessly indicated that Rosalind, too, should sit. Then he studied her, the strangest expression on his face.

'Freddie? What does she say? Is it Nell? Do please tell me what is wrong.'

'There is nothing wrong with Nell, but I fear you will dislike the news.'

'Sir Peter has come for her!'

Freddie threw back his head and laughed. 'Rosalind! No, it is not Sir Peter. You really do have the most lurid imagination. Do you imagine I should be so calm if *he* were the problem? No. The news is that her ladyship has broken her leg and is therefore unable to fulfil her role as chaperon to Nell.'

'Oh! But—' Rosalind fell silent in response to Freddie's raised hand.

'Allow me to finish. She asks…no…she *insists* that we go to London in order that Nell can still have her Season. You, my dear Ros, are to be Nell's chaperon.'

Everything froze. Time itself appeared to stand still. Then the air whooshed from Rosalind's lungs and her heart thudded painfully against her ribs. *Leo!*

'No! I cannot.'

Freddie gave a puzzled smile. 'Of course you can. There is nothing to fear.'

'But…but…'

'Come, my dear. This is Nell. Our *sister*. We cannot allow fear of our Hillyer relations to prevent us from helping when she has need of us.'

'I am not afraid of *them*.' She spoke unthinkingly.

'Then you can have no objection to spending a few months in London. We agreed how important it is that Nell should find a husband. I shall be with you for moral support and we can laugh together at the pompousness and the self-importance of these people who have done nothing to earn their privilege other than be born to the right parents. It will be our private joke.'

Rosalind stared helplessly at her brother. She had not even begun to think about her maternal relations and their arrogant friends…her first thought, her *only* thought, had been how on earth she could face Leo—and his wife, and his children—if she were expected to attend balls and parties and all the other society events to which Nell would surely be invited.

And what of Nell? If Rosalind's immoral behaviour became known…

How can I bear it? I have been so wrong about him. What if I was also wrong in believing he will say nothing of our…of my…?

She could not even complete that thought as sick dread welled up inside. She tried to summon up hatred and defiance against Leo, but her heart and her emotions still… just…*wanted.*

Freddie leaned over and caught her hand in his. 'Is there something else, Ros? What are you not telling me?'

She shook her head. 'I'm not… I have… I cannot… Oh, heavens! I cannot string more than two words together at a time.'

She rubbed her forehead with her free hand. Hauled in a deep breath. She must endure. She had no choice. A few short months…surely she could bear so brief a time? She gathered her thoughts.

'There are practicalities, Freddie. Step-Papa left us financially comfortable, but our income will not stretch to the expense of a Season. If we are to accompany Nell, we must dress the part.'

'You always look elegant, Sis, whatever clothes you wear.'

Freddie winked at Rosalind, offering her a cheeky grin, and love for him flooded through her. At least she still had Freddie. Life without him would be so very dull, especially when Nell did wed.

'Lady Glenlochrie has already offered to stand the cost of a new wardrobe for you,' Freddie continued. 'She says—' he consulted the letter, then read out in a high-pitched, perfect imitation of her ladyship's well-modulated tones '"—Rosalind will stand as my representative in society and therefore I shall expect her to uphold the Glenlochrie name and position during her time in London". She also says she wants us there as soon as possible even though Nell's ball is not until after Easter.' He bent his head, studying the letter with a frown. 'It seems several families are already in town and there are some private parties to which Nell is invited. The carriage will be here on Saturday and we are to travel to London on Monday.'

'But what about Hector?'

'Hector?'

'Yes. And Susie. We have responsibilities. I cannot imagine Lady Glenlochrie will be enthused at the thought of a dog the size of Hector in her home, let alone a stray child such as Susie. I fully intend that, in time, she will become a polite and accomplished young lady, but even I cannot pretend she fits that description as yet.'

Freddie scowled. 'You know my opinion on *that* subject, Rosalind. Removing a child from her natural place in society can never be fully successful. You of all people should know that.' He paused, then thumped his fist into his open palm. 'Of course! Boyton will be in London. We shall make enquiries about getting her a place in that orphan asylum he mentioned.'

'No!'

'Come, Ros. The slights we have endured through our parentage will be as nothing compared to Susie's plight when she realises the stigma of illegitimacy.'

Rosalind stood up, smoothing her skirts. 'You cannot change my mind, Freddie, so you may as well give up now. Susie will remain with us.'

'You are being selfish, Ros. And you know it.'

Rosalind walked to the door. She refused to listen to another one of Freddie's lectures. She would not abandon Susie to an uncertain life of hard toil, not when she could provide a home and love and some hope for her future.

'And as for Hector...' Freddie's voice floated through the door before she could shut it behind her '...he is part of this family. Where we go, he goes, too, even to London for the Season.'

Chapter Fourteen

Four days later, they left Stoney End. Rosalind, Freddie, Penny and Hector all travelled inside the Lydney carriage, which had come to convey them to London. Susie, who had begged and begged until Rosalind had finally relented, was well wrapped up and sitting up on the box with the coachman, and Kamal was tethered to the back of the coach for the thirty-nine-mile journey to London. Sir William had set out for the north a few days before, with the promise of staying in touch to let them know how he fared at his daughter's house.

It was over a fortnight since Rosalind had last seen or heard from Leo and, try as she might, she had been unable to banish him from her thoughts. Sleep had evaded her night after night as she relived the time they had spent together and now… Gloomily, she peered through the rain-spattered window as the carriage bowled through the outskirts of London—a grim, grey mid-March scene to match the weather and to echo the state of her heart and her mind, both weighted with dread at the thought of that inevitable meeting with Leo.

What would she say when she saw him? Would he imagine she had followed him to the metropolis? Would he reveal her immorality? A blush of shame heated her cheeks.

If only she could turn the clock back.

If only he had called upon her just once after that disastrous afternoon.

If only he had not simply disappeared back to town as soon as he had fulfilled his carnal lusts.

If only…if only…

If only I had not so stupidly, recklessly given in to my basest desires.

Lust. Pure and simple.

Well, I have learned my lesson well.

But the very worst of her worries was: what if her actions harmed Nell? When she had lain with Leo, she'd been confident that Leo would never…*could* never…connect her with Lady Helena Caldicot. But now…

She sighed. If only she could have resisted Lady Glenlochrie's summons, but that had been impossible. She knew if she did not help Nell now, it would be as good as abandoning her to Sir Peter Tadlow's machinations.

She heaved another sigh and tore her gaze from the rainsoaked streets to the hands that twisted in her lap.

'Why the sighs, Ros?'

How long had Freddie been watching her? Her brother was far too observant. He must suspect there was more to her distress than the simple fact they had been forced to change their plans and come to London.

'It is nothing, Freddie. I am tired. I had trouble sleeping last night.'

'Again?'

'Is it any wonder, with the prospect of meeting Mama's darling sisters, not to mention Sir Peter?'

'You might also meet Mr Boyton again,' Freddie remarked in a casual tone as he gazed out of the window.

Rosalind knew that seemingly simple statement concealed a wealth of meaning. She glanced at Penny, seated opposite, but she was sound asleep, mouth agape as she snored quietly, oblivious to their conversation. Nevertheless, Rosalind lowered her voice.

'That is an eventuality I view with complete and utter indifference.'

Freddie's muffled *humph* reached her ears.

'Freddie! Please believe me. He was a pleasant gentleman, but I have no desire to further our acquaintance.'

'"The lady doth protest too much" comes to mind. You gave every appearance of enjoying his company when he called at Stoney End.'

Rosalind shrugged, lifting her nose. 'His company was a welcome distraction. He alleviated the tedium of only having my aggravating younger brother with whom to converse.'

'Ouch! And the lady bites back. You had better watch your place, Hector, old lad.' Freddie leant down to pat the dog, who was stretched out with his head on Freddie's feet. 'Who needs a guard dog when they have a ferocious sister?'

'Oh, Freddie!' Despite her worries—and her irritation with him for seeing too much—Rosalind had to laugh. 'I am sorry, you know I did not mean that but, please, I beg of you, do not read more than it meant into a passing acquaintanceship. You know yourself that a new face and new conversation is welcome from time to time. It meant nothing.'

The carriage slowed, and turned into a residential street. Rosalind leaned forward, glad of the opportunity to change the subject.

'Look, Freddie. Here we are, South Audley Street.'

Rosalind gazed around the staircase hall of Lady Glenlochrie's town house, awed by the magnificent stone staircase, complete with elegant wrought-iron balustrade, and the intricate and ornate plasterwork that decorated the ceiling and cornices. The sprawling Lydney Hall, where they had lived for over twenty years, had always seemed grand to her, but to compare its appearance to this was to compare a plough horse to a highly bred racehorse.

Penny and Susie had already been despatched upstairs to begin unpacking, one footman had been sent to apprise Lady Glenlochrie and Lady Helena of their arrival and a second had been detailed to take charge of Hector.

'Ros! Freddie!'

Nell's voice brought Rosalind back to the realisation she was staring around open-mouthed. That would never do in front of the starchy butler who had opened the door to them. He had peered down his pointy nose when given their names, clearly having already relegated them to the status of poor relations. Even though he was right, Rosalind was determined the servants should treat them with due deference. After all, they were Lady Glenlochrie's guests. It was not as if they even wished to be there.

Nell ran lightly down the stairs, an imperious voice floating in her wake.

'*Walk*, Helena. Walk! You are a young lady.'

Nell did not slow, but launched herself at Rosalind, throwing her arms around her.

'Thank you for coming, dearest Ros. I know what a trial this must be for you.' She released Rosalind and hugged Freddie. 'And thank you, too, Freddie, although I suspect you will enjoy London and its sights far more than Ros. Are you completely exhausted after your journey?'

'It was not as tiring as the journey from Lydney to Foxbourne.' Rosalind suppressed her shudder, recalling their fear that Sir Peter would catch them and force Nell to go back with him. 'I should not care to live through that again.'

'Neither should I,' Freddie said, with a grimace. 'Will you take us to pay our respects to her ladyship, Nell?'

'Of course.' Nell led the way, taking the stairs slowly to accommodate Freddie. 'I should warn you that Aunt Susan has hired a lady's maid called Elspeth for you, whilst you are here, to help with your toilette and to dress your hair à la mode. And a valet and a footman to assist you, Freddie.'

'But there is no need—'

'Hush. Do not let my aunt hear you say that.' Nell stopped on the stairs and struck a pose. 'Whilst you reside in *my* house your conduct and your appearance shall be paramount. Never forget that you are my representative in society.'

'Nell! Lady Glenlochrie has been very good to you. Do not mock her,' Freddie hissed. 'It does you no credit.'

Rosalind bit back a smile, recalling Freddie's own mockery of her ladyship.

Nell sobered. 'I am sorry, Freddie. I did not mean to appear ungrateful.'

They eventually reached the second floor.

'Aunt Susan is confined to this floor, but she is able to use her boudoir during the day,' Nell said as she tapped on a door and opened it, revealing a feminine room decorated in shades of pink and cream, with a pretty sprig design wallpaper.

'Aunt Susan, Rosalind and Freddie have arrived.'

Lady Glenlochrie reclined on a chaise longue by a window. Solidly built, with ash-grey locks covered by a lace-edged cap, she was dressed in a purple day dress, with a shawl covering her legs and another draped around her shoulders. She raised a lorgnette to peer at her visitors.

'Lady Glenlochrie...' Rosalind dipped into a curtsy '...I was very sorry to hear of your accident. I do hope your leg is healing well?'

Humour gleamed in the lady's grey eyes. 'I have no doubt of your being sorry, Rosalind, for I know how much you will dislike chaperoning Helena over the next few weeks.'

Their eyes met and Rosalind smiled at the understanding she read. Lady Glenlochrie might be formidable, but she had always been kind, if a touch patronising, in her dealings with Rosalind and Freddie.

'I dare say I shall cope well enough,' Rosalind said. 'It is only a few weeks. I shall endeavour to avoid any of our Hillyer relations and thus afford them no opportunity to snub me.'

'That's the spirit,' Freddie said. He bowed. 'Your servant, Lady G. Looking as ravishing as ever, I see.'

'You never change, Frederick, you wicked boy,' Lady Glenlochrie said, with a pleased smile. 'I have every expectation that you will provide me with a little diversion whilst your sisters are occupied with their frivolities.'

'Indeed I shall and I shall enlist the help of Susie as I foresee that I must become her main tutor whilst my sister is out gallivanting.'

'Susie?' Her ladyship's voice boomed in the sudden silence.

Rosalind frowned at Freddie, who raised a mocking brow in response. She had hoped to introduce Susie's presence herself. Diplomatically. She explained how they had discovered Susie and her desire to help the child better her prospects.

Lady Glenlochrie raised her lorgnette again and glared through it at Rosalind. 'Raised by *farmers*, you say? Humph! You had better ensure the child learns her manners fast. The woman you brought with you can have charge of her, and I shall review the situation after I have met her.

'I cannot say I think your decision wise, but I dare say you think to fill the gap left by your sister, once she weds.'

Rosalind bridled at her ladyship's words, not trusting herself to respond, but Freddie's nod of agreement made her wonder if her ladyship was right. Was that why she was so adamant Susie should stay? Because she dreaded losing Nell? *Was* she clinging to Susie as a replacement? Freddie had accused her of being selfish. Mayhap he was right. But what would be the purpose of her life when her brothers and sister no longer had need of her? Jack might still be only fourteen years old, but he was growing fast. A young man—an earl—would have little use or time for an older stepsister such as she.

At least Freddie was unlikely to ever leave, even if they did seem to spend more and more time bickering.

'Well, I cannot wait to meet her,' Nell said stoutly. 'And I have not yet seen Hector. You did bring him, Freddie?'

'Hector?' Lady Glenlochrie's voice was filled with horror. 'You have brought that hellhound to *my house*?'

'Now, now, Lady G.' Freddie patted her ladyship's shoulder. 'I shall make certain you see neither sight nor sound of him. He is very well-behaved, don't you know... You will barely know he is here.'

'But he is so big, Frederick. And he will need exercise! You are not to take him to the park during the promenade hour, do you hear? Oh, why could you not have a dainty little lapdog as other people do?'

'We had no choice but to bring Hector,' Rosalind said. 'There was nowhere else for him to go. I enjoy the exercise walking him, as Freddie is unable to, and I promise I will only take him out at the times you deem suitable.'

Lady Glenlochrie appeared mollified. 'Such a pity you are unable to walk him, too, Frederick. You must suffer with being so housebound.'

Freddie's jaw set, but his reply was determinedly cheerful. 'You do realise, my lady, that you and I are now bound together by our infirmities? Although I suggest that you are in a worse case than I, for I may still hobble about whereas I wager your physician has advised you to rest until your leg is healed.'

Lady Glenlochrie sighed. 'He has indeed. I am not to venture out for several weeks. Now, Helena, my dear, you may show Rosalind to her chamber.' Her sharp gaze raked

Rosalind. 'I have ordered an appropriate wardrobe for you, in order that you will not shame us when you attend the various functions in my stead. Helena, fortunately, knew your measurements so there will only be a few minor adjustments before the clothes are ready to be worn.'

'There was truly no need—'

'No.' Her ladyship held up her hand, cutting off Rosalind's protest. 'There was every need. If we left you to your own devices, you would no doubt go out looking an utter drab.

'Now, there is a party tonight that Helena *must* attend. It is a private affair for a few young ladies who are about to make their debuts, to accustom them to dancing with other couples before they are let loose in a crowded ballroom. The Duke has two adult sons and they will bring some of their friends to the evening to provide partners.'

'The Duke?'

'The Duke of Cheriton, Ros. I am bosom friends with his daughter, Lady Olivia, who is coming out this Season, as well.'

'But…tonight? I had thought—'

'Your invitation is for eight,' her ladyship continued, 'so you should go to your bedchamber now and rest. You will soon become accustomed to town hours, but we cannot have your first foray into polite society attended by yawns and dark circles around those lovely eyes. Although…' her ladyship leaned closer to Rosalind and tutted '…I fear the dark circles are already present. No matter. Elspeth will know how to disguise those so you look your best. Frederick will remain and keep me company, so there is no need for any obligation on your part, my dear. Now…tonight… there is a pretty green evening gown in your wardrobe that will be perfect for the occasion and Elspeth will make any final adjustments to ensure it fits perfectly. I expect you to visit me here before you leave so I can give you my final approval.'

Lady Glenlochrie waved a dismissive hand at Rosalind. 'Run along now, my dear. I shall see you later.'

As Rosalind left the room, she heard her ladyship say, 'Now, Frederick, pull up that chair and tell me what you think of your first sight of London.'

My goodness.

Rosalind stared around the grand entrance foyer of Beauchamp House in wonder. She had thought the Glenlochrie town house magnificent, but this...*this* was true opulence. How did anyone have enough wealth to live in this utter luxury? She and Nell followed a liveried footman, complete with powdered wig, up a wide, marble staircase, lit by a glittering chandelier suspended high above, to the first floor where they were shown through a pair of intricately carved doors into a salon thronged with strangers.

A swarm of butterflies invaded Rosalind's stomach as she smoothed her gloved hands down her skirt and then patted at her beautifully coiffed hair. She had joked with Elspeth, the maid appointed to her, that her appearance was fine enough to attend a real ball. Now she understood the woman's enigmatic smile as she continued to diligently comb and tweak and pin Rosalind's locks. Now, Rosalind could see that—compared with the bejewelled glitter of many of the ladies present—her appearance was positively restrained. She raised her hand to her simple locket. She had never needed fine necklaces.

And I will not covet them now.

She thought of her mother, who had been born into a world such as this and had been unable to adjust to a simpler, more basic life, even for love. She rubbed her locket between finger and thumb and thought of her father, and then of her grandfather. Her heart ached. So many years ago. Was Grandpa still alive, even? Rosalind pictured Grandpa as she had last seen him, stooping over his workbench, pouring his love into what was, for him, an extravagant gift for his only granddaughter for her sixth birthday.

That was her reality. Not this.

'We shan't be announced, as this is an informal gathering,' Nell whispered, as they paused a short way into the salon.

Sheathed in silvery lilac, Nell looked beautiful and poised and at home in this world as she searched the faces of the other guests with a confident smile. They'd had little time to talk since Rosalind's arrival, but she could see that Nell—*Helena! I must become accustomed to calling her Helena*—had changed in subtle ways since coming to town.

'Look, Ros. There is Olivia and her aunt, Lady Cecily.'

A slender young lady in a white gown, pink flowers woven into her raven hair, had emerged from the crowd and now hurried in their direction, a happy smile lighting her face. She was followed, more sedately, by a graceful, chestnut-haired lady, dressed in blue silk with a single strand of pearls around her neck and matching eardrops. Rosalind's mouth dried even as her palms grew damp inside her evening gloves and she envied Nell for her careless confidence as she greeted her friend.

What will they think when they find out Papa was a mere soldier?

As soon as the thought arose, Rosalind quashed it. She would not be intimidated. She had loved her papa and she would not tarnish his memory by being ashamed of him now. She was not pretending to be something she was not— she was here solely to chaperon Nell.

'Lady Cecily, Lady Olivia, I should like to introduce my sister, Rosalind Allen.'

Rosalind bobbed a curtsy and returned the other ladies' smiles, suppressing her jolt of surprise at the familiarity of

Lady Olivia's silver-grey eyes fringed by black lashes...the image of Leo Boyton's. She forced her wandering thoughts away from that wretch. Many people had black hair and grey eyes. Would she freeze with shock every time she encountered one?

'I am pleased to meet you,' Lady Cecily said.

'And I,' Olivia said. 'Nell has told me all about you and your brother, Miss Allen. And I cannot wait to meet Hector.'

'And who, might I enquire, is Hector?' Lady Cecily had stiffened and her well-modulated tones acquired a sharp edge. 'Olivia, please remember what I have told you.'

'Please do not worry, Lady Cecily,' Rosalind said, with a smile. 'Hector is our dog.'

The other woman visibly relaxed as Olivia said, 'There, Aunt Cecily. You may see I *can* be trusted. May Nell and I go and talk to Lizzie now?'

'You may.'

The two young girls went away, arm in arm, chattering. Rosalind watched them go with a touch of envy for their youth and the possibilities that lay in their futures.

'Olivia,' Lady Cecily said, 'will be the death of me. I am grateful that she has developed such a close friendship with Helena, Miss Allen, for I have grand hopes that your sister's genteel behaviour will prove a moderating influence upon my niece.'

'Helena is my stepsister.' There must be no misunderstandings. When Rosalind's maternal relatives learned of her presence here in town, she had no doubt her father's humble beginnings would become common knowledge. The Hillyers would not allow their position in society to be contaminated by association with Rosalind and Freddie. 'We are not related by blood.'

'I am aware of that, but I also know you have done more for Helena and her brother than many a natural sister might have in the same circumstances. I have looked forward to meeting you, for you and I have much in common and I hope—like our youthful charges—we shall find ourselves becoming friends.'

Much in common? She is a duke's daughter, a duke's sister. Whereas I...

'I should like that.' To do other than agree would be ungracious in the face of the other woman's warmth.

'I understand from Olivia that you travelled up to London today? You must be exhausted... I make no doubt you would rather be resting than being dragged here to chaperon Helena. I did offer to watch over her myself, but Lady Glenlochrie would not hear of it.' Cecily signalled to a footman. 'Bring us some wine, please.' She glanced over at the doorway, frowned, then gestured towards the knot of guests standing nearest to them. 'Come, let me introduce you to some of our other guests and then, once the dancing has started, we can find a quiet corner and become better acquainted.' She paused before adding, a touch diffidently, 'If you should care to do so, that is.'

The remainder of Rosalind's misgivings melted in the face of the other woman's uncertainty. Lady Cecily appeared warm and friendly and it would be pleasant to have a friend—an ally—in London.

Rosalind smiled at Cecily. 'I should like that very much indeed.'

Cecily's face brightened, her green eyes creasing at the corners. 'The truth is that I have not spent much time in London myself over the years and I soon become bored with the usual topics of conversation, whether that might be the latest fashions or the most eligible suitors and the size of their fortunes.'

They moved further into the room, pausing again as the footman brought their wine.

Cecily glanced again at the doorway and her lips firmed before she returned her attention to Rosalind.

'Helena has already made the acquaintance of most of the people here tonight.' She indicated a group of younger guests—Olivia and Nell amongst them—standing apart from the others present. She sipped her wine. 'Of a certainty she knows all the young people and, after all, the rest of us are of little consequence.'

'That would appear to be true,' Rosalind said, with a laugh, responding to the twinkle in Cecily's eyes. 'I do beg your pardon, ma'am, but is there anything amiss?'

Cecily's gaze snapped from the door to Rosalind, all contrition. 'I do apologise, Miss Allen. I am on the lookout for my wretched brothers. Really, it is too bad of them. Cheriton knows the party is tonight and how important it is to Olivia, yet he needs must go out of town at some perfectly ridiculous hour this morning—heaven only knows where—and has not come back.'

Rosalind couldn't help but wonder where Olivia's mother, the Duchess, might be but didn't like to ask, fearing such a question would be impertinent.

They moved again and Cecily introduced Rosalind to Lady Tubthorpe, rotund and rosy, before excusing herself, leaving Rosalind to exchange small talk.

'You must meet my daughter, Elizabeth, or Lizzie as everyone calls her,' Lady Tubthorpe said. 'She is great friends with Lady Helena. There…' She pointed to a plump young lady who was chatting to Nell and Olivia. 'There she is. Come, let me introduce you.'

As they joined Nell and her friends, Rosalind became aware of a subtle stir in the room behind her. The low murmur of conversation faded and she could see heads swivelling towards the door of the salon. Rosalind followed suit, but Lady Tubthorpe's bulk blocked her view of the door. She sidestepped at the exact moment the chatter in the room resumed, louder than ever, a suppressed air of excitement pervading the room.

Two men stood framed in the doorway.

Rosalind had eyes for only one of them.

Leo.

Chapter Fifteen

The room, its occupants, the hubbub of conversation all faded into the background. It was as though a bank of fog had rolled in, leaving a narrow tunnel with Rosalind at one end and, at the other, Leo Boyton—devastatingly handsome in black evening clothes as he stood in the open doorway of the Duke of Cheriton's salon, gazing at the room with a bored expression.

Rosalind absorbed this in a single glance before tearing her attention away. Nell, Olivia and Elizabeth—deep in conversation—seemed oblivious to the change in the atmosphere in the room. Rosalind's knees trembled as her breath caught in her lungs and her vision blurred.

'Are you quite well, Miss Allen?' Lady Tubthorpe cupped Rosalind's elbow. Her voice appeared to come from far away. 'You are exceedingly pale.'

Rosalind felt her glass of wine being removed from her unresisting grasp.

What is he doing here?

She knew she must face him at some time, but...

Please...not now. I am not ready.

She felt herself sway, her lungs burning.

Breathe! Keep breathing!

Lady Tubthorpe's anxious expression swam into focus

and Rosalind forced a smile, conscious that Nell and her friends had fallen silent and were watching.

'I apologise. It has been a long day. I am tired and I felt faint for a moment.' She retrieved her wine glass from Lady Tubthorpe and gulped a large mouthful, heedless of her manners. 'I am recovered now. I shall not spill the wine, I promise.'

Lady Tubthorpe beamed. '*Such* a relief, my dear. Now, this is my daughter, Elizabeth. Elizabeth, this is Lady Helena's sister, Miss Allen.'

The girl's plain face creased in a smile. 'I am pleased to meet you, Miss Allen. Call me Lizzie, everyone does.'

Rosalind stretched her lips into an answering smile even as her heart battered at her ribs and her knees continued to tremble. To her relief, the three girls resumed their discussion about a new hat Lizzie had purchased that very afternoon and Lady Tubthorpe soon joined in with her opinions, diverting their attention away from Rosalind. She fired another swift glance in the direction of the door.

Mayhap I am overtired and imagined him? It cannot be him.

It was.

Why would he attend a private party for young girls not yet out? She could understand the presence of the younger men, but a man of his maturity? Perhaps he wouldn't stay... unless...she recalled Lascelles's claim that Leo had a family. Was his daughter here? Worse, was his *wife* here? Bile rose to scour her throat. If only she could leave, but Leo remained in the doorway and no power on earth could persuade her to move in his direction.

She cast a casual glance around the salon. There was another door, but it was closed, and to reach it she must cross the room in full view of Leo, should he happen to look in that direction. Her courage failed her. She remained still.

She snatched another glance at the doorway, recognising Vernon Boyton at his brother's side. As she watched, he leaned towards Leo and passed a comment. Leo, who had until that moment been looking rather sombre, laughed, his gaze sweeping the room as he did so. Despite the distance, Rosalind could feel the potency of those silver eyes and a shiver of longing trembled through her. How did he still have the capacity to make her feel so...so alive? So tempted? So *needy*? She tried to summon her anger over the way he had walked away without a backward glance once he'd satisfied his lust, but all she felt was longing: for his smile, his touch, his kiss.

I am weak-willed and foolish. An utter disgrace.

If her conduct should become known, how might that harm Nell? She must—even though the very thought terrified her—speak to Leo and beg him not to expose her. If the Duke should find out, he might even forbid the friendship between his daughter and Nell, and poor Nell would be tainted along with Rosalind.

She drained her glass, her gaze glued to the two men. Lady Cecily now stood before them, her hands waving elegantly as she spoke. She grasped Leo's sleeve as she stepped closer, and he looked down into her face with an unreadable expression as he replied.

A stab of...*was that jealousy?*...wrung a gasp from Rosalind.

Then, the haughty butler who had greeted them at the front door entered the room, halting by Leo's side. Leo turned his head slightly and the butler spoke into his ear. Leo replied, then moved his hand in a dismissive gesture. The butler bowed and left the room.

Rosalind absorbed all this as though she were viewing a play on the stage and it made about as much sense to her addled brain as a play with no dialogue. Then a sharp exclamation caught her attention and Lady Olivia was hurrying across the room in a most unladylike manner. As

she reached the group by the door Lady Cecily appeared
to reprimand her, but Olivia simply laughed as she gracefully pirouetted before Leo and Vernon, both watching her
with indulgent expressions.

Rosalind's brain—slowly, reluctantly—began to analyse the evidence of her eyes. She sank her teeth into her
lower lip to prevent any sound escaping as speculations
and conclusions arose, one after the other, faster and faster.

Lady Olivia's physical resemblance to Leo was undeniable. If they were related that could mean his wife was
somewhere in this room. Not only that but, seeing Vernon
and Lady Cecily side by side, she could not miss the resemblance between them. Leo was far more highly con-
nected than she had ever imagined. Nausea flooded her
and a whimper escaped her lips despite her best efforts.
Nell, next to her, took her arm.

'What is it, Ros? You have gone white again. Oh, we
should never have plagued you to come tonight. It was too
much for you after that journey. Shall we leave?'

Lady Tubthorpe and Lizzie were, thankfully, now en-
gaged in conversation with a beefy young gentleman and
had noticed nothing untoward.

'No. I shall not leave. Not yet.' Rosalind braced her
shoulders and stood tall. It was time to face Leo. Putting
it off would only cause her more turmoil. It might as well
be tonight. 'I shall be fine, Nell. It is only the slightest of
headaches.'

Nell squeezed Rosalind's arm before releasing it. 'That
is a relief, for Olivia has promised to introduce me to her
papa. She was so worried he would not arrive home in time
for her party. She has told me all about him… Only imagine, Ros, having a father who is a *duke*.'

That artless comment hauled Rosalind from her thoughts.
'Why should a title make any difference? A peer is a man
like any other, only more spoilt and more privileged.'

She immediately regretted snapping at Nell. Rosalind's disdain for the aristocracy was not Nell's fault. And now she must contend with the knowledge that the man she had imagined she was in love with was related to a duke: the highest and most powerful rank of the peerage.

'Papa was not spoilt,' Nell said, quietly.

'Oh, Nell, of course he was not. He was the best of men. And both Freddie and I are eternally grateful for what he did for us. But, I beg of you, do not make the mistake of believing just because a man has a title it makes him an honourable man. And, yes…' Nell's lips had opened '…I do know you are about to accuse me of being prejudiced, but—'

Rosalind bit off her tirade as her brain, once again, scurried to catch up. Father? *Duke?* She forced a swallow through the sudden constriction in her throat and she massaged her temples.

'Did you say that the Duke has arrived?'

'Why, yes. He is over by the door with Olivia and her aunt.' Nell giggled. 'Lady Cecily will have scolded Olivia for running across the room like that. She is always saying Olivia behaves like a hoyden.'

Rosalind barely heard Nell's words as she shot another swift look at the group by the door.

'But, Nell…' she lowered her voice to a whisper '…surely…those gentlemen with Lady Cecily are Mr Boyton and his brother?'

'Mr Boyton?' Nell frowned, her lips curving in a puzzled smile. 'I do not know a Mr Boyton, but that is definitely Olivia's father. And her Uncle Vernon. Olivia *told* me.' A faint sigh whispered from her lips. 'They are both so handsome, are they not, Ros? 'Tis a pity they are so *old.*'

Rosalind choked back a horrified laugh. *Old?* She supposed they would appear old to an eighteen-year-old. Another bubble of laughter fizzed up and she clamped her lips to prevent its escape. Carefully, she moved, presenting her back to the room, and faked an absorbed examination of a group of portraits on the wall. Even they mocked her. Male and female alike, the same cast of features stared down at her impassively. She again gulped down the urge to laugh and pinched the tender skin on the inside of her arm. Now was not the time to lose control.

A *duke*! She had fallen in love with a duke. *Her!* The woman who despised the aristocracy, with their air of superior entitlement, their disdain for those of lesser birth and their outright *cruelty* in their inability to forgive transgressions.

As her wits started to reassemble, Rosalind's spine stiffened and icy rage began to pump through her veins. What a complete, gullible *fool* she had been. She had already come to terms with the fact he had deliberately set out to seduce her, interested in her only because he thought her a widow, but now…to discover he had lied to her about his *identity*…that was a more painful cut. Deeper. It slashed to the very heart of her.

She was so far beneath him in her station that he had not even viewed her as a person worthy of the truth. She had been a convenience—a common vessel upon which to slake his lust. Everything—*everything!*—had been a lie.

His concern for Susie. A lie.

His sweet words and compliments. A lie.

His promise to call upon her. A lie!

All with one end in mind. Details of each time they met flitted through her brain and revulsion for her own part in the charade fuelled more rage. She had *allowed* it to happen. How he must have laughed at her. Her disgust of him now was real, surpassed only by her own self-loathing, but she was *damned* if she would let *the Duke* know how well he had fooled her. Or how much this hurt.

What was that Nell said? Rosalind glanced sideways. Nell's attention was on someone behind Rosalind.

She heard Olivia's voice. 'Papa, this is my very best friend, Lady Helena Caldicot.'

A becoming blush coloured Nell's cheeks as she dropped into a curtsy. 'Your Grace.'

'I am delighted to meet you, Lady Helena.'

That well-remembered voice—dark, rich, sonorous— sent shivers racing up and down Rosalind's spine.

This is it.

'And this is Helena's sister, Miss Allen.'

Rosalind sucked in a deep breath, curved her lips in a gracious smile and turned.

Leo curbed his impatience at being forced to do the pretty with a gaggle of giggling ingénues and their chaperons. It was not Olivia's fault his mood was as black as it could possibly be and he had no wish to cast a cloud over her party.

Where is she?

He had woken early that morning knowing he must finally surrender to the compulsion to return to Buckinghamshire and confront the woman he had been unable to banish from his mind and, yes, his heart. He still thought about her. Constantly. He dreamt about her: the warm smile that lit an unquenchable fire in his blood, her soft skin like silk to his touch, the honeyed taste of her lips and her jasmine scent.

And the taste and the scent of *her*...the essence of woman.

But when he arrived at Stoney End, it was deserted. Not a sign of life, in the house or in the stable. She had gone and when, in desperation, he had driven to Foxbourne to ask her whereabouts, Sir William Rockbeare had already left for his daughter's house in Cheshire. No one could, or would, tell him where he could find Rosalind Pryce.

He had driven back to London with a leaden heart. No matter how many times his head told him it was for the best, his heart would not listen. He had been wrong about her motive for lying with him. If she *had* planned to trap him into marriage, surely she would not simply vanish.

And now Alex had gone missing. Again. Cecily might be convinced Alex only meant to avoid having to attend Olivia's party but, still, the news had rattled Leo. Fortunately, Vernon had offered to go back out and try to track Alex down, leaving Leo to concentrate on his daughter.

Leo pushed his troubles aside as he crossed the salon with Olivia, bubbling in her eagerness to introduce her new friend, Lady Helena Caldicot. Cecily had told him Lydney's daughter seemed a perfect friend for Olivia and Leo's first impression agreed. She was serene and well mannered, with an innocent charm that he hoped would prove a good influence on his irrepressible daughter. They certainly made a striking pair, with Olivia's beauty and Lady Helena's silvery-blonde hair and English-rose complexion. And he had not forgotten his promise to Rockbeare about this daughter of Lydney's and her young brother. He had already set Medland to making enquiries about Sir Peter Tadlow.

He barely noticed the lady with her back to him, standing a little behind Lady Helena, until Olivia introduced her and she began to turn.

His senses came alive, his nerve ends tingling at the instinctive recognition of her slender neck, with the feathery brown curls that caressed the nape, the sensitive spot below her ear, where he had delighted in kissing her, the curve of her cheek. His unguarded heart leapt with joy, but all too soon it plummeted again as he took in her expression. There was no hint of surprise in those wonderful golden-brown eyes when they met his. Her smile did not waver and there was an air of challenge about her. Those lurking suspicions reared up once more: she had not disappeared after all. She was here and, seemingly, perfectly aware of his identity.

Then Olivia's precise words registered. Allen. Not Pryce. *Miss* Allen, what was more. Not a widow. Never a widow. And she was Lady Helena's sister. And here, then, was the proof that Rockbeare *had* conspired with her. If he had not, what reason could there be for him to conceal the connection between the Lydney children, whom he had begged Leo to protect, and the so-called Mrs Pryce and her brother?

So many lies.

Since Margaret's death thirteen years before, Leo had adroitly avoided all such traps only to fall straight into one baited with a thirty-year-old country spinster.

What a bloody fool!

But there was guilt as well as fury. She had been a virgin and she was a gentlewoman. He had, in effect, ruined her, albeit unknowingly. As a gentleman, he *should* do the honourable thing and marry her, but every fibre of his being rebelled at surrendering to such a low trick. Besides, he had his family's position and his children to consider. He could not marry just anyone. He knew nothing about Rosalind Allen other than that she was a liar.

Years of experience in navigating the treacherous undercurrents of society came to his aid. He donned his ducal mantle and bowed as Rosalind dipped into a curtsy.

As she arose, she said, 'Good evening, Your Grace. I trust I find you well?'

Leo captured her gaze, as he sifted this new information. Miss *Allen*. Not Caldicot. So she was not Lydney's daughter. Perhaps she and Lady Helena shared the same mother? But, no. Had Rosalind not told him her mother had died when she was nine years old?

But how could he believe a single word she had told him?

'Mrs... I beg your pardon, *Miss* Allen.' He allowed his gaze to slide with calculated insolence over her silk-clad body to her green satin shoes and then drift up again, to her face. 'I am relieved to see you in such fine fettle following our previous encounter. The exercise clearly agreed with you.'

Her eyes flashed and she inhaled deeply, which had the effect of thrusting her chest out, the creamy expanse of her décolletage all too tempting, despite his utter rage. His fingers itched to slip inside that low neckline and explore.

'Papa! What a joke. I did not know you were acquainted with Miss Allen.'

Olivia's guileless comment jerked Leo back to a sense of their surroundings and he swallowed his bile. The accusations he longed to fling at this scheming hussy must wait until they were private. And that, he vowed, would be before the evening was out. *Miss Allen* would be left in no doubt as to what he thought of her lies and deceit.

'We met once or twice whilst I was in Buckinghamshire. Miss Allen and her brother are neighbours of Cousin Anthony.' A devil inside prompted him to add, 'We shared a most enjoyable ride the afternoon before I came home.'

Rosalind's heightened colour suggested she was all too aware of the double entendre that passed both Olivia and Helen by. Silently, he applauded her acting skills. Not by a flicker did her expression alter from one of polite interest.

'Indeed we did.' Her voice was smooth as molten honey. 'Although the ride was neither so vigorous nor so satisfying as I might have liked. I fear your father views members of the fairer sex as delicate beings unable to withstand the rigours of hearty exercise, Lady Olivia.'

Every muscle in Leo's body hardened. Before he could slap down her boldness, however, Olivia gurgled with laughter.

'I am delighted to hear you say it, Miss Allen. Papa and Aunt Cecily are constantly telling me I may not do what my brothers have done since they were schoolboys. They are allowed such freedom compared to me. It is so unfair.'

Leo's tension wound a notch tighter as Rosalind responded to Olivia's words with a sympathetic smile.

'*Ladies,*' he said, 'are expected to exhibit restrained and elegant behaviour at all times, Olivia. Remind me again, Miss Allen, what *precisely* is the familial relationship between you and Lady Helena? Lydney, I collect, was not your sire?'

'We are sisters, Your Grace.' Helena's voice quaked as she spoke up on Rosalind's behalf. 'Rosalind raised my brother and me after our mother died.'

Rosalind placed her hand on Helena's arm. 'It is all right, Helena. There is no need to leap to my defence. I am not ashamed.' Her eyes met Leo's, defiance in their depths. 'My mother married Lord Lydney after she was widowed and his lordship raised Freddie and me after my mother died. He then married Helena's mother, so Your Grace's inference that we are not related by blood is correct.'

'Your father's name was Allen? I do not recall the family.'

'My father was a soldier and *his* father was a silversmith. Your Grace will appreciate that the family did not move in your circles.'

He had said it to hurt her, to humiliate her. She had responded with dignity and pride and he, a peer of the realm, had emerged from that exchange as less than a gentleman.

'I see.' He needed to put some distance between them before he lost control of the anger roiling his insides. 'Excuse me, ladies, I must greet our other guests before the dancing commences.'

He bowed and strolled away, pretending an indifference entirely at odds with the turmoil raging in his gut. He joined the nearest group of guests and responded to their greetings by rote even as his thoughts revolved ceaselessly around his one overriding goal.

How can I get her alone?

He was no nearer a solution when the pianist signalled the start of the dancing by playing a few chords. He thrust down every thought of her as, proudly, he claimed Olivia's hand in the first dance. As other couples formed the set behind them, he allowed his gaze to roam the room. Rosalind stood aside with Cecily and the other chaperons. And then Dominic was before her, bowing, and she smilingly accepted his hand and Leo watched his son lead Rosalind into the set. Leo tore his attention from her and concentrated on the intricate steps of the dance, carefully guiding Olivia when her natural exuberance threatened to overflow and she was in danger of colliding with the neighbouring dancers.

After that first dance, he waited. His patience was finally rewarded when, after three dances—during which she smiled and talked as though she had not a care in the world—Leo noticed her speak to Cecily and then slip from the room. He followed. She climbed the stairs, a figure of elegance and poise, sheathed in green silk that accentuated the roundness of her bottom as she raised her skirts clear of her feet. His heart yearned for her, but he concentrated on her lies and his simmering fury.

She disappeared from sight, in the direction of the chamber designated as the ladies' retiring room. A quick glance around ascertained no one other than servants in sight. Taking the opportunity, Leo ran up the stairs two at a time and strode along the landing.

Allowing no time for second thoughts, he thrust open the door and walked in.

Chapter Sixteen

On the far side of the room Rosalind sat before a mirror. Mary—the maid tasked with assisting the female guests with their toilette—stood behind Rosalind, fussing with her hair. Unnecessarily, in Leo's opinion. Her hair looked perfect as it was.

Rosalind's gaze snapped up as the door clicked shut behind him. Her eyes widened and her jaw dropped as she met his gaze in the mirror. Mary glanced around and an audible gasp escaped her. She spun round to face him and dropped into a curtsy.

Rosalind frowned. 'You cannot come in here. This room is for the ladies.'

He advanced into the room. 'You think to tell me where I may or may not go in my own house? You can go for your supper, Mary,' he added, without breaking eye contact with Rosalind, 'and not one word of this, mind, if you want to keep your job.'

'No! Do not go.' Rosalind caught the maid's hand. 'Please—'

Mary snatched her hand from Rosalind's grasp and mumbled, 'Yes, Your Grace.'

She skirted around Leo and scurried from the room.

'I am hungry, too.' Rosalind stood, and took a hesitant

step in his direction, followed by another. 'Lady Cecily said supper is soon to be served. You can say whatever it is you wish to say to me then.' She took another step, but Leo did not step aside and she halted her progress at a distance of several feet, uncertainty flickering in her eyes. 'I will not stay in here with you, creating a scandal.'

'You should have thought of that before you invited me into your bed.'

Leo narrowed the gap between them. He could see her steeling herself to stand her ground but, at the last minute, she stepped back. A dull ache invaded Leo's jaw and he became aware he was clenching his teeth.

'I did not invite you into my bed.' Her voice was a breathless squeak.

'I was speaking metaphorically.'

He flicked an imaginary speck of dust from his sleeve. When he met her gaze again, her expression had changed from apprehension to narrow-eyed suspicion. Drawing on years of practice in repressing the pretensions of others— ever eager to ingratiate themselves with him merely because he was a duke—Leo looked down his nose at her and lifted one brow, in full knowledge that he would appear both arrogant and unapproachable.

Her eyes narrowed still further. 'Why are you here?'

She tilted her head, appraising him as one corner of her mouth quirked up. With a start of fury he realised she was challenging him, mocking him.

'This is *my* house,' he growled.

'I am aware this is—' she flicked her fingers '—*your* house.'

Her voice dripped sarcasm, and Leo bristled. Who the *devil* did she think she was talking to?

'What I meant was...why are you *here,* in this room?' Her hands rotated as she opened her arms wide, as elegant as a ballerina. 'Is it customary for dukes to accost their lady guests in such a manner? Why, you are no better than your cousin!'

Leo felt his lips draw back in a snarl. He curled his fingers into his palms to prevent him from reaching out... from grabbing her...from *shaking* her...

With a muttered curse, he strode across the room to stare from the window into the night, but all he could see was the room behind him, including Rosalind, reflected in the glass. She had a point. Why *was* he here? Why had he followed her? Why had it mattered so very much that he speak to her alone? The unpleasant thought hovered that he had been prompted by an urge to punish her.

'You tricked me,' he growled. 'That is why I am here. To inform you that your scheme did not work.'

'My *scheme?*'

'Your scheme to trap me into marriage.'

'*Trap* you?' Her reflection moved out of sight and he turned as she paced the room, her countenance livid. 'Why on earth would I want to trap *you* into marriage?'

'Do not think you are the first to try it. A man in my position becomes accustomed to such importunities, but I have never before encountered any lady so desperate that she would gamble her *actual* virtue.'

She halted in front of him, her eyes sparking fire as she spat her reply. 'You really believe I would stoop so low as to...?' Her chest expanded as she hauled in a deep breath. 'You forget, *Your Grace...you* lied about *your* identity. To me, you were Leo Boyton—nothing more, nothing less. Besides—' she frowned, shaking her head '—you make no sense. How could I trap you into marriage? What about the Duchess? You are in no position to speak to me of schemes—I was mortified to discover from your cousin that you are a married man.'

'Married? Lascelles said that I was married?' Leo's head was spinning.

'He told me of your son, your family.'

'I am a widower, Miss Allen, as I am sure you are aware.'

Rosalind's face was the picture of bewilderment. 'I didn't know. I didn't even know you were a duke!'

A bitter laugh escaped him. 'You really expect me to believe that? I watched you as Olivia introduced us. There wasn't the slightest sign of surprise on your face: you planned the whole thing.' In his mind's eye he saw again that hurried whispered conversation between Rockbeare and Rosalind, the furtive glances in his direction. 'As soon as Sir William told you my real identity, you couldn't wait to try and trap me into marriage. That *very afternoon*, Miss Allen.'

Rosalind's jaw dropped before snapping shut again. Her lips tightened as she heaved in a breath, swelling her creamy, oh-so-enticing breasts—and how was it they could fire his blood even now, when he was so consumed with fury?

'Why, you arrogant, contemptuous *coxcomb*! How *dare* you suggest I would plan such a thing? And what about *your* behaviour? You satisfied your lust and then slunk away without a word. No doubt a duke believes he may act as he pleases, without any regard for the feelings of those so far beneath him. I wouldn't marry you if you were the last man alive. I want nothing more to do with you.'

Slunk away? How *dare* she? He would not give her the satisfaction of explaining himself. Alex had needed him, but his son's escapades were nobody else's business.

Rosalind spun from him and marched to the door.

'Who was your mother?'

She jerked to a halt. Rotated slowly to face him. 'My *mother*? Why do you ask…?' Her upper lip curled. 'Oh, I understand. What you wish to know is—was she someone who *mattered*?'

Leo had meant exactly that, but hearing it from her lips forced him to acknowledge his own arrogance. He shoved his fingers through his hair. He could not back down now. He had his pride.

'Well?' His voice rasped in his dry throat. 'I must know who I have despoiled.'

'Why must you?' She glared at him, challenging...and then her shoulders slumped. 'It cannot make any difference.' Weariness laced her tone as all her fight appeared to trickle away. She stumbled to a nearby chair, sinking on to it as though her legs could no longer support her.

'It makes a difference to me.'

A frown carved a deep slash between her brows and her hopeless laugh huffed into the silence of the room.

'And *my* assertion that this knowledge will make no difference is of no consequence?' She bent her head. Heaved a heartfelt sigh. 'Very well. I make no doubt you will discover the truth before long, even if I refuse to tell you. If any of my maternal relatives are in town, they will ensure my full parentage—and their disowning of Freddie and me—is made public knowledge. As I said, my father was a soldier, the son of a silversmith. My mother was the daughter of Lord Humphrey Hillyer. They eloped.'

Hillyer?

'You are related to the Duke of Bacton?'

'He was my grandfather.'

Thoughts tripped over one another as Leo tried to work out how he felt at this revelation. He raked his hand through his hair again. He might not be sure of his feelings, but he was damned certain of his responsibility.

'Then your plan has succeeded.'

Rosalind stared. 'Plan? Did you not hear what I said? There was no plan.'

'Then why did you give yourself to me?'

Rosalind shot to her feet. 'My judgement of your character was clearly shockingly amiss. I was wrong about you being as bad as your cousin. You are worse. At least he was open about *his* intentions, whereas you...*you* intended exactly the same, but you achieved it through lies and deceit.'

'You talk to me of lies and deceit, *Miss* Allen? You pretended to be a widow.'

'To protect my sister. For no other purpose. I was Mrs Pryce before ever I met you.'

'You could have told me the truth.'

'And *you* could have told *me* the truth. But you did not.'

'And if I had?' Leo paced to the window and back again, to stand before her. 'If I had told you I was a duke, do you really expect me to believe you would have told me your true identity?'

She stilled, holding his gaze. 'No. You are correct. I would not have told you, but I would never have given myself to you, had I known.'

'You surely do not expect me to believe that?'

She moved her head in a slow, deliberate, negative motion, a scornful smile on her lips, and Leo fumed at her sheer effrontery.

'You really *are* insufferably arrogant,' she said. 'Not all people are dazzled by the brilliance of your position in society, Your Grace. *Some* of us set greater store by the character of a man than an accident of birth.' She thrust her face closer to his. 'I told you before and I tell you again: I want nothing more to do with you. Now, if you will excuse me, I am here to chaperon my sister and I should be with her.'

'Not so fast.' Leo grabbed her wrist. She tugged to free herself and he tightened his grip. 'You cannot expect to impugn my character and not allow me the right of reply.'

Rosalind stopped struggling and bowed her head. 'Very well. Say what you have to say, but then, please, allow me to return to Nell.'

'You are…were…a gently born virgin whom I have ruined. I am a man of honour and, therefore, we will be married—'

She gasped and began once more to struggle. 'No!'

'Oh, have no fear, Miss Allen. It will be a marriage in name only, but we *will* be married. I suggest you accustom yourself to the notion. No matter who your father was, your mother was the granddaughter of a duke and my duty is clear—'

'There is no need.' Her words tumbled out, her eyes haunted. 'My mother's family disowned her—until she married Lord Lydney—but still they have never even acknowledged my existence. No one will beat upon your door demanding you make an honest woman of me. No one but you and I know what happened. And as far as I am concerned, no one else will ever know.'

Her words should have been as welcome as rain upon a desert, but they were not. And for the first time, Leo wondered if he was mistaken. She sounded so sincere. If she was the scheming hussy he accused her of being, would she not leap at his offer of marriage? The fire of anger that had driven him thus far began to fade.

He needed time to think—time alone to work through this whirlwind of events and to understand this confusion of emotions.

'There is every need.' He held her gaze. 'We *will* be married, Rosalind. You can be certain of that.'

The man was insufferable. Did he *never* listen to what was said to him? Rosalind snatched her arm from Leo's unresisting grasp and drew herself up to her full height.

'You are too accustomed to having your own way.' *Arrogant swine!* 'Duke or not, you cannot force me to marry you. And you cannot one minute accuse me of plotting to entrap you and then in the next expect me to meekly accept the prospect of marriage to a man careless enough of my feelings to disappear without a word after…after…'

To her horror, his face began to blur. 'I must go to Nell,' she blurted out. 'She will wonder where I am.' And she stalked past him to the door.

This time he made no attempt to stop her. Outside the retiring room she paused to dash away the tears that dared to spill, wetting her cheeks. Tears of anger and frustration, she told herself furiously as she rounded the corner on to the wide landing at the head of the imposing marble staircase, where she cannoned straight into a wide, muscled chest.

'Whoa, there.'

Two strong hands clasped her shoulders, steadying her. She found herself looking up into the green eyes of Lord Vernon Beauchamp.

'Why, Mrs Pryce. Good evening.' A frown drew his brows together. 'I was not aware you were coming up to town.'

Her stomach clenched. She had forgotten the other three men from Halsdon Manor. What a tangle. It would only take one slip from one of them for it to become known Nell had fled her guardian's protection. People wouldn't care about the reason. They would simply condemn.

'It is Miss Allen.'

'*Miss* Allen?' Vernon's lips pursed in a soundless whistle. 'Pray, forgive my bluntness, but you are here tonight because…?'

Rosalind lifted her chin. 'I am here to chaperon my stepsister, Lady Helena Caldicot. I… That is… My lord… There is a very good reason why I gave a false name but… I can explain… I *will* explain… Just…'

She cast an anxious glance over her shoulder. The door to the ladies' retiring room remained closed. It could only be a matter of time, though, before Leo—

'Just not at this moment in time, am I correct?'

She smiled shakily. 'Thank you. Yes. And, in the meantime, I beg of you…please forget you ever knew me as anything other than Miss Allen.'

Somehow, she realised, she must also speak to Mr Stanton and Mr Lascelles, and persuade them to keep her secret. Cold dread prickled her spine at the thought of asking the latter for any favour.

Vernon took half a step backwards and executed an elegant bow. 'Your wish is my command, ma'am.'

'Thank you.'

'Now, have you by chance seen—ah.' His gaze settled on something over Rosalind's shoulder and, this time, the tingles racing down her spine were not of dread, but of awareness. She had no need to look to know Leo had appeared behind her. Vernon's raised brows and the dawning comprehension on his face confirmed it.

'*There* you are, Leo.'

Rosalind bridled at his blatant amusement. *Now he believes we have been meeting clandestinely…which, of course, we have, but not in the way he clearly thinks… and—*

'Here I am,' Leo drawled. 'Miss Allen and I have been discussing our future.'

Vernon's brows shot up again, and if she hadn't been incandescent with rage at Leo's arrogance, Rosalind might have laughed at the sight.

'There is no "our future".' She forced the words through gritted teeth.

'Rosalind…' There was a wealth of warning in Leo's voice, which she chose to ignore. He could not dictate her life.

'If you will kindly excuse me, gentlemen, I must take up my duties as chaperon.'

'Perhaps…' Vernon pivoted smoothly on his heel and

captured Rosalind's hand, tucking it into the crook of his arm '…you will allow me to escort you downstairs, Miss Allen? I fear my brother does not take kindly to having his wishes thwarted.'

'Vernon.'

Leo's voice was a growl and Rosalind sneaked a look at him as Vernon led her resolutely to the head of the staircase. Leo's forbidding expression sent her nerves into a tizzy and she tightened her fingers on Vernon's sleeve. He looked down at her and grinned.

'Don't let him intimidate you,' he whispered.

'But…you just said…'

'That, my dear Miss Allen, was said purely to aggravate him.' They began their descent. 'He *is* accustomed to having his own way, but he is no ogre. As I'm sure you will discover in time.'

Rosalind snatched her hand from his arm. 'I have no wish to discover anything more than I already know about the Duke. I am here to chaperon Helena and I am not… not…'

In her agitation, Rosalind had halted on the stairs. Vernon stopped, too, and gently retrieved her hand to place it back on his sleeve.

'I know,' he said, soothingly. 'And I understand. He is an arrogant tyrant and you want nothing to do with him. I wonder…might it interest you to know that Leo took a trip into Buckinghamshire today?'

'B-Buckinghamshire?'

'And he was not a happy man when he returned.'

'I s-see.' That meant nothing, though. He could have gone anywhere.

'In fact, according to my sister, Leo has been nigh on impossible to live with since he came back from Halsdon Manor and I doubt that's entirely due to Alexander's latest caper.'

'Oh.' A tiny ember of hope glowed into life at Vernon's words.

Alexander. Alex. That was the name Lascelles mentioned.

'Alexander is the Duke's son?'

'Yes, his second son and as different from Avon as he could possibly be.'

'Is he here tonight? I have met Lord Avon, but not Lord Alexander.'

Vernon barked a laugh. 'He is not, despite orders to attend. I've tried to hunt him down but without success, I fear.'

Rosalind found herself torn between questioning him further and the stubborn refusal to reveal any further interest in the subject. Curiosity won.

'Mr Lascelles mentioned that the Duke was called back to London unexpectedly because of Lord Alexander. I do hope it was nothing too serious.'

Vernon's jaw cocked to one side and, above, his green eyes twinkled. 'No. It was nothing too serious. Or at least, nothing Leo could not remedy, once he tracked him down.'

Rosalind lifted her brows in query and he cupped her elbow and steered her away from the other guests before continuing, 'Silly chump went into hiding after a…shall we say, a difference of opinion with Leo's secretary over a matter of finances. It is all resolved now, however.'

The dance had finished and, after declining Vernon's offer to partner her for the next, Rosalind wandered over to sit with the older married ladies, presuming that even Leo would be unlikely to accost her in their presence. She had much to think about and the remainder of the evening passed in a blur of confusion and surreptitious observation of Leo as he played host.

* * *

It was not until she and Nell were ready to leave—awaiting their pelisses and hats in the entrance hall with several other guests—that he approached her.

'Miss Allen, may I beg a moment of your time before you leave?'

Conscious of heads turning in their direction, Rosalind could not refuse. Leo gestured towards an area where they could not be overheard and Rosalind, with as much grace as she could muster, walked ahead of him.

As soon as they were out of earshot of guests and servants alike, Leo said, 'We need to talk. I shall call upon you at Lady Glenlochrie's house at noon tomorrow.'

'We have nothing more to say.' Her unthinking rebuttal prompted a firming of those sensual lips. Her gaze fixed on them…remembering…stirring a cauldron of longing, excitement and fear deep within.

'Rosalind…'

His deep voice and the wealth of resolve she detected in that one word sent a wave of pleasurable anticipation rippling right through her, the resultant shiver prickling her skin. She swallowed and tore her gaze from his mouth to focus on the dark sapphire pin that nestled within the perfect folds of his neckcloth.

'I shall call upon you and we will talk. I expect you to be there to receive me. Twelve noon.'

He had moved closer, crowding her. His body shielded her from the eyes of the people at the front door and she shivered as he trailed one finger down the bare skin of her arm, to the scalloped edge of her evening glove. The musky scent of his cologne, with its remembered undernotes of orange and cinnamon, pervaded her senses, catapulting her back in time to that afternoon in the shepherd's hut. A lump formed in her throat and she swallowed past the pain.

'I cannot,' she breathed. 'I cannot.'

'Then you must tell me why.'

His voice was a comforting rumble. His caressing finger continued to stroke her arm discreetly, making its hairs stand on end. She heard his breathing quicken.

'You must make me understand what there is to fear, Rosalind.'

Longing intertwined with doubts deep in the pit of her stomach as his eyes searched hers.

'You are only pressing me because you cannot abide being gainsaid,' she whispered. 'You do not...you *cannot*... wish to marry me. And I cannot marry a man who—' She choked back her words and averted her face.

'A man who...?'

Rosalind shook her head.

'I shall persuade you. Tomorrow. There is nothing to fear. And you are not to worry about my cousin or Lord Stanton. I shall make sure they are aware of your real name. They will not spread gossip.'

'*Lord* Stanton?'

'Ah, yes...he is an earl, I'm afraid.' Another thing he had omitted to tell her. 'Until tomorrow then. At noon.'

He turned from her and the spell was broken. They rejoined the others, Rosalind resolutely ignoring Nell's questioning look as her thoughts whirled.

In the carriage, as soon as the door had been shut by the Duke's footman and before it was in motion, Nell said, 'What did the Duke say to you, Ros?'

'He merely wished to explain why he introduced himself as Mr Boyton in Buckinghamshire.'

Nell settled back against the squabs. 'Is that all? Olivia told me he often travels as Mr Boyton. He is Viscount Boyton, you know. It is one of his minor titles. She said ladies are always in pursuit of him because he is a duke, so sometimes he likes to be anonymous.'

Another one of the barriers Rosalind had erected against Leo crumbled. She now knew why he had given her a false name, why he had left so suddenly and also—and it was this that fanned that little glow of hope until it burned with a small but steady flame—that he had gone back to Buckinghamshire.

But it did not change the fact he was a duke and she an utter nobody.

Nell suddenly sat upright with a gasp, jerking Rosalind from her thoughts.

'He must have known you by the wrong name, too, Ros. Oh, what fun. I cannot wait to tell Olivia.'

'Nell! You must not mention it to Olivia. We must take care not to fuel even the slightest gossip about our time at Stoney End. The fewer people who know I removed you from your guardian, the better.'

'You did not take me, Ros. We agreed we must leave. We had no choice.'

Rosalind sighed. 'We may know that, Nell, but there will be those who will delight in making mischief for us, such as my Hillyer relations. They will not hesitate to distance themselves from Freddie and me, and what better way to achieve that than by denouncing our actions and, thus, our characters? *Your* character and reputation will be tarnished by association and that will not help in your search for a husband.'

'Olivia will stand by me. She will not listen to such tittle-tattle.'

It was true. A little of the burden eased from Rosalind's shoulders. Association with the Duke of Cheriton and his family would do much to protect Nell against spiteful gossip and rumours. For the first time that evening, Rosalind found herself grateful for Leo's position in society...but only because it might secure her beloved sister's future.

Chapter Seventeen

The following morning Leo sat down at his desk early in the hope that dealing with the mountain of correspondence that had piled up since he dismissed Capper, his secretary, would distract him from Rosalind and their forthcoming interview.

Interview? Conversation!

He scrubbed an impatient hand through his hair. Interview, indeed. What was he thinking? That he would set out a list of requirements for his Duchess and tick them off one by one?

An unsettled night, passed in the company of several glasses of brandy, had left him tired, crabby and feeling uncomfortably vulnerable.

Can I trust her? Am I about to make a huge mistake I will live to regret?

He shoved his chair back and paced over to gaze unseeingly from the window, bracing his arms against either side of the frame.

What was the alternative? Let her go? The very idea of losing her again shook him to the foundations of his soul. How had he moved from bitter blame—believing the very worst of her and her motives—to this…this *neediness*? It went against every rule by which he had led his life since

Margaret's death. But that sleepless night had resulted in one huge, shocking insight: he was in love with Rosalind Allen. He was willing to risk, once again, trusting a woman. He would no longer allow Margaret and her lies and infidelity to sour his chance of happiness with another woman. Another wife.

In the first few seconds after Rosalind had turned to greet him last evening, a calming peace had flooded through him. And then his defences had rolled into place, that voice of doubt in his head reawakening all his old suspicions. His honour drove him to offer marriage and it was only her stubborn refusal to accept the inevitable that had convinced him to re-examine his distrust and begin...hesitantly, *fearfully*...to believe he might be mistaken.

He pushed away from the window with a derisive snort. Fearfully, indeed. It was fortunate nobody other than he could read his thoughts. The idea of anyone getting a sniff of such weakness sent a judder down his spine. He crossed his study to his desk and stared down at his correspondence. Damn Capper. If only he had not refused Alex the monies to pay off his gaming debts, Alex would not have gone into hiding, driving a frantic Cecily to beg Leo to come back to London. Leo would not have left Rosalind without a word and he would still have a secretary.

Perhaps he should put Alex to work on this lot... Leo straightened, a solution suddenly presenting itself to him.

Freddie! Perfect!

It would solve Leo's immediate problem and, hopefully, demonstrate to Rosalind that his intentions—contrary to his threat of a marriage in name only—were honourable and that he would take care of her family.

He glanced at the clock on the mantelshelf. Eight o'clock. Still four hours to wait and too early to call upon Lascelles or Stanton. He strode to the door and sent a message to the mews to saddle Conqueror and have him brought round.

A ride in the park at this quiet hour was exactly what was called for.

Even the weather had brightened. From the grey drizzle of the past week, this day had dawned clear, with barely a cloud to mar the pristine blue of the sky. The sun still hung low, but the temperature was definitely on the rise. Spring, with all its promise, was in the air. Leo trotted Conqueror along Upper Grosvenor Street to the Grosvenor Gate and through it into Hyde Park. He turned the horse's head to the south and allowed him to break into a canter.

Half an hour later, Leo reined Conqueror to a halt at the sight of a rough-haired, fawn-coloured hound lolloping across the grass near to the Serpentine. There surely could not be another dog that size in London. He stood in his stirrups and scanned the park—almost empty at this time in the morning apart from a few grooms exercising their masters' horses. There: emerging from the far side of a clump of bushes, was Rosalind, clad in an ankle-length amber pelisse and matching bonnet, a maid by her side. Leo grinned, picturing her disgust when told she must not venture out unaccompanied. In London society a lady did not walk alone, particularly in a public park.

Hector bounded up to Leo, who curbed Conqueror's first impulse to gallop away. Once he had his horse under control again, he looked up to see Rosalind now headed in his direction. Hector, seeing this, whirled in a circle, then galloped back to Rosalind, tail waving like a flag. Leo dismounted, pulled Conqueror's reins over his head and walked to meet her. Rosalind hesitated, then spoke to the maid, who dropped behind her, out of earshot.

Perhaps Rosalind, too, had calmed down over night? Had the shock of meeting again driven her, too, to say things she did not mean? Or was this meeting destined to be as fractious as that of yesterday evening? A flash of insight suggested that instead of dictating their future—as was his natural inclination—perhaps he might behave more as Leo Boyton rather than the Duke of Cheriton.

'Good morning, Your Grace.'

Rosalind halted several paces away. Hector trotted over to Leo and pushed at his gloved hand to encourage Leo to fondle his ears.

'Good morning, Miss Allen. I am surprised to see you out walking so early after your late night.'

She smiled and his heart turned over in his chest. There was a hint of apology in that smile.

'And I, you.' She came closer. 'I spent a restless night.'

He smiled ruefully. 'As did I.' He crooked his arm. 'Would you care to walk with me?'

'Thank you. Yes.'

She placed her gloved hand on his sleeve and they began to walk, Conqueror plodding quietly on Leo's other side. A quick glance over his shoulder confirmed the maid maintained a discreet distance, but her eyes bulged with curiosity.

'We need to talk about—'

Rosalind fell silent as Leo covered her hand with his, gently squeezing her fingers.

'Hush. The sun is shining and the birds are singing. May we not just enjoy our walk and these beautiful surroundings?'

'Very well.' Her doubt was audible. After a short pause, she said, 'But, after last night, I did want to say—'

His hand still covered hers and he squeezed again. 'And *I* wish to say that, at this moment, I want nothing more than to haul you into my arms and kiss you until you are breathless.'

She gasped and her fingers tightened on his sleeve. A sidelong look revealed a wash of pink colouring her cheeks. 'Y-you cannot say such a thing.'

'Can I not? I thought I just had. After everything we have shared, are we to pretend a mere casual acquaintance even in private conversation?'

A smile trembled on her lips. 'Perhaps not. But do not think I am ignorant of your quite blatant attempt to distract me.'

'Was it successful?'

She pursed her lips and a dimple appeared in one cheek. He had missed that dimple.

'Somewhat,' she said. 'But I do wish to…'

'Hush,' he said again but, this time, she continued to speak.

'Please allow me to finish.'

Leo inclined his head. He could not continue to press her into silence if she was determined to have her say. He only hoped they could discuss whatever was on her mind without it becoming a clash of wills. She was one of the few women of his acquaintance who did not hesitate to disagree with him if her opinion differed from his. It made a refreshing change from those women who, in their eagerness to curry favour, would agree with him if he were to assert the sun was green.

'My apologies. Please continue.'

'Thank you. It is about Susie. I dare say you have forgotten all about her, but I think it only right I should tell you what I have decided about her future.'

'I confess she slipped my mind last night, but I had not completely forgotten her. When I…'

He paused, his instinct to conceal any hint of weakness coming to the fore. But had he not sworn to be Leo Boyton today, and not to hide behind the invincible, infallible guise of the Duke of Cheriton? He must be truthful, however much the very idea shook him.

'I returned to Buckinghamshire yesterday. To find you.' His voice cracked at the remembered pain when he had arrived at Stoney End and found it deserted. 'Afterwards, I did wonder what had become of Susie. Do I understand she is still with you?'

'She is.'

'What did the vicar discover about her?'

They had reached the banks of the Serpentine and they strolled along its bank as Rosalind's voice revealed her anguish for Susie as she narrated the little girl's history.

Poor child. Destined to suffer because of her father's sins. At least my uncle did not disown Lascelles, even if he did refuse to wed his mother.

'I shall speak to my son, Avon,' he said to Rosalind after she completed Susie's story. 'He is a patron of Westfield, that orphan asylum I told you about, and I am sure—'

'No!'

Leo halted and raised a brow. Conqueror took advantage and lowered his head to nibble the grass.

Rosalind flushed. 'I am sorry. I did not mean to be brusque. I must tell you… I have decided to raise Susie myself and to give her an education. I cannot bear the thought of her going into service. She… It is not her fault her father was a scoundrel.'

Her feelings about Susie echoed his own, but, as for her plan to raise her…

'You are mistaken if you believe she will be happier in our world,' he said. 'If her birth becomes known, she will be ostracised.'

'Our world? There is no such thing. She will not be of *your* world, but of mine,' Rosalind said.

'And if it should become our world?'

Rosalind set off again, at an angle across the park, away from the water's edge. Leo pulled a reluctant Conqueror's head up and followed. He caught her up several strides later, and then kept pace.

'I gave you my answer last night,' she continued. 'There

is no need for us to marry. No one will ever know what happened.'

'And if there are consequences to our lying together? Will you be happy bringing another Susie into this world?'

She halted. 'Then mayhap I shall have to think again. But I shall never be happy in this world. I do not belong here.'

'You arrived in London only yesterday. How do you know how you will feel in another week? Another month?'

She raised a sceptical brow, her eyes bleak. 'I *know*.'

Her voice carried such conviction he had to believe her. Or at least, he must accept that *she* believed what she said was fact.

'Allow me the chance to make you happy,' he said. He would do all in his power to change her mind.

Her eyes dulled before her lids lowered, masking her thoughts. 'I cannot.' More conviction, but tinged with regret. Leo took heart.

'If it wasn't for your maid, I would take you in my arms right now and kiss you.'

'Then for the first time I appreciate Lady Glenlochrie's insistence that I should not walk in the park unaccompanied,' she said, her smile wry.

'And a kiss is not all I desire, my sweet Rosalind.'

Pink tinged her cheeks and her breathing quickened, igniting his blood. Their path had led them alongside a clump of shrubs to their right and the empty park stretched away to their left. A quick look affirmed that the maid had halted several yards behind them.

Leo lowered his voice. 'That afternoon is seared into my memory, sweetheart. *You* are seared into my memory and on to my soul: your image, your scent, your taste.

'We belong together and sooner or later you will accept the truth of it.'

She stared up at him, wide-eyed, seeming not to notice as he surreptitiously nudged Conqueror around so the horse's body blocked them from the maid's view.

'You are exquisite, my darling Rosalind…' Swiftly, he cupped her chin and bent his head to hers, capturing her lips.

Her gasp took his breath and he seized the chance to explore the sweet heat of her mouth as she swayed towards him, her luscious curves pressing against his chest. He should not succumb, he knew. He should have a care of her reputation, just as she—though her gold-brown eyes were at this moment soft and dazed—should have a care of her sister's good name. Shielded as they appeared to be, this was still a public park and the town was full of eager gossips.

Sweet Lord! How I want her!

He struggled to regain control of both his mind and his body. Using every ounce of his mental strength, Leo tore his mouth from Rosalind's, almost panting with the effort required. He held her by her upper arms and supported her until he was sure her legs would not buckle.

'That,' he whispered, 'is why you *will* be my Duchess.'

An inarticulate cry erupted from her lips and, in the swiftest of changes, Rosalind stiffened, her expression hard. 'No.'

That one swift word—so resolute—winded him, robbing him of speech. He could do nothing but stare as Rosalind pulled away from him.

'Bessie! Come. His Grace has recalled an urgent appointment and it is time you and I returned home.'

Bessie was still out of sight, behind Conqueror. Leo grabbed Rosalind's arm.

'Why? You owe me an explanation.'

She stared at him, cool as the Serpentine on a winter's day. 'I owe you nothing.'

'I shall call on you at noon. As arranged.'

'There is nothing more to discuss.'

Stubborn, infuriating woman!

'Quite apart from our own future, we have yet to come to an agreement about Susie's. You should at least visit Westfield before making such a momentous decision. The decision to raise a child you know nothing about is a serious one.'

'I have experience of raising children, Your Grace, and I will not abandon Susie to some…some *institution*.'

Rosalind tilted her chin, spun on her heel and marched away, Bessie trotting along in her wake. Hector—who had been foraging in the bushes—emerged and bounded after them, leaving Leo to wonder how the hell that had gone so very wrong. His former sense of well-being had dissipated and he rode back to Beauchamp House plagued by uncertainties.

Why was she so adamant she would not marry him? It made no sense. She had given herself to him. That kiss proved she was not indifferent and she could not deny the material benefits of marrying him. Did she distrust him? He sifted through ideas to prove to her that she could trust him and rely upon him. He would visit Lascelles and Stanton, as he had promised, and then…more than ever, he was convinced the way to her heart would be through her family.

As soon as he arrived home he would send for Medland and find out what he had discovered about Sir Peter Tadlow. And, later, he would speak to Freddie and offer him the role as his secretary—he knew in his bones that bored young man would leap at the opportunity.

Her insistence on raising Susie might prove more of a problem, however. His determination to wed Rosalind—driven equally by love and honour—did not mean he would meekly agree to a course he believed to be wrong. He would reserve judgement until after he had seen the child again and he would persuade Rosalind to visit Westfield and see the place for herself. Ultimately, if he agreed to raise Susie, then the child would become a member of his family and *no one* in society would then dare to cut her.

Cheered by the prospect of taking action, he handed Conqueror over to a footman to take round to the mews and ran up the steps to his front door. Rosalind would soon see he was neither as arrogant nor as untrustworthy as she appeared to believe.

Chapter Eighteen

Rosalind's first instinct was to be anywhere but at home when the clock struck noon.

Arrogant, interfering man! Who does he think he is, giving his orders and meddling in my life when it is none of his business?

But common sense and practicality eventually prevailed. If she antagonised Leo, it might set him even more against her plan to keep Susie and could prompt him to disapprove of the friendship between Nell and Olivia. Twelve o'clock, therefore, found Rosalind sitting with Susie in the drawing room, awaiting Leo's arrival, her insides twisting with nerves. She could not get used to his high position in society. Leo, a *duke*! She had forgotten that fact this morning, distracted by his kiss, until his alarming declaration that she *would* be his Duchess. Now, with the benefit of quiet contemplation, she found it hard to believe he was still willing to wed her despite her father's humble beginnings, even though a proud voice inside her head insisted on reminding her that Leo seemed not only *willing* to wed her, but actually eager to do so.

You are seared into my memory and on to my soul.

That came very close to declaring his love. And, oh,

what if it were true? His feelings for her…about her…were vital: she could not bear to be wed out of duty.

And yet…

Mama and Papa must have loved one another once, to take that drastic decision to elope. Love had not endured in their case: unable to survive their different expectations of life, it had disintegrated into indifference and even dislike in Rosalind's recollection of her childhood.

And what of her responsibilities: to Jack, still only fourteen, to Nell, to Freddie and, now, to Susie? The voice of reason reminded her that, if she wed Leo, she would be in a much stronger position to help them all—unless, of course, Leo happened to disagree with her over how to help. The ultimate decision would be his. Not only because he was a duke, but also because of his sex.

And what if Leo grew to regret shackling himself to a wife of lowly birth? He had been quick to believe the worst of her last night. It was not only Susie who would risk being ostracised. She glanced fondly at the child, laboriously copying a sampler given to her by Lady Glenlochrie, her tongue emerging between her lips as she plied her needle. How would Leo look at Rosalind once her poisonous aunts became aware she was in London and would be attending many of the same balls and parties? The gossip would fly through the *ton* and people would view Rosalind with either pity or contempt.

Restless, she stood and crossed the room to the window, which overlooked the street. A carriage, with a painted crest upon its door and driven by a uniformed coachman, pulled up outside the house and Rosalind's stomach performed a slow, sickly somersault. She was no nearer deciding what she would say. Or how she should behave. Was it time she capitulated, or would she live to regret not listening to that sixth sense of hers, the one that clamoured at her to run?

A hand crept into hers, jerking her from her thoughts.

'Why are you sad?' Susie looked up at Rosalind, her eyes huge with worry. 'Have I got to go back home?'

Rosalind crouched down and hugged the girl to her, marvelling at how far she had progressed—in appearance, behaviour and speech—since that day they had found her cowering in the corner of that store, terrified and half-starving. 'No, Susie. You do not have to go anywhere. Your home is here with us.'

And just let anyone *try to take her away.*

The sound of a throat being cleared attracted her attention. Keating, the butler, peered down his nose as Rosalind released Susie and regained her feet, keeping hold of her hand. Let him disapprove! Only then did she see Leo behind Keating. Would he be as judgemental as the butler? She did not care. She stiffened her spine and regarded the butler down her own nose.

'Yes, Keating?'

The Duke of Cheriton. For you, miss.' Disbelief coloured his every word.

'Thank you, Keating. Please ask Lady Helena to join us here.'

She had warned Nell her presence would be required to sit with Rosalind when the Duke called, causing Nell some amusement at the idea of chaperoning her own chaperon. She had also been desperately curious as to the reason for Leo's visit, but Rosalind had told her, with some truth, that it was in order to discuss Susie's future. Nell could also occupy Susie whilst she and Leo talked.

Leo strolled into the room, filling it with his presence, but before Rosalind could even greet him, Susie tore her hand from Rosalind's and hurtled across the room, her brown curls bouncing in a cloud around her head. 'Mr Boyton! Mr Boyton!'

Rosalind froze but Leo caught Susie under the arms and swung her around.

'Susie! What a surprise, meeting you here.'

'I live here now. With Miss Allen and Mr Allen and Lady Glenlo-loch…and Lady Helena and Penny and—'

'Yes, yes, poppet. I believe I understand the gist of it.' His silver-grey gaze sought Rosalind's, his smile sending a warm glow right through her. 'You live with lots and lots of people. And are they kind to you?'

He plopped her on to the floor, where she bobbed up and down, keen to keep his attention.

'Yes! And I eat a *lot* and no one says that is enough and no one steals it from my plate and—'

'And I think it is time to calm down, Susie.' Rosalind ruffled the little girl's curls. 'Lady Helena is coming to sit with you whilst I talk to the Duke…er, Mr Boyton.' Susie stared up at Rosalind. 'And do you remember what Lady Glenlochrie told you about speaking more slowly so you can hold a proper conversation with adults?'

Susie nodded.

'Good girl.'

'She has improved beyond all recognition,' Leo murmured as Nell entered the room, distracting Susie. 'You have worked very hard with her.'

He and Nell exchanged greetings, then Nell took Susie to sit by the window whilst Rosalind and Leo crossed to sit on the sofa where they could talk without interruption.

'It did not take much effort on my part,' Rosalind said. 'She is eager to please and receptive to lessons in good manners, although she is, as you have seen, a little over-exuberant at times.'

Tension once more held her in its grip. If Leo repeated his belief Susie should go to the orphan asylum, would she, Rosalind, really be able to withstand the decree of a duke? His expression gave nothing away. Which man was he today? Leo, the gentle, teasing man she had fallen in love with, or was he the powerful Duke of Cheriton, accustomed to having his every whim obeyed?

'I have been thinking over our earlier conversation,' Leo said. Rosalind held her breath. 'Now I am reacquainted with Susie, I understand your eagerness to help her but, before we make the final decision, I should like to take you to Westfield, so you may see the place for yourself. You will see that the children there are happy and well cared for.'

'I do not need to see the place. Any child, surely, must be happier raised in a home, and with a family, than in an institution, no matter how well run.'

'But you do not consider the happiness of a child raised in a world that does not forgive illegitimacy?'

'I shall protect her. She *will* be happy.'

Leo shook his head even as one corner of his mouth quirked up.

'You are an obstinate woman, Rosalind. I have not said no.'

'But it is not for you to grant permission, Your Grace. The decision is, surely, mine?'

Far from being angry at her opposition, his eyes danced with delight. He reached for her hand and enfolded her fingers in his. 'It *will* be your decision, Rosalind. I simply wish you to be acquainted with all the facts before you make it.'

He then remained silent, watching Nell and Susie sitting together at the other end of the room, his expression giving away none of his thoughts. Rosalind took the opportunity to study his profile. There was an ageless strength in his features that projected power and nobility, together with an unquestioning acceptance of his birthright: his influence in society and his place in the world. It was that innate assurance that had attracted her to him at first meeting, but his boldness that morning in stealing a kiss from under the eyes of her maid had shaken her. She had enjoyed his kiss, but his sheer audacity in manipulating the scene to his advantage—that spoke of a man accustomed to getting exactly what he wanted.

Did he even know what it was to be filled with doubt and fear and insecurity?

He was the Duke of Cheriton.

He was a stranger.

But…she remembered Leo Boyton, and their time together. That man, surely, was still somewhere inside the Duke. If she were to agree to wed him she must ensure she could find Leo Boyton again—that he had not been created for the sole purpose of seducing her.

After a time that seemed like an eternity, Leo's chest rose as he inhaled. He released his breath with a sigh.

'Susie is not the only matter I have considered since we met in the park. Our meeting last night was a shock for both of us. May we agree to view last night's exchanges as words uttered in the heat of the moment, to be forgiven and forgotten?'

His silvery eyes met hers and she felt again that tug of connection, deep down inside, as their gazes fused.

'Yes.' Her throat was dry and she wished she'd had the foresight to ask Keating to send in refreshments. 'I agree.'

He smiled. 'We belong together, sweetheart. This morning's encounter only served to strengthen *my* conviction, but I cannot deny your reluctance.'

He circled her palm lazily with his thumb. Rosalind forced herself to concentrate on his words and away from the sparks of desire shooting up her arm and heating her body, tightening her skin.

'Last night and again this morning you said, "I cannot". You did not say no. You did not say "I will not". *I cannot.* Why can you not marry me, Rosalind? I know you are not indifferent to me. Tell me what you are afraid of and I will banish your fears.'

So full of self-confidence: an intrinsic part of him, but the trait that also made it hard to confide in him.

Uncertainty held her tongue.

'Well, I shall not press you for your answer.' Leo stood, towering over her. 'You have only just arrived in town and everything must feel strange. I will give you time to think over what I have said. You need time to adjust and I hope you will come to see that I only have your best interests at heart. I shall see you soon.'

He bowed to Rosalind and again to Nell, and left the room, leaving Rosalind's head spinning with indecision. She sent Nell and Susie upstairs to visit Lady Glenlochrie and used the quiet to try and decide whether her feelings for Leo were enough to overcome her fear of such an unequal marriage and her distaste for the society he represented. *He* showed no hesitation over their different places in society, so why did she waver? It did not follow that, because one such marriage had been unhappy, every such union would suffer. Had she allowed her anger with her maternal relatives and, more recently, Sir Peter Tadlow and his cronies to sour her opinion of all aristocrats? After all, Step-Papa had been kindness itself to her and Freddie, even after their mother died. Nell and Jack's mother had accepted them and even Leo's family did not appear to think any the worse of her.

Perhaps her long-held prejudices were wrong.

Half an hour later, the door opened and Freddie limped into the room with Hector at his heels. Her brother's cheeks were flushed above a huge grin. When had she last seen him so excited? She sent him a quizzical look.

'Ros! You will never guess what has happened.'

His delight was infectious and Rosalind put aside her troubles. 'No, I dare say I never shall. Will you tell me?'

'The Duke asked to see me after he left you. Ros…he

needs a secretary and he offered *me* the position!' He struck a pose. 'I am now employed by the Duke of Cheriton. Oh, I still cannot get used to calling him that. Is it not strange we were befriended by such a high-born aristocrat and yet we had no idea of it?'

Rosalind stared. 'Employed? By the *Duke*? Is this a jest?' She pressed her hands to her stomach in a futile attempt to quell the turmoil within. 'You have no need to work, Freddie. Step-Papa left us both enough income to live comfortably.'

'Stuff living comfortably! Just think. I shall be privy to all manner of information. Cheriton sits in the Lords, you know. And he said that if I am interested in politics and show an aptitude, I could become a Member of Parliament. What do you think of that, Ros? Your brother, a Mem— Ros? What is it? You've gone very pale.'

Hot tears scalded behind her eyes, but Rosalind forced a smile, shaking her head.

'I thought you would be pleased for me, Ros.' Freddie sat beside her, and clasped her hand in both of his. 'You know how bored I have been. I know we have enough income from the trusts Step-Papa set up, but it is not about the money. I will finally have some purpose to my life.'

What about me?

She longed to scream the words, to use the air that was trapped in her burning lungs to power her protest into the atmosphere, but she swallowed both words and emotion down. She could not dampen Freddie's joy by revealing the panic that enveloped her, banishing any hope for the future from her heart. *Her* future which—whatever happened to Nell and Jack—had always included Freddie.

You are being a hypocrite. Not ten minutes since you were contemplating marrying Leo. What of Freddie then?

Freddie would have come with me. I would never have left him.

But he will be with you now, if you do marry Leo.
And if I do not? What will happen then?

Her options had shrunk alarmingly with this news.

'Of course I am pleased for you,' she said. 'It was something of a shock.' A ray of hope flickered. 'Is your employment to be temporary, whilst we are in London?'

'I should say not! It is a permanent post, Ros. And I am to live at Beauchamp House whilst the Duke is in town and at his estate in Devonshire when he goes to the country.'

He has stolen my brother from me.

Anger stirred as Rosalind's scurrying thoughts slowed and steadied. How *dare* Leo come here and break her family apart? Was this his way of ensuring she accepted his offer, by enticing Freddie away with an offer he could not refuse? He *knew* how close she and Freddie were. Freddie needed her. No one could care for him like she did. She had been as a mother to him, not a sister. But as quickly as that anger flared, it fizzled out again. She loved Freddie. She wanted him to be happy. And he was. She must accept what had happened, but that did not mean she had to be happy about the *way* it had happened. Why, Leo had not even had the courtesy to mention his plan to her, let alone discuss it.

Did she not have a right to know? Was this what she might expect if she accepted his offer of marriage? A future of arrogant, high-handed decisions made without reference to or consultation with anyone? With *her*?

She smiled at her brother. Her questions and resentment were for Leo, not him.

'It sounds very exciting, Freddie. When do you start?'

'Immediately. I'm off to tell Nell and Lady G, and then I shall pack my valise. Cheriton is sending his carriage for me at two.'

Chapter Nineteen

The Lydney carriage deposited Rosalind and Nell, together with a footman to carry their purchases, outside Grafton House on the corner of New Bond Street and Grafton Street. The pavement was thronged with pedestrians, the road itself crammed with all manner of vehicles, from elegant carriages to lumbering coal wagons. Rosalind viewed the scene with distaste, in the mood to find fault with everything after waving goodbye to Freddie half an hour ago.

After their excitedly waving brother had disappeared from view, Nell had taken one look at Rosalind and enveloped her in a hug.

'We shall go shopping. *That* will take your mind off Freddie.'

She had refused to take no for an answer, harrying Rosalind without pause until she finally capitulated in sheer desperation.

Their first call was Wilding & Kent, where Lady Glenlochrie had commissioned them to purchase a length of Irish poplin on her behalf, as she had a fancy to have a new day dress made up. Despite her misery, Rosalind could not help but marvel at the sheer number of beautiful fabrics available to purchase. The shop heaved with customers, beleaguered shop assistants running hither and thither in their efforts to satisfy their customers' every demand.

'It appears we shall have a long wait,' Rosalind said, as she and Nell worked their way further into the shop.

Eventually, they emerged from Wilding & Kent and made their way along New Bond Street, where the crowds were mercifully thinner.

'Helena!' A round, smiling face appeared before them. 'And Miss Allen. How do you do?'

'Lizzie, what a lovely surprise.'

'Good afternoon, Miss Tubthorpe.'

As the two girls chattered, Rosalind scanned the nearby faces until she located Lady Tubthorpe, standing to one side in conversation with a stout, fashionably dressed matron. Lady Tubthorpe caught sight of Rosalind at the same time and waved her over.

'Here is Miss Allen, newly arrived in town. Allow me to introduce you. Lady Tring, Miss Allen.'

Rosalind's mouth dried and her hands turned clammy inside her gloves. This was her worst nightmare: a face-to-face introduction to her mother's eldest sister. If only she had realised whom Lady Tubthorpe had been talking to.

Her Aunt Henrietta—the Countess of Tring since her marriage—looked her up and down.

'Miss Allen?' Her gaze narrowed, flitting past Rosalind to where Nell still stood with Lizzie Tubthorpe. Her nostrils flared and she stepped back, actually sweeping her skirts aside with one hand. Lady Tubthorpe's expression changed to one of bewilderment as Lady Tring continued, 'This is an introduction I cannot accept, Louisa. Pray, excuse me.'

'Well, I am sure I cannot see any objection to Miss Allen,' Lady Tubthorpe said. 'Not when we made her acquaintance at Beauchamp House last evening.'

Her words prompted Lady Tring's eyebrows to shoot skywards.

'Lady Tring.' Nell was by Rosalind's side in an instant, dropping a curtsy. 'I trust you are well?'

Her ladyship hesitated and Rosalind took pleasure at her predicament. She could not cut Nell—Lady Glenlochrie would not take kindly to her niece being snubbed.

'Lady Helena. Good afternoon,' she said in a strangled voice.

'My dear sister, Rosalind, has come to town to chaperon me for my come-out, after my Aunt Glenlochrie broke her leg,' Nell said. 'Is that not kind of her?'

Stone-faced, Lady Tring inclined her head. At that moment, a masculine voice intruded.

'Miss Allen, is it not?'

The contents of Rosalind's stomach curdled, leaving her queasy. Lascelles. Could this day get any worse? She forced a smile as he moved to stand between Nell and Lizzie and bowed to each of the group in turn.

'I beg your pardon for the interruption, ladies, but I was unaware until earlier today that Miss Allen was in London and, having spied her from the other side of the road, I could not resist crossing over to pay my respects.'

Miss Allen. Leo must have kept his promise and warned him of my change in name.

'How do you do, Mr Lascelles,' Lady Tring said.

Rosalind stared at the warmth in her voice. It was clear both she and Lady Tubthorpe were previously acquainted with Lascelles. Rosalind performed the introduction to Nell, her brain churning.

So neither Freddie nor I are respectable enough for my aunt to acknowledge, but Lascelles, who was born out of wedlock, is perfectly acceptable?

This encounter would not have been Rosalind's choice but, now it had happened, she was unable to resist a mischievous urge to further discompose her aunt.

'Your nephew, Freddie, is also in town,' she said, facing her squarely, chin up. 'And, as of this afternoon, he is employed by the Duke of Cheriton as his secretary. Is that not splendid news?'

'*Nephew?*' Lady Tubthorpe's mouth hung open.

'Indeed.' Rosalind warmed to her role. This would teach her aunt to disown Mama all those years ago. 'My mother was Lady Tring's younger sister.'

'You must be proud of your young relatives, my lady,' Lascelles drawled. 'When my Cousin Cheriton informed me Mr and Miss Allen had come up to town, he made particular mention of their Hillyer connection and how delighted you will be to renew your acquaintance with them.'

Lady Tring turned puce under her orange turban. 'I do declare—'

'Well, of a certainty she is delighted,' Lady Tubthorpe said, looking anxiously from Rosalind to Lascelles to Lady Tring and back again. She linked her arm through that of Lady Tring. 'I do beg your pardon, but I fear we must take our leave. It has been a pleasure to see you again so soon, Miss Allen. Come, Lizzie. Say your goodbyes to Lady Helena. Good day, sir.'

She nodded at Lascelles and then bustled Lady Tring away. Lizzie, with a shrug of her shoulders at Nell, followed. Rosalind bit back a laugh as she watched them go.

'Thank you, Mr Lascelles.' It went against the grain to thank him, but he *had* done her a service. 'Your arrival proved most timely.'

'Horrid woman,' Nell said. 'I wonder that *you* did not give *her* the cut direct, Ros. And I add my thanks to my sister's, sir. That was a splendid notion, mentioning the Duke. Did you see her expression?'

'No need to thank me, ladies. It was my absolute pleasure. May I offer you my escort to your next destination?'

She could hardly refuse, but Rosalind remained wary,

their very first encounter stamped upon her memory. She pretended she did not notice Lascelles's proffered arm as they all three strolled along New Bond Street.

'Is this your first visit to London, Miss Allen?'

'It is, although my sister has been before, when she was younger,' Rosalind said. 'This is her first Season, however.'

'And I cannot wait for my come-out ball and to be presented to the Queen,' Nell said. 'Oh! *Look*, Ros. Are those parasols not *darling*?'

She darted across the pavement and almost pressed her nose against a nearby shop window. Rosalind and Lascelles followed slowly in her wake.

'If your sister's aunt is incapacitated, how is Lady Helena to be presented at Court? I assume—forgive me—that you will not be able to do so?'

'You assume correctly, sir. We are lucky in that Helena has formed a close friendship with your cousin's daughter, Lady Olivia. Lady Cecily has offered to present both girls in the Queen's drawing room.'

'Ah, Cousin Cecily. That is lucky indeed, but it is unfortunate you will be forced to miss the occasion.'

'As I expected to miss Helena's entire Season, I am not disheartened by my exclusion from that particular event.'

She paused. Should she broach such a subject? Curiosity got the better of her.

'I hope you will not object to my next question, sir, but I was puzzled that my Aunt Tring appeared more accepting of you than she is of her own sister's children.'

Lascelles laughed; a bitter sound. 'Oh, I am tolerated in some circles. Cheriton deigns to notice me and others, keen to toad-eat my cousin, follow his lead, but I do not fool myself that I shall ever be fully accepted in society.

'You and I have something in common, Miss Allen. We are condemned for ever to be on the outside looking in.'

'Except that I, for one, have no desire to be on the inside, sir. I am content with my life.'

At Nell's urging they entered the shop, where she purchased a pretty pink parasol, edged with Honiton lace.

'It is a gift for you,' Nell said to Rosalind, as she handed the package to the footman who still silently dogged their heels.

'But…Nell…I have no need of another parasol,' Rosalind said. 'I already have one and—'

'One is not enough. You cannot carry the same one every day.'

Rosalind raised her brows at Lascelles, who shrugged as he held the door open for Rosalind and Nell to exit the shop. 'Your sister is a lively young lady,' he said, low-voiced, as Rosalind passed.

Out on the street once more, Rosalind said, 'Is she *too* lively? Ought I to contain her high spirits?'

'I am hardly the person from whom to seek advice about correct behaviour,' Lascelles said. 'Particularly that of young ladies. If you feel in need of guidance, there can be no better person to consult than my Cousin Cecily.'

'We have arranged to meet her and Lady Olivia in the park later,' Rosalind said. 'I shall take the opportunity to ask her advice.'

'Speaking of my cousins,' Lascelles said, 'I was surprised to hear Cheriton had appointed your brother as secretary. I wonder what happened to Capper?'

'Capper?'

'Cheriton's secretary… Former secretary, I should say, as he is clearly no longer employed by my illustrious cousin.'

The sarcastic note in his voice as he spoke of Leo stirred a warning deep within Rosalind—within just a few short minutes she had again been in danger of forgetting this

man's true nature. How had his superficial charm so readily overridden her former caution?

'I am afraid I have no idea,' she said, as repressively
as she could.

'Nor I. One can only hope Cheriton did not dismiss
Capper merely to provide an opening for your brother. You
will miss him, I make no doubt. I trust you will not be too
lonely. I know my cousin and he will expect his secretary
to be at his beck and call at all times. Has he moved to
Beauchamp House yet?'

'He left earlier, before we came shopping,' Nell said.
'And Rosalind will not be lonely. She still has me, sir.'

'But you no doubt hope to wed, Lady Helena. Who,
then, will keep your sister company?'

'I still have Susie,' Rosalind said.

'Ah, Susie. Poor, unwanted child. I had forgotten all
about her. You have brought her with you to town, Miss
Allen?'

'I have. And she is not unwanted. She has me. The circumstances of her birth are hardly her fault.'

'Indeed not and I am delighted to hear such sentiments
fall from your lips. She is a fortunate child.'

Nell had once more stopped to examine the contents of
a shop window and Rosalind and Lascelles paused, waiting for her to catch them up.

'I do hope my cousin approves of your plan.'

'Susie is no longer the Duke's concern,' Rosalind said.

Lascelles leaned towards Rosalind, bending so his lips
were close to her ear, the smell of bay rum filling her nostrils. 'Do I detect a touch of resentment when you speak
of my cousin?'

A shiver of warning tracked across her skin.

'Resentment? Why should I resent your cousin, sir?'

'Why, he has enticed your brother away, has he not?
That cannot be an insignificant occurrence.'

'Insignificant, no, but I dare say I shall become accustomed to it. There is no need for resentment.'

The lie slid readily from her tongue, but his words revived her angst over Freddie leaving and, at Lascelles's knowing smile, Rosalind knew she had failed to conceal her distress. She marvelled at the man's ability to manipulate others' feelings.

He inclined his head. 'My mistake, ma'am.'

Nell joined them at that moment and Lascelles continued, 'I fear I have monopolised you enough, dear ladies—I know from experience that shopping is one activity at which the male of the species is distinctly de trop.' In one smooth movement, he captured Rosalind's hand and she braced herself against the impulse to snatch it away. 'Might I beg your leave to call upon you tomorrow, Miss Allen?'

His eyes were hard, even though his lips curved in a smile, reminding Rosalind of the danger of antagonising him. But she could not bring herself to give him encouragement.

'I am sorry, but I must decline, sir.' Rosalind tugged experimentally at her hand, but Lascelles did not relinquish his hold. 'My sole reason for being in town is to chaperon my sister, not to pursue my own social agenda.'

He bowed over her hand, then released it.

'But you shall not deny me, Mrs P—I mean, Miss Allen.' Those few softly spoken words sent apprehension rippling through her. 'I bid you both good afternoon.'

He walked away, disappearing around a nearby corner into a side street. Rosalind's shoulders sagged as the breath left her lungs.

'Well, I am pleased he has gone,' Nell said. A frown creased her brow. 'I am sorry, Ros, and I cannot say why, for he *seemed* polite, but there is something about that man that makes me feel...uncomfortable.'

The habit of protecting her sister was so ingrained, Rosalind shrugged off Lascelles's threat.

'Oh, he means no harm, Nell, but if he does make you uncomfortable we shall try to avoid him in the future.'

Chapter Twenty

After Lascelles left them, Rosalind and Nell returned to South Audley Street. The delights of shopping could no longer distract her—Rosalind's head was bursting with the accusations she longed to throw at Leo. As soon as they were home, Rosalind sent for Penny to accompany her to Beauchamp House.

'I wish you would not go, Ros,' Nell whispered as they waited for Penny. 'I recognise that expression. You will only say something you will later regret. Besides, you promised we would go to the park.'

'I shall be back in time to go to the park. I merely wish to speak to the Duke about—'

'About Freddie. Yes, I know. But Freddie is excited and happy, Ros. If you upset the Duke, he might change his mind and Freddie would *never* forgive you.'

'I shall be on my best behaviour, I promise.'

It was a short walk to Grosvenor Square, situated at the opposite end of South Audley Street from Lady Glenlochrie's town house.

'Good afternoon. My name is Miss Allen. I should like to speak to the Duke, if you please.'

The superior butler from the previous evening puffed

out his chest as he peered down his nose at Rosalind. 'His Grace did warn me you may call, Miss Allen.'

His tone left Rosalind in no doubt as to his disapproval and she felt Penny, standing close behind her, bristle. Really, the effrontery of the man! Although, of course, he could no doubt sniff out a commoner at a hundred paces. The thought amused her, banishing her irritation.

'Please inform him I am here.'

The butler stood aside and allowed Rosalind and Penny—who sniffed audibly as she passed—to enter. He crossed the hall with a measured tread and disappeared through a door to their left.

'A body might think *he* was the Duke,' Penny hissed.

'Shh. Someone might hear.'

But there was no one around *to* hear. The great house was still and silent: an oasis of calm in contrast to the busy square outside. Without volition Rosalind's hand rose to tuck and tidy any stray wisps of hair into her bonnet then, recalling the reason for her visit, she stopped. She would not primp and preen in deference to a man who had stolen her brother, even if he were a duke.

The butler reappeared.

'His Grace will see you in his study.'

As Rosalind and Penny began to follow the butler, he halted. 'His Grace asked that your maid wait here. He said you will not be here for long.'

Rosalind stiffened, but then a bubble of reluctant laughter formed in her chest. Leo was a step ahead of her and not for the first time. She had silently rehearsed her verbal attack during the short walk to Beauchamp House but now, if she followed her plan to ring a peal over his head and then walk straight out, she would merely prove him right. Or she could prove him wrong by lingering—and *that*, no doubt, was his intention.

As she approached Leo's study, she wished she had

heeded Nell's plea not to come here whilst her temper was still frayed. Scolding him would doubtless only serve to amuse him, but he had still stolen her brother from her without a word of warning. She would treat him with cool civility at the same time as leaving him in no doubt as to what she thought of his underhandedness.

The butler announced her and she entered a surprisingly light and airy study. She had expected a dark and masculine room, with heavy furniture, stacks of papers and an oppressive air. Instead, the walls were papered in pleasing light green and fawn stripes above light oak wainscoting. Sunlight streamed through the two tall windows.

Leo rose from his chair behind his mahogany desk, every inch the nobleman, self-assured in his domain as he came to greet her. Rosalind's heart, annoyingly, skipped a beat whilst nerves coiled in the pit of her stomach. Much as she wanted to discount his status and still treat him as Mr Boyton, she could not entirely dismiss his status and she found herself intimidated and attracted in equal measures.

'Miss Allen. Good afternoon. Please, take a seat—' he manoeuvred a chair into place so it faced his across the desk '—and tell me how I may be of assistance.'

'Good afternoon, Your Grace.' She sat. 'I wish to discuss my brother. I understand you are now his employer?'

'Ah.'

Leo returned to his own chair in a leisurely fashion. She gritted her teeth. How very provoking! She folded her hands in her lap and waited for him to speak.

'Not quite,' he said, eventually, once he had settled.

Her eyes flew to his. 'Not quite? I do not understand.'

He tipped his head to the side and gave her a benign smile that set her teeth on edge. 'Have you forgotten your question already? You said you understand I am now your brother's employer, and I replied, "Not quite".'

'So—' her brows squeezed into a frown '—Freddie is not to be your secretary after all?'

'I did not say that.'

'You are speaking in riddles, sir.'

'Your Grace,' he said softly. 'I am a duke. Had you forgotten that as well, Rosalind?'

'Your Grace.' She forced it out through her still-clenched teeth. 'And *my* name is Miss Allen.'

His lips compressed—he was trying not to laugh, the wretch.

'*Is* Freddie, or *is he not*, employed by you as your secretary?'

'Today, the answer is no. Tomorrow, it will be yes. He is settling into his quarters today and he will start tomorrow.'

'Why?' The question burst from her lips.

One dark brow rose. 'Why? Well, you must ask your brother why, but I presume he wishes to familiarise himself with the house and its occupants before he begins his duties.'

He scraped his chair back and stood up. He rounded the desk: tall, dark and imposing, radiating confidence and natural authority. He had always been thus, she realised. It had been his uncompromising attitude when he had given Lascelles short shrift that had first attracted her. And now, to discover he was a duke…the highest rank of peerage in the land…utter confusion boiled inside her.

Leo perched one hip on the desk, so near to Rosalind that his boot brushed her skirts as he swung it to and fro. She swallowed, her gaze riveted to his breeches-clad thigh. His cologne and, beneath that, his own unique scent pervaded her senses. Her breath grew short. He was so…so…

He was Leo. The man she had given herself to because she had fallen in love with him. Her heart twitched as the past…*their* past…invaded her mind. In her memory, Leo rose above her, silvery eyes dark with passion. Her skin tingled with the memory of his tender touch and her fingers tangled again amongst the coarse dark hair that covered his chest. Her lips throbbed with the remembered onslaught of those sensual lips. She felt again the safe and solid weight of his body...of Leo...as he loved her.

Her throat thickened and she tore her gaze from him. She plaited her fingers together in her lap to prevent the fidgets and concentrated on steadying her breathing.

'I wish to understand,' she said, 'why you did not deem it necessary to inform me of your intention to offer Freddie a job?'

Leo folded his arms across his chest, his gaze unwavering. Silence reigned.

'Well?'

Leo quirked a brow. 'Why I did not deem it *necessary* to inform you of my intention to offer your twenty-five-year-old brother a job? Hmm.'

'You know what I mean!' Rosalind leapt from her chair and stalked across the room to stand by a window. 'We were speaking only minutes earlier, but you did not breathe a word of it.'

'Frederick is not a boy. He is a grown man. I do not have to explain, but I shall as you appear unable, or unwilling, to understand. The reason I did not tell you...the reason I told *no one* before I made Frederick that offer is because it is no one's business but his, and—to be honest—I wished to see his reaction *without* any outside influence. He does not need his sister's permission to receive an offer of employment. I thought you would be pleased that he is so happy.'

Rosalind moved to stand at the opposite end of the desk from where Leo still perched. She pondered his words. Is that what angered her: the fact he had taken away any chance of persuading Freddie to refuse? If Leo had forewarned her, would she have tried to convince him not to make the offer and, if she failed, would she then have interfered and encouraged Freddie to refuse? Was she really that overbearing?

'It is only because I care about him,' she said.

Leo's heart went out to Rosalind, she looked so forlorn. He slid from the desk and in two strides he was by her side, her hands in his as he ran his thumbs across her knuckles.

'I know, sweetheart.' Her sweet jasmine scent enveloped him, making his blood sing and his head spin with memories. He had expected her to rip up at him and so she had begun. But her readiness to listen and to try to understand only increased his love for her. 'You will see this is for the best. Frederick needs a purpose and he needs some independence.'

'Independence from me.'

'Yes. It would be wrong of me to pretend otherwise.'

She hung her head. Leo popped a finger beneath her chin, tilting her face to his.

'There is no need for shame. You have always cared for Frederick and he knows that. Your only failure is to discount the passing of the years and the effect of that upon your brother. He is a man and is ready to make his own way in the world.'

She met his gaze, her beautiful golden-brown eyes shiny with unshed tears. One trembled on her lower lashes and Leo dipped his head, catching the salty drop on his tongue. Her gasp, innately feminine, set his pulse thundering and, helpless to resist her, he enfolded her in his arms and placed his lips on hers, kissing her, moulding her warm curves to him as his hands roamed her back and bottom. She fitted perfectly against him. She belonged in his arms. She was here, in his house, and he felt at peace. All too soon, though, the clamour of his body for more rang a cautious bell and, reluctantly, he caressed her lips one more time before ending their kiss. She gazed up at him, bonnet askew, moist lips parted, eyes dark with passion, and he fought to cling to his control. He untied her bonnet and flipped it on to his desk, then took her hand.

'You know...' He led her, unresisting, to his chair, sat down and tugged her on to his lap. She squirmed a little, then snuggled against him as Olivia used to when she was a child needing comfort. He put his arms around her, resting his cheek on her hair. 'If you would only accept me, this upset about Frederick would be immaterial. He would still be a part of your daily life.'

Her breath hitched. 'Is that why you have given him a job? To persuade me to accept?'

'No. I offered him the job because I have need of a secretary, I like your brother and he impressed me with his knowledge of Parliamentary affairs, despite never having been to London in his life.'

'What happened to your former secretary?'

'We agreed to part company.'

She leaned back against his arm and searched his face. 'Your brother told me there was trouble between him and your son Alexander.'

'There was, but it is all resolved now. You have not met Alex, have you?'

'No.'

'I tasked him with showing Frederick around the house earlier,' Leo said. 'I assume you would like to see your brother before you leave? They should be finished now. Shall we go and meet them?'

He clasped her waist and lifted her from his lap, then took her hand as they walked to the door. Leo gestured to Penny to remain seated and led Rosalind through to the staircase hall. They were halfway to the foot of the stairs— and in full view of Freddie and Alex, as they descended— before Rosalind realised what he was doing. She snatched her hand from his with an impatient click of her tongue, and Leo bit back his grin.

There was more than one way to help Rosalind reach her decision and where better to begin than raising expectations within their own families? Sitting passively and waiting for a decision—from *anyone*—was not his way.

In an unexpected bonus, Cecily and Olivia followed Alex and Freddie down the stairs. If Olivia suspected an attachment between Leo and Rosalind, she would tell Helena and Rosalind would very soon find herself affianced to Leo, whether or not she had actually said yes.

'You did that deliberately,' Rosalind hissed.

Leo spread his hands as he shrugged. 'How could I possibly have known half my household would be coming down the stairs at that precise moment, sweetheart?'

She narrowed her eyes at him. 'Do not call me sweetheart.'

'But I *like* to call you sweetheart. Come, allow me to introduce you to Alex.'

He ushered her towards Freddie and Alex, who reached the bottom of the stairs at the same time as Cecily and Olivia.

'I see you have all met Mr Allen,' he said. 'Alex, this is Mr Allen's sister, Miss Rosalind Allen. Rosalind, please meet my younger son, Alexander.'

Cecily caught his eye, her own eyes wide and questioning, and Olivia smiled knowingly, but Rosalind herself appeared oblivious to his casual use of her Christian name.

'I am delighted to meet you, Lord Alexander,' she said.

Alex bowed. 'Likewise, I'm sure. I'm givin' your brother the guided tour.' He winked at Freddie. 'Saved the best till last—the kitchen and so forth. You won't need to go there much, but at least you'll know where the larder and the wine cellar are, for midnight raids.'

Leo watched, bemused, as his normally taciturn son grinned, and nudged Freddie, who laughed.

'I suspect I might not last long in your father's employ if I indulge in schoolboy pranks,' Freddie said, 'but I should like to see them, nevertheless. And meet the rest of the staff. You go on ahead, Alex, and I shall join you in a minute. I'd like a private word with your father first, if I may, Your Grace?'

'But of course,' Leo said.

He glanced at Cecily and flicked his head to the stairs.

She nodded her understanding, smiled at Rosalind and said, 'I shall look forward to meeting you in the park directly, Miss Allen. Come, Olivia, it is time you and I changed our gowns.' And she ushered a protesting Olivia back up the stairs.

Alex had already wandered off towards the back of the house and the servants' stairs that led to the basement and Rosalind remained at the foot of the main staircase, watching suspiciously as Leo and Freddie moved out of earshot.

'Am I correct that my sister has been alone with you in your study?'

'You are indeed.' Conflicting expressions chased one another across Freddie's features. How torn the poor lad must be—so excited by his new job and yet intent on protecting his sister's virtue. Little did he realise that bird had already flown.

A slash of colour appeared high on Freddie's cheekbones. 'Do not think I am ungrateful for your offer of employment, but I must say this and if, after hearing me out, you feel compelled to withdraw that offer, then so be it.

'I have to inform you that I object in the strongest possible terms to your placing my sister in such a compromising position. I should like to know, sir, what you—'

'Freddie?' Rosalind appeared at Freddie's shoulder and she touched his arm. 'There is no harm done. I—'

'There is *every* harm done, Ros. I read the newspapers. I know all about the gossip and the tittle-tattle that can ruin a lady's reputation. Is that what you want?' He lowered his voice. 'You were alone together in his study, and the entire household is aware of it. Think how it will impact Nell. I acquit *you* of anything other than naivety, but His Grace was very much aware of the implications and… *Where is your hat?*'

Rosalind's hands flew to her hair and her cheeks blossomed pink. 'Oh!' She hurried back across the hall to the study.

'Allen,' Leo said, 'I am pleased you take your duties as a brother so seriously and you have my word I shall never do anything to harm your sister. I knew I was not mistaken in your character.'

Freddie's jaw clenched and Leo placed a placatory hand on his arm.

'My intentions are entirely honourable. It is your sister who has yet to make up her mind.'

Freddie stared at him, then at Rosalind, who had emerged from Leo's study, bonnet now firmly on her head. Leo waited for the young man to catch on to his meaning. After several seconds, Freddie visibly relaxed. His lips pursed and his eyes creased.

'Well, I wish you luck if you think to force her hand, Your Grace,' he murmured. 'Although, had you thought to ask my advice, I could have told you my sister is *doubly* resistant in the face of any form of coercion.'

'Coercion? You misunderstand, dear Frederick. I am merely helping her to appreciate that my way is the best way. Now, perhaps you would be so good as to go and finish your tour with Alex whilst I smooth your sister's ruffled feathers?'

Freddie sucked in one cheek and shook his head, grinning. He kissed Rosalind goodbye and then went to join

Alex. His scepticism did little to dent Leo's confidence. He could barely recall the last time he did not get what he wanted. One of the many advantages of being a duke, he supposed. And he wanted to marry Rosalind. The sooner she realised it was inevitable, the better all round.

'Why were you so ready to believe the worst of me?'

Leo started. What bee had she trapped beneath that bonnet of hers? 'I beg your pardon?'

'Last night,' she said. 'The minute you saw me, you believed I had set out to trap you into marriage. I want to know why. What makes you so cynical?'

Margaret's image drifted into his head. What indeed? Past experience. But he did not wish to sully his relationship with Rosalind with the memory of Margaret and her infidelities.

He forced a nonchalant shrug. 'I have come to expect attempts to either cajole or trick me into marriage. There are plenty of females in the *ton* for whom the lure of being a duchess overrides *any* other consideration.

'Now, is it not time you returned to your sister?' He cupped her elbow and steered her in the direction of the entrance hall, where Penny still patiently waited. 'You will no doubt wish to change your clothes in readiness for your outing to the park.'

Rosalind gave a puzzled smile, then glanced down at her gown. 'I do not need to change. This gown is perfectly adequate.'

Leo tutted and shook his head, pleased his distraction had worked. 'You will soon find that no lady can be expected to manage without at least four changes of clothing per day. You should prepare yourself for Lady Glenlochrie's insistence that you change your gown before walking in the park.'

'Well, that,' Rosalind said, 'seems not only a waste of

time but also exceedingly extravagant.' She halted just out of earshot of Penny. 'What about your wife?'

'My wife?' He used his most forbidding tone.

'Yes. The mother of your children. Will you tell me about her? Was it she who made you so distrustful?'

Stubborn, infuriating woman. What good would talking about it do? It was history. He had no need to discuss it. He gazed into the depths of her wide eyes, close enough to see the golden flecks in her irises, and all he wished for was to haul her into his arms and kiss her senseless.

'Not now, sweetheart. That must wait for another day.'

Chapter Twenty-One

'Papa?'

Leo tore his attention from the papers on his desk. It was Freddie's first day of work and already he had cleared much of the backlog of correspondence that Capper had left behind, leaving Leo to read through the documents and sign where required.

'Yes, Olivia?'

Leo laid his pen aside, pushed his chair away from the desk and stretched his arms above his head as Olivia crossed the study and sat down.

'You have been at your desk all day,' Olivia said. 'I thought you might like to accompany Aunt Cecily and me on our walk in the park.'

Her gaze travelled around the room with a studied air of nonchalance. Leo bit back a smile as his daughter avoided catching his eye. She was up to something.

'I am not certain I can spare the time—'

'But, Papa, you are constantly telling me how important it is to go out into the fresh air and take exercise.'

'And so it is. But I think I should prefer to ride rather than walk and have to make polite conversation with—'

'But you *must* come with us.'

'Must?'

Olivia pouted. '*Please*, Papa. It is important.'

'Then why do you not tell me why it is of such importance and allow me to judge for myself?'

A frown wrinkled Olivia's brow and her lips pursed. Leo waited.

'I *could* tell you,' she said, at length. 'After all, I only promised not to say a word to Aunt Cecily.'

Leo tensed, but forced himself to remain outwardly relaxed. The idea that anyone was encouraging Olivia to keep secrets from her aunt... All kinds of suspicions slithered through his thoughts. If he tried to force the information from her, however, she might clam up and then he would never know.

'Would it help if I promise not to tell anyone you told me?'

Relief flooded her face. 'Yes, for I should not like Helena to think I cannot be trusted, but with you and Miss Allen being such...well...*particular* friends—'

'Livvy,' he growled.

Olivia's eyes widened. 'Well, you are, Papa...and I like her, too, Papa, very much, so you need not worry...and that is why I think you should know what Helena told me, but it was in confidence and, if you will agree to walk with us in the park this afternoon, you would see it for yourself and also if Cousin Anthony makes a nuisance of himself again then you could stop him, because he listens to you even if he doesn't like you, so Aunt Cecily and Uncle Vernon say, and—'

'Whoa!'

Olivia snapped her mouth shut.

'Slow down and tell me what it is I need to see for myself. Although, first—what do you mean, Aunt Cecily and Uncle Vernon told you Cousin Anthony doesn't like me?'

Surely they would not discuss Lascelles with Olivia. His daughter caught her bottom lip between her teeth.

'They might not have told me, precisely,' she said. 'But they were speaking *very* loudly in the parlour, just as I happened to be passing, and—'

Olivia fell into silence in response to Leo's raised hand. He might have known. There was little that went on in his household that his inquisitive daughter did not know about. He stifled a sigh. Not for the first time, he wished he could turn back the clock and make her ten again. She was much easier to manage then. The thought of the havoc she might wreak once loose in society made his heart quail.

'Enough,' he said. 'I have the gist of what happened there, Olivia. Now, tell me what Helena told you.'

She eyed him for a moment. 'When you were in here with Miss Allen yesterday did she tell you about Lady Tring?'

The mention of Lady Tring set Leo's mind racing. She was the daughter of Sir Humphrey Hillyer and, therefore, Rosalind's maternal aunt.

'No.'

'Helena said they met Lady Tubthorpe when they went shopping and she was with Lady Tring, and she was nasty to Miss Allen—Lady Tring, that is—and then Cousin Anthony came up to them and she had to be...well, less nasty...and then Miss Allen felt obligated to Cousin Anthony and he escorted them along Bond Street and he asked if he could call upon Miss Allen, and she said no, but then he said "You shall not deny me" and Helena said his voice made her cold.'

She paused for breath and Leo sorted through what she had said.

'And why do you believe that necessitates my presence in the park this afternoon?'

Olivia cast him a reproachful look. 'I have not finished yet, Papa. Anyway, Helena said Cousin Anthony was nice on the surface, but she didn't really like him and she is worried her sister trusts him too much and then, yesterday afternoon in the park—after Miss Allen came to visit you, Papa—Lady Tring gave Miss Allen the cut direct, even though she spoke to me and Aunt Cecily and Helena, only Aunt Cecily was talking and *she* did not notice, but *I* did and that's when Helena told me all about it and *she* says…' she inhaled before rushing on '…that Miss Allen *pretends* it doesn't matter that her mother's sisters disapprove of her, but they are the only family she has apart from her grandfather, although he might be dead, and she says Miss Allen only pretends not to care because she does not want Helena to be upset, and so she says things like "I shall give them something to gossip about", but she does care, really…' Olivia heaved in another deep breath '…and then afterwards, I saw her—Lady Tring—speaking to other ladies and gentlemen, and they all looked at Miss Allen as if she were a…a…doxy, or something, and—'

'Olivia! Where did you hear a word like that? It is not a term a lady should use.'

'Well, Alex says it—'

'That is enough. You know you should not listen to Alex.'

Leo pushed his fingers through his hair. He had noticed a few silver strands at his temples in the mirror that morning… It was a wonder he wasn't completely grey-haired by now, having to cope with both Olivia and Alex. Thank God Dominic had a level head.

'I was right to tell you, Papa, was I not? You can only make it right if you know about it—that is what you always tell us.'

She looked at him so trustingly Leo's heart turned over in his chest. Suddenly, she was a child again, not a young lady on the brink of her come-out. He *had* always told his children that they could rely upon him to solve any problems they might have and they had grown up knowing they could confide in him.

'You were right to tell me, Livvy. What time do you leave?'

'Aunt Cecily has ordered the carriage for quarter to five. We have arranged to pick up Helena and Miss Allen from Lady Glenlochrie's house and then drive to the park, where we shall walk.'

'In that case, I shall meet you in the park.'

It was but a short walk along Upper Grosvenor Street from Grosvenor Square to the park. Leo was beginning to understand Rosalind's way of thinking. If he were to arrive with Cecily and Olivia this afternoon, she would most likely interpret it as him pressing her to come to a speedy decision. If, however, he were to meet up with them, quite by chance, and offer Rosalind his arm—why, that would convey two messages at the same time. It would not only signal to Lady Tring and any others inclined to follow her lead that Rosalind Allen had the full approval of the Duke of Cheriton, but it would also fuel speculation about his intentions towards her.

And *that* could only further his cause.

Olivia smiled—a far-too-satisfied smile for Leo's comfort... How did his daughter get to be so knowing and manipulative?—and rose to her feet.

'Thank you, Papa. I shall see you in the park.'

'Livvy,' he said, before she left the room.

'Yes, Papa?'

'Do not forget to be surprised when we meet later, or Helena will guess you have told me.'

'Yes, Papa.'

'I fail to see why we needs must walk, when we have any number of perfectly good horses eating their heads off in the stables.' Vernon twirled his cane as he strolled by Leo's side through Hyde Park.

'The walk will do you good. And, if we are on horseback, we would need to dismount if we are to converse with all the interesting people we may meet.'

'Converse? *Interesting?* Who, may I ask?' Vernon swished his cane horizontally, indicating a wide swathe of parkland where the *haut ton* walked, rode and drove in order to see and be seen at this time of day.

They passed a group of four young women promenading in the opposite direction. Leo merely tipped his hat, but Vernon paused, raised his hat and bowed.

'Good afternoon, ladies.'

His greeting oozed seduction. Leo glanced back. His brother was gracing the group with his most charming smile, provoking blushes and trills of giggles from the ladies.

Leo did not break his stride and, before long, Vernon caught up with him.

'Do you care to enlighten…? Ah, *now* I understand.'

Leo followed his brother's gaze to where several people strolled along the bank of the Serpentine. He recognised Rosalind at once. She held Susie by the hand as she approached three ladies, one of whom he identified as Lady Tring.

'What *does* she think she is about?'

Olivia's words came back to haunt him: *I shall give them something to gossip about.*

Thankfully, Cecily and Olivia were nowhere to be seen and nor was Helena. It was just Rosalind and Susie. As he watched, Lady Tring halted before quite deliberately turning her back upon Rosalind. He now recognised Lady Tring's companions as Lady Slough—Rosalind's other aunt—and her daughter. They, too, cut Rosalind. Then a tall dark figure separated from a group passing nearby, waved his companions onward and went to Rosalind, bowing over her hand. Every muscle in Leo's body hardened. Lascelles. *What the hell does he think he's doing?*

Protecting Rosalind, even from her own folly, was Leo's role. He changed direction, heading directly for the group on the bank.

'Leo? Who is that child? Is she Miss Allen's…?' Vernon caught up with Leo and now matched him stride for stride.

'No! That is the child I told you about. Susie.'

'The little runaway? Isn't she a bastard?'

'She is.'

'But…does Miss Allen not realise what will be said about her if she parades the girl around in public?'

'I *believe*,' Leo said, through gritted teeth, 'she is only too well aware of it.'

Vernon emitted a disbelieving whistle and then there was no time for more, for they were almost upon the small gathering.

'An utter disgrace to the Hillyer name,' Lady Tring was proclaiming in a shrill voice, her back still to Rosalind.

'My name,' Rosalind said, quite calm, 'is Allen. And this is Susie, my protégée.'

'Protégée?' This from Lady Slough. 'Is *that* what you call her? No decent person will—'

Lascelles intervened. 'Lady Slough,' he said, his voice smooth but steely, 'I should be most careful how you phrase what I suspect you are about to say. As you may witness, *I* am happy to acknowledge Miss Allen and I am certain you would not care to insult *any* member of the Beauchamp family, no matter which side of the blanket they were born on.'

Rosalind's pulse raced and skittered, but she refused to back down in the face of her aunts' deliberate snub. Susie's hand was hot in her grasp and she could feel the little girl tremble as she pressed close. Why had she not stopped to think what effect this confrontation might have on an innocent child? It was too late for regrets, but what on earth had she hoped to achieve?

You wanted to prove to your aunt that you don't care a jot for her opinion of you. Instead of which, all you have done is made a spectacle of yourself and risked tarnishing Nell by association.

Nell, who had tried so hard to persuade her to wait for Lady Cecily and Lady Olivia to collect them in their carriage as arranged.

Oh, why didn't I listen to her?

God help her, she was actually relieved to see Lascelles when he appeared. Her relief was cut short, however, by Leo's arrival, his eyes icy. With one glance she understood his fury was directed in the main at her, not at her aunts. Her insides shrank and shrivelled. He was, rightly, disgusted. This was not how a lady should behave.

'Good afternoon, Miss Allen,' Leo said. Then, he said to his brother, 'Keep them moving along, Vern, will you?' And he indicated the small knot of onlookers who were gathering.

Rosalind had no chance to reply. With a squeal, Susie ripped her hand from Rosalind's and launched herself at Leo, wrapping her arms around his thighs.

'Where's Conqueror?' she shouted. 'Can I ride him again? Please?'

Rosalind's aunts, and her cousin Amelia, turned as one, mouths agape.

'Susie!' Rosalind pried her loose from Leo as she tried to convey her apology with a look. 'You must not do that. You must curtsy to the Duke when you see him.'

Vernon laughed outright. 'Oh, indeed. A duke must be afforded due deference at all times.'

Rosalind shot him a scathing look, which merely served to widen his grin.

'Do not scold the child,' Leo said. 'It is not her fault her upbringing failed to prepare her for how to behave in polite society.'

Rosalind bit back the retort that hovered on her lips, irritated to realise he was right. A few weeks' tuition in good manners could not override years of neglect in the way to behave.

'I am sorry,' she said. 'You are right.'

Lascelles stirred. He was so close by her side, his sleeve brushed hers and she could smell the bay rum cologne he favoured. 'You have no need to apologise, Miss Allen. The child has as much right as you or I to walk in the park on a pleasant afternoon.'

His words prompted a shocked response from her aunts and a murmur of disapproval from the small knot of onlookers, still hovering despite Vernon's best efforts. Rosalind wished Lascelles had not said something that seemed designed to put them—together with Susie—on one side of a divide and everyone else on the other.

'Lady Tring.'

The words were softly spoken, but an immediate hush fell over all present, the attention of every one of them, Rosalind included, focussed on Leo.

This was his power: his quiet strength, his presence, his poise. This was how people responded to him—what Rosalind loved, but also what she feared.

'I gather you have something to say regarding those who choose to associate with Miss Allen?'

He waited, brows raised, gaze unwavering. Lady Tring's face bloomed beetroot red and Rosalind felt the beginnings of sympathy stir deep inside. She would not care to be on the receiving end of that penetrating stare or that menacing tone.

'You do not know the whole, Your Grace,' Lady Tring said. 'This woman's father was a common soldier. She is not fit to mix with decent people—and now, to discover she has a child and her not even wed! I cannot countenance her behaviour. It is more than my conscience will allow, family or not.'

'I must say, I cannot fathom what so upsets you about Miss Allen's presence. She has come to London to chaperon her young sister, Lady Helena Caldicot. What can be so troubling about that? To be perfectly frank, madam, I find your attitude to your niece incomprehensible.'

'But her father, Your Grace. He was—'

'So you said before. And yet, her father was married to Miss Allen's mother, *your* sister. I venture to suggest that if my family and I are happy to accept my cousin here then you have no grounds for shunning your niece. Or, come to that, your nephew who, as of this very day, happens to be in my employ and resident within my household.'

'But...Your Grace...the *child*...'

'Was a runaway. I happened to be with Miss Allen when we found her and she has been in Miss Allen's care a matter of weeks only. I am very much afraid *I* cannot countenance your continuing objection. I bid you good day, madam. If you will not acknowledge your own legitimate flesh and blood that must be your right. But it shall be my right to decide not to—'

'No!' Lady Slough stepped forward, urging her daughter with her. 'Surely, Your Grace, that is unnecessarily harsh? It has been a shock to my dear sister. I am sure we shall come to terms with our niece's presence given time to adjust.' She stretched her lips, directing a somewhat sickly smile at Rosalind. 'There is no need for any unpleasantness.'

'Quite,' Leo said. 'Good afternoon, ladies.'

It was a blatant dismissal and Rosalind's relatives took

the hint. They nodded to Rosalind, and walked away, followed eagerly by their audience, presumably intent on learning more.

Leo's attention did not waver from Rosalind's face as he said, 'Vern, be a good chap and walk ahead of us with Anthony, will you? I wish to have a word with Miss Allen. Oh, and take Susie with you. We shall follow behind.'

Rosalind swallowed at the steely gaze that promised dire consequences if she dared to object. Vernon, with a flashed smile of sympathy at Rosalind, slung his arm around Lascelles's shoulder and reached for Susie's hand.

'Come, tiddler. Let us go and find some swans to watch.'

Lascelles glared at Leo, but nevertheless went with Vernon. Everyone had fallen in with what Leo decreed without a murmur of protest.

Leaving Rosalind facing Leo.

His power—it was intoxicating but also terrifying. Was this what married life would be like—him commanding and her obeying, without any chance to have her say?

Leo proffered his arm and Rosalind laid her hand on his sleeve.

Chapter Twenty-Two

Leo and Rosalind strolled in the wake of the others.

'Where is your sister?'

'I left her at home. Lady Cecily and Lady Olivia were to collect her in their carriage.'

'And you chose not to wait for them? Would you care to tell me why?'

Her own shame made her sharp. 'I do not answer to you.'

An exasperated noise erupted from Leo and she sneaked a sideways look at him. He captured her gaze and their steps faltered.

'I am not,' he said, 'trying to force you to my will. If you would only lower those prickly defences of yours for a minute or two, you might realise I am trying to help.'

She tore her hand from his sleeve and faced him. 'And if I declare I do not need your help?'

'If, my dearest Rosalind, you do not see that you need *someone's* help, then you are not the intelligent woman I believe you to be. Your aunts' opinions are nothing. There was no need to agitate them by appearing with Susie. Did you not stop to think of the connotation they would put upon her existence?'

'I do not care what they think of me. They disowned Mama—until she remarried a man with a title. She was so

happy her family received her again, it didn't matter to her
that they refused to acknowledge m-me and F-Freddie.' Her
voice had risen throughout her speech and now it cracked
and a painful lump lodged in her throat.

'Oh, sweetheart. What am I to do with you?' Leo shook
his head, captured her hand, placed it back on his sleeve
and began once more to stroll. 'You cannot battle the world.
You cannot force others to hold a particular opinion when
they are determined they are in the right. All you can do is
leave them to their lives whilst you continue with yours.'

'I *am* continuing with my life. Or I was, until I was
forced into coming *here*.' She swiped a lone tear from her
cheek with her gloved hand. 'What was I supposed to do,
when my Aunt Tring was so foul to me yesterday?'

Leo halted. He nudged her chin up so she must look into
his face. She settled her gaze on his lips. She could not cope
with those all-seeing silvery eyes of his.

'You *could* have confided in me.'

'And what would you have done? Scolded them and
f-forced them to be nice?'

His lips curved slightly, then pursed as though he were
trying to conceal his grin. She was being childish, she
knew, but her wits had scattered to the wind and she did
not *wish* to be sensible and logical.

'I am a duke, my darling girl. Where I lead, society
follows. I have no need to force anybody to do anything.
With me and my family on your side there is not a house
in London that would deny you access.'

How must it feel to be so…so *sure*?

'Have you any idea how arrogant that sounds?'

He quirked a brow and shrugged. 'It is how it has always been. Just as you have grown up with the shadow of
your mother's disgrace, and have carried that burden, so I
have grown up with the privilege and authority of knowing
I would follow my uncle and my father to the dukedom.'

'Your uncle? Was that Lascelles's father?'

'Yes. He was the Duke, as the elder of the two brothers. He never married, so the title passed first to my father and then to me.'

No wonder Lascelles is so bitter. She had known Lascelles was illegitimate, but not that his father had actually been the Duke.

'Come, we had better keep walking or I shall not be responsible for my actions.'

'What actions?'

They began to stroll once more. Ahead of them, Vernon, Lascelles and Susie had paused on the bank. Vernon and Susie watched the swans, but Lascelles was staring in their direction.

'Why, that I shall not be able to resist kissing those luscious lips of yours, my sweet Rosalind. We do not wish to set tongues wagging more than they are already, do we?'

Rosalind heaved a sigh. 'I realise I was wrong, confronting my aunts like that.' She hated to humble herself, but the truth must be said if she were to retain her self-respect. 'I allowed my emotions to overrule my good sense. I felt so small and, somehow, *unclean* when they cut me yesterday in the park. I was determined to prove their opinions did not matter to me, that I did not care.'

'When, in actual fact, all you have done is proved how very much you *do* care.'

'I see that now and I do regret it.'

'Promise me in future you will come to me for help.'

'I promise.'

'I do wish, however, that you had not so recklessly dragged Susie into such a public altercation.'

Rosalind hung her head, guilt swirling. She would make it up to Susie.

'Perhaps,' Leo went on, 'you can now see why she would

be happier going to Westfield, where her origins will not cause comment.'

'I have not changed my mind,' Rosalind said. 'Susie will stay with me.'

'But that is entirely illogical. You have your own experiences to tell you that.'

'It is not about logic, it is about the heart. I will not— oh, *no*!'

Rosalind snatched her hand from Leo's arm.

'Rosalind? What is wrong?'

'It is Sir Peter Tadlow. Nell's guardian.'

'And there—' Leo pointed at the path ahead of Sir Peter '—if I am not mistaken, is Helena herself, together with Cecily and Olivia. How opportune.'

'Opportune?' Rosalind glared at him. 'What if he…? Oh! You would not understand. I must go.'

She half-expected Leo to try and stop her as she left the pathway they were following and hurried across the grass, but he did not. When she reached Nell, she glanced over her shoulder to where Leo followed in her footsteps, taking his time, his hat set at a rakish angle as he gently swung his cane. Then he paused, to allow Vernon, Lascelles and Susie to catch him up.

Rosalind swallowed her *humph* of disgust. For all his fine talk of confiding in him and allowing him to help, he was not there when she needed him. Facing Sir Peter was a far more daunting prospect than facing her aunts.

'Good afternoon, Lady Cecily, Lady Olivia,' Rosalind said, puffing slightly after her quick dash across the grass. 'Thank you for bringing Nell to the park. Nell, do not be alarmed, but Sir Peter is approaching.'

'Sir Peter? Oh, Rosalind, what if he makes me go with him?'

Olivia moved closer to Nell and put her arm around her. 'He shan't take you, Nell,' she said. 'We shall not let him.'

Rosalind stepped in front of Nell, shielding her from Sir Peter, her legs shaking at his overt fury. He stopped in front of her, too close for comfort. She steeled herself not to retreat.

'Well, sir?'

'I wish to speak to my ward.'

'Say what you must, sir. Lady Helena is able to hear you quite adequately.'

'What? Are you afraid I might snatch her? I would be within my rights, you know.'

'Forgive my intervention…' Cecily moved alongside Rosalind, standing shoulder to shoulder '…but it is my understanding that you are unmarried, Sir Peter, in which case you are unable to present Lady Helena to society. I should have thought you would be grateful Lady Glenlochrie has undertaken that duty.'

'Helena has no need for a come-out. I have a husband lined up, ready and waiting for her…and an excellent match it is too. A viscount, no less. And who are you, madam, to busy yourself in matters which are no business of yours?'

'She is,' interjected a calm voice, 'my sister.'

Sir Peter's gaze swivelled to take in Leo and the others, who had now joined them. Rosalind smiled to see him blanch. That was the advantage of having a duke on your side. But then Sir Peter's expression turned mutinous.

'Lady Helena Caldicot is my ward,' he said. 'I am sure you will agree with me, Your Grace, that a ward's affairs should be under the sole control of her rightful and legal guardian.'

'Oh, indubitably so,' Leo murmured.

Rosalind stiffened in dismay.

I might have known! How could *he?*

Sir Peter's darting, triumphal look followed by Nell's quiet moan from behind her set Rosalind's pulse pounding.

'You shall not take her,' she cried. 'She will not be sacrificed to that...that...*scoundrel*, Bulbridge.'

Sir Peter thrust his face into Rosalind's and, despite her
best efforts to stand her ground, she stumbled back and she
heard Leo emit a low growl.

'She will do as I say, madam.' Spittle flew from Sir
Peter's lips, landing on Rosalind's cheek. 'You are fortunate I do not haul you before the courts to answer for
your actions.'

In a daze, Rosalind reached to wipe her cheek, but was
beaten to it by Leo, who cleaned away the saliva with a
dab of his handkerchief.

'Stand aside, my sweet. Leave this to me.'

He set his hands to her shoulders and gently pushed her
back to stand next to Helena, then turned to face Sir Peter.
Nell's hand crept into Rosalind's and clung tight. It went
against the grain to relinquish control of her family business to Leo, but she had to admit she had no idea how she
could withstand Sir Peter if he would not agree to Nell remaining in the care of Lady Glenlochrie.

'I have no quarrel with you, Your Grace. Hand over my
ward and I shall forget Miss Allen's part in all this.'

'How very generous.'

Leo's voice—low, menacing—sent a shiver snaking
down Rosalind's spine. She cast a surreptitious glance
around. Once again, everyone appeared mesmerised, their
full attention on the Duke. Sir Peter retreated a couple of
steps. Leo followed.

'All I want is my ward.' Tadlow's voice trembled. 'You
agreed that a ward should obey her guardian.'

'Ah but, you see...' Leo cocked his head to one side
'...I am very much afraid you are no longer Lady Helena's guardian.'

Nell clutched harder at Rosalind's hand and they exchanged startled glances.

'*What?*' Sir Peter shook his head in denial. 'You jest, Your Grace.'

'Oh, trust me—I am in no mood to jest with you, Tadlow.'

'But...but...'

'And whilst I am correcting your misconceptions, I should also inform you that neither are you any longer the guardian of the young Earl of Lydney.'

Rosalind released Nell's hand and started forward. What was going on? A large hand closed around her upper arm. Vernon. He shook his head, mouthed *shh* to her and tugged her back to take her place next to Nell, exactly where Leo had placed her.

Humph! Despite her irritation, however, she stayed put whilst Sir Peter blustered about his rights.

'I have the papers to prove my guardianship, signed by the Lord Chancellor himself,' he said.

'And I am very much afraid *I* have papers—signed by Eldon only yesterday—transferring the guardianship of both Lord Lydney and Lady Helena Caldicot to me.'

'*You?*'

'Me.'

Leo was now Nell and Jack's guardian? Rosalind struggled to draw breath.

'But...but...'

'You sound confused, Tadlow, but there really is nothing to puzzle over,' Leo said. '*You* abused your position of trust over those two youngsters and *I* was asked to take action to protect their interests.'

'You?'

'As I have already confirmed. Do not ask me to repeat myself.'

'But how?'

'I do have a certain amount of influence with both Eldon and Sir William Grant, you understand.' Leo's confident stance belied the note of apology in his voice. 'I… er…*persuaded* them to expedite my petition.'

'This is preposterous, sir!'

'No! What is preposterous is an uncle fleecing his young nephew and attempting to marry off his young niece in order to reduce his own debts. That, sir, is preposterous and I suggest that a prolonged sojourn in the country would be to your great advantage.'

Sir Peter, shoulders slumped, swung his head from side to side in bewilderment. 'I cannot believe this,' he muttered. He straightened. 'Where is the proof?'

'Come to Beauchamp House tomorrow at ten and you shall see the papers.' Leo's voice was laced with boredom. 'Good day, sir.'

As soon as Sir Peter was out of earshot, Rosalind said, 'Is this true?'

'Of course it is true.'

'But who asked you to take over the guardianship?'

'Sir William Rockbeare. He asked me to investigate Tadlow upon my return to London,' Leo said. He studied Rosalind's expression. 'Cecily, would you walk on with Olivia and Helena, please?'

'But I want to know—'

'Livvy. You will do as I say. And take Susie with you. Miss Allen and I have matters to discuss.'

'Come along, girls,' Cecily said. She threw a swift smile at Rosalind, gathered the younger element and walked on.

'Well—' Lascelles looked from Leo to Rosalind, and back again, with a smirk '—it would appear my cousin has behaved true to form and not consulted you in any of this, Miss Allen.'

'No, he did not.'

The implications of the last few minutes were still sinking in. Her whole family. He had taken them over. Freddie, Nell and Jack. Panic swirled inside. What was she to do?

I still have Susie. He has not taken Susie from me. He said it would be my decision.

Except…she had seen him in action now…if he did not want her to raise Susie, would she *really* be able to withstand him? Anger and confusion churned Rosalind's stomach, nausea threatening to overwhelm her.

What should I do? What can I say?

'Vern?'

Rosalind caught the flick of Leo's head in Lascelles's direction. He was doing it again. Manoeuvring everyone to suit his purposes.

'I should prefer Mr Lascelles to remain.' She challenged Leo with her stare.

Every plane in his face hardened and then, with a flick of his brows, he granted permission. A solid weight of anger lodged in Rosalind's chest. She did not *need* his permission.

'It would appear, my dear Coz, that Miss Allen has experienced sufficient of your individual attention for one day.' Lascelles sauntered across to stand by Rosalind's side.

Leo's attention remained solely on Rosalind and she was, contrarily, comforted by Lascelles's presence. Vernon remained several feet distant, watching them with every evidence of enjoyment.

'Why did you not tell me?' She would not wait for him to dictate the conversation. He was just a man. She must not be intimidated by his title or his power. 'You have done this—' she waved an agitated arm '—behind my back. Why? First you lure Freddie away and now you have taken control of Nell and Jack.'

Just saying the words brought that roil of panic back into her insides. *My entire family!*

'Have you already decided to take Susie, too? Do you imagine by taking my family I shall have no choice but to accept—'

She stopped with a gasp. Lascelles stirred next to her.

'No choice but to…?' he murmured. 'Oh, do tell, Coz. Have you fallen *that* hard for the Delectable Dorcas?'

'That is none of your concern, Lascelles,' Leo growled, the intent in his silver gaze—still riveted to Rosalind's face—sending thrills of nervousness, coupled with anticipation, up and down her spine.

'There was neither need nor time to consult anyone,' he said. 'My man Medland dealt with the matter and—'

'You could have *warned* me what you were planning.'

'And if I had?'

'Then I would have—'

She bit her tongue. What *would* she have done? Begged him to leave Nell and Jack under Tadlow's control? Was Leo not the better bet as their guardian? Frustration seized her. There was *nothing* she could have done, had she had the time and opportunity to think it through. As a female, she could not be appointed guardian and Tadlow was Nell and Jack's only male relative.

'Quite.'

The fact that Leo was right only incensed her further. She thrust her nose in the air and averted her gaze.

'Mr Lascelles, would you kindly escort me to my sister? I wish to go home.'

'With pleasure, ma'am.' He crooked his elbow.

'Rosalind…' There was dire warning in the way Leo enunciated her name.

'Your Grace?' She placed her hand upon Lascelles's arm.

'We have yet to finish our discussion about Susie and her future.'

Without volition, Rosalind's fingers clutched at Lascelles's sleeve. Gone was the slightest vestige of intimacy or warmth in Leo's expression or his voice. Had she lost his good opinion entirely? Indecision rendered her speechless.

'You wish to leave this uncertainty hovering over you?' Leo bit the words out into the silence.

No, she wanted to cry. The thought of not knowing was dreadful indeed, but she could not cope with any more. Not now. Her nerves were shred to ribbons and confusion fogged her brain. Before she could even begin to reply, though, Leo spoke again.

'I shall call upon you at two tomorrow. We shall take Susie to visit Westfield. Once you have seen the place, we shall decide what is best to be done...for *all* concerned.'

Chill fingers clutched at her heart. He was every inch the intimidating Duke: remote and severe. Leo was nowhere to be seen. He did not wait for her reply, but spun on his heel and strode away. Vernon, with a lift of his brows and a nod of his head, followed.

Rosalind silently castigated herself as they left. Her obstinacy over the guardianship bordered on the irrational— she was aware of it and yet—as with her aunts—she had not been able to bring herself to back down.

'My cousin has ever been thus,' Lascelles said, patting her hand. 'He listens to no opinion but his own and he has the power to ensure his will is always served. I pity you, my dear lady, for he will not relinquish control of your family now he has them where he wants them.'

And now she was left with Lascelles—the very last man she wished to associate with—and she had no one to blame but herself and her own stubbornness.

'I have no need of pity, sir.'

'But what is to become of you, my dear, with all your family now under his control? And there is that poor, sweet, innocent girl, to be tarnished by the circumstances of her birth for ever. My cousin will for certain decide to send her away.'

'I will not allow it.' Why would Lascelles not be silent? She needed to think.

'I very much fear, once my cousin decides upon a course of action, he is not easily swayed. Why, even I find it impossible to stand against him and I am not only a man but two years his senior. What hope have you of withstanding his decree?'

'I will take whatever steps I must to prevent Susie being sent to that place,' Rosalind vowed. 'The Duke will not get his own way this time.'

Chapter Twenty-Three

'A gentleman caller for you, Miss Allen. A Mr Lascelles.'

Rosalind set aside her novel with a sigh and glanced at the over-mantel clock. One o'clock. She'd barely taken in a single sentence in the past hour, her mind constantly wandering to her impending appointment with Leo and the likely outcome of their visit to Westfield. That was more than enough of an ordeal for one day. The last thing she felt like coping with was Anthony Lascelles and his faux sympathy.

'Did you show him into the salon?'

'Yes, miss.' Keating, as usual, peered down his nose at her.

Rosalind rose. She could not receive Lascelles on her own, but Helena was upstairs reading to Lady Glenlochrie and Penny was occupied with Susie. She had no wish to encourage any sort of acquaintance between the little girl and Lascelles.

'Send one of the maids to sit with us, will you, please?'

Keating trod ahead of Rosalind to the door of the salon and opened it for her, before disappearing towards the servants' stairs.

'Good afternoon, Mr Lascelles.' Rosalind halted just a few steps inside the open door. If she did not sit, then Lascelles could not and, hopefully, he would take the hint and leave all the sooner.

'My dear Miss Allen.' He crossed the room with hasty strides and, before she realised his intention, he clasped her hands. 'Or may I have your permission to call you Rosalind?'

Rosalind tugged her hands free. He stood so close to her, she now had no choice but to venture further into the room. She walked to the fireplace, then faced him. He had closed the door. Her hands clenched by her sides and she prayed the maid would come quickly. At least Lascelles had remained by the door and not followed her.

'I fear that might be unwise, sir. It might prove all too easy to forget oneself in company.'

His face darkened. 'I note my cousin uses your name with impunity.' He strolled towards her.

'And that proves my point.' Rosalind wandered over to stand behind an armchair, resting her hands on the back. It provided a convenient barrier between herself and her visitor and gave her the comfort of something solid to hold on to. 'Your cousin, as you yourself have warned me, follows his own agenda. He has not asked permission to call me by my name and I have granted no such licence.'

'I have not come here to discuss my cousin.'

'Indeed? It was you, sir, who brought his name into this conversation. I certainly have no wish to discuss him.'

Lascelles barked a laugh. 'I stand corrected.'

He approached another few paces and Rosalind's heart picked up pace, thrumming in her chest.

Where is that maid?

'I have come to offer a solution to your dilemma over Susie, Miss Allen.'

He smiled, a smug smile, brimming with confidence. Rosalind's temples throbbed a warning.

'Pray, continue, sir. As you are aware, your cousin is due to collect Susie and me very soon.'

'Where is the little angel?'

Angel indeed. Rosalind concealed her exasperation. Did the man truly believe she would fall for such mendacious nonsense?

'She is with Penny.'

Penny had taken Susie upstairs to try and distract her from their visit to Westfield. The poor child was convinced she was to be sent away and Rosalind—fearing exactly the same—had found it impossible to properly reassure her. Susie's fears gave Rosalind even more determination to withstand any attempt to send her to the orphan asylum. She hoped when Leo saw Susie's dread of leaving Rosalind, he would agree she might remain, although she still agonised over whether her own reckless behaviour yesterday had already persuaded him she was unsuitable to raise the child.

'That is a shame,' Lascelles said. 'I had hoped to become better acquainted with her.'

'She is preparing for our visit to Westfield with the Duke. Now, sir...you spoke of a solution?'

'Marry me, Rosalind.'

Those three words stole the air from her lungs. She stared at him, open-mouthed. Marry *him*? Marry Lascelles?

'It is the perfect solution, my dear. Think about it. You and I will deal very well together. I enjoy a woman with spirit and you will have the security and position of my name. Think of the advantages to our union,' he urged. 'I am a wealthy man and I am generous to those who please me. And we can provide a home for Susie. Who else, after all, could have a better understanding of what the poor child will have to endure? Not my cousin, that is for certain. He is set on shutting her away in that orphan asylum and she will face a future of servitude.'

'*Marry* you?'

Suddenly, he was by her side. She hadn't even noticed him move. She shrank from him, but he took her by the shoulders, holding her fast.

'You do me a great honour, sir, but…' Her words faltered as his black eyes blazed. She hauled in a deep breath. 'But I must refuse.'

His fingers dug into her flesh and, before she realised his intent, his lips were on hers. She clamped her jaw tight, resisting his questing tongue. He lifted his head.

'Open for me, dear heart. I will show you pleasure you have never dreamed of.'

Did he not hear me refuse? Fear squirmed in her belly and she struggled to free herself, but he was too strong. He backed her against the chair that only a few moments ago had given her the illusion of safety.

'Release me, sir! What if someone comes?'

He laughed. 'No one will come. I slipped the butler a guinea to ensure we are not disturbed—he is well aware there are some occasions when a man requires privacy. When you know me better, dear heart, you will find it is not only my cousin who can arrange matters to suit his purpose.'

One arm encircled her shoulders and he clamped her jaw with his free hand, squeezing.

'Come, my love.' His breath was hot on her cheek, his cologne choking her lungs. 'Enough of this maidenly protestation. You chose me over my stuffy cousin yesterday. I can provide for you and the child—you will want for nothing.'

Her flailing hands beat uselessly at his arms. She opened her mouth to scream and he kissed her again, this time invading her mouth with his tongue. He pressed the full length of his body into hers, flexing his hips so she could not mistake the hard ridge of his arousal. She gagged and her knees started to buckle. He tore his lips from hers and placed them close to her ear.

'I told you once before that you would not deny me, Rosalind. It is up to you whether you accept me now or whether you make me work a little harder to…*persuade*… you.'

The insinuation in that one word chilled her very bones.

'Either way, now my mind is set I shall not give up.' He laughed, stepped back and bowed. 'My cousin and I are also alike in that respect.'

Dazed, Rosalind rubbed at her swollen lips, tasting blood in her mouth. She stumbled as she tried to put more distance between them and he was at her side in an instant, cupping her elbow, steering her solicitously to the sofa to sit down.

'I shall leave you to consider my offer, Miss Allen… and the alternative. I anticipate your grateful acceptance by the end of the day.'

He bowed again and left.

Rosalind stared blankly into space. The man was mad. How on earth did he imagine *that* little display of charm would persuade her to have anything at all to do with him, let alone *marry* him? She shuddered. She must ensure she was never alone with Lascelles ever again. Her heart rate gradually steadied to normal and she stood up on still-trembling legs. She must go to her bedchamber and tidy herself ready for the visit to Westfield.

Twenty minutes later, she emerged from her bedchamber, having changed her gown, donned her pelisse and re-pinned her hair. She met Penny on the landing.

'Is Susie ready?' she asked. 'The Duke will be here to collect us shortly.'

'She went downstairs a little while ago, ma'am. To look

for you. Poor lamb could not settle, so I changed her dress and sent her down to wait with you.'

'I have not seen her.'

They descended the stairs together, but Susie was nowhere to be found in the rooms on the first floor. Rosalind sent Penny back upstairs to search and continued down to the ground floor. Again, there was no sign of Susie, nor of anyone else. The door leading to the basement stairs was ajar and, as she approached it, Keating strolled out.

'I am looking for Susie, Keating. Is she downstairs?'

'No, miss.'

'How long has the hall been empty?'

'A mere matter of moments, miss,' he replied stiffly.

Rosalind hurried up the stairs and met Penny once again on the landing.

'Well?'

'She's not in any of the bedchambers. I even went in to Lady Glenlochrie, but neither she nor Lady Helena have seen her.'

'But where can she be, Penny?'

'Oh, madam, do you think she has run away?'

'But why would she run away?'

'She hated the idea of being sent to that school. She ran away from her other home, after all.'

Voices floated up the stairs from the hall below. Penny peered over the balustrade.

''Tis the Duke! Oh, what will he say when he finds out we've lost Susie?'

Rosalind clutched Penny's sleeve. 'We must not tell him, Penny. It will only convince him I am not capable of caring for her.'

'But he is expecting Susie to visit the school with you.'

'I know.' Rosalind thought fast. 'You keep looking. I shall tell the Duke that Susie is unwell.'

* * *

Leo climbed the stairs behind the butler. There was the sound of a scuffle overhead and as his head came level with the floor he saw Rosalind, dressed in an amber pelisse, clutching at Penny's arm and whispering urgently into her ear.

Suspicions aroused, he continued up the stairs. Penny disappeared up the stairs to the next floor.

'Good afternoon, Miss Allen. I am pleased to see you are ready to leave.'

He searched for words of conciliation, but they would not come. He still smouldered over her rejection of every damned thing he had done to try to help her and her family. Every time he thought she was beginning to see things his way, something else came along and blew their tentative accord into the sky. He could no longer dismiss the suspicion that it was *him* she was rejecting, not merely his help. The image of her choosing Lascelles—*Lascelles* of all people—over him had plagued him all night and only the consumption of half a bottle of brandy had finally allowed him to sleep.

'Where is Susie?'

'I'm sorry, Your Grace. I am afraid Susie is not well. Our visit will have to be postponed.'

She would not meet his eyes. Her gaze darted hither and thither, settling nowhere for longer than a second.

'What is wrong with her? Shall I send for a physician?'

'No! That is unnecessary.'

Rosalind was more flustered than he had ever seen her. She had grabbed hold of the balustrade with her right hand and her knuckles shone white.

'She needs to rest, that is all.' She met his gaze now, her golden-brown eyes accusing. 'She has worried herself into a fever of apprehension over this visit to Westfield.'

'So…it is my fault?'

Rosalind's gaze slipped from his. 'Yes.'

There was more to this than she admitted. He knew it in his bones. 'Susie need not come,' he said. 'You and I can still visit Westfield.'

'No!'

'But we must come to a decision over Susie's future.'

'I have made my decision.'

Leo moved closer to her and she retreated along the landing, her hand sliding along the rail.

'I need to get back to Susie.' Her lips were tight, her whole demeanour strained. 'We can discuss this another time, if you still insist upon it.'

'What are you hiding? Is Susie really ill?'

Again, her eyes gave her away, skittering all over the place.

'I am trying to help, Rosalind. All I intended was for us to take a look at Westfield. Why do you persist in believing the worst of me?'

'I know what is best for Susie and it is not being raised in that institution.'

Exasperation exploded through him. With two strides he was upon her. He clasped her shoulders and she winced, even though he knew he had not grabbed her hard. Then… he stilled. The hairs on the back of his neck lifted. Bay rum. She reeked of it. He tilted her face to his, his fingers beneath her chin, and her guilty expression told its own tale. And her lips… They looked swollen.

'Who has been here?'

'No one.'

Frustration growled in his throat. She lied. She was no different from Margaret. He spun on his heel and stalked down the stairs. In the hall below he waited in a fever of impatience as the butler fetched his hat, gloves and cane.

Then he saw a letter on a console table and recognised the heavy, spiky lettering that read 'Miss Rosalind Allen.'

He glanced up the stairs. Rosalind was nowhere in sight.

'When did that arrive?'

'It has just this minute been delivered, Your Grace.'

'I see it was written by my cousin, Mr Lascelles. That is most odd... I understood it was his intention to call upon Miss Allen earlier today.'

'Oh, he did call, Your Grace. About an hour ago.'

He would wash his hands of her. If Lascelles was her choice, then pity help her.

Outside, he jumped into his carriage and gave orders to drive to Beauchamp House. Once home, he stalked through the front door, growled 'I don't want to be disturbed under any circumstances, Grantham' as he passed the butler and slammed into his study where he slumped into his chair and thrust both hands through his hair.

He'd thought all this *angst* was long behind him. He'd *thought* he was too shrewd to fall for the lies and trickery of *any* woman, let alone some countrified old maid who had never even set foot in London until a few days ago.

He reached for the brandy decanter and a glass.

Some time later there was a tap at the door and it opened.

'I *said* I don't want to be disturbed,' he roared.

'So Grantham said.'

Cecily closed the door behind her and advanced across the room. One look at her face was enough. He didn't want...didn't *need* her sympathy. What did she know about anything?

'Say your piece and leave me alone,' he growled.

Cecily pulled up a chair and sat opposite him. He fixed his gaze on his glass and the scant quarter inch of brandy that remained.

'I thought you were going to Westfield with Miss Allen?'

'Plans change.'

'You did go to Lady Glenlochrie's house?'

He lifted his gaze. Held hers. 'Why the interest?'

'I saw Miss Allen leaving just now. You will be pleased to hear Grantham denied her.'

'I pay him to obey my orders.' He snatched up his glass and drained it. 'Why are you telling me this?'

'Evidently she then asked for her brother, but he is not here. Leo... Miss Allen... She seemed distressed. She did not even notice me as she rushed past.' Cecily put a folded sheet of paper on the desk and slid it across the surface towards him. 'She left this.'

'What does it say?'

Cecily raised a brow. 'It is addressed to you, Leo, so I do not know.'

He eyed the note with distaste. 'Whatever it says, it is too late. I have tried to help her, but she has made her choice.'

'Choice?'

Leo surged to his feet and crossed the room. He flung open the door.

'More brandy!'

He returned to his desk. Cecily had not moved. She sat in the chair opposite his, calm and composed as always, hands folded in her lap.

'What choice did Miss Allen make, Leo?' she asked as he sat down.

'She has rejected my every attempt to help her and her family. It seems she would prefer to rely on Anthony Lascelles.'

'I know you are not so foolish as to believe that.' Cecily leaned forward and reached out her hand. 'She is simply trying to prove she can manage without your help. She has cared for her family all her life, and now you have come along and she feels...*unnecessary*.'

The emotion she put into that one word jerked Leo from his anger.

'You sound as though…' The similarities between Rosalind's life and Cecily's had occurred to him more than once. 'Cecily? Is that how you feel? Unnecessary?'

She caught her lip between her teeth. 'Not precisely. But, once this Season is over, and when I think about my future…yes, that is my fear. And so I understand exactly how Miss Allen feels and I cannot condemn her for wanting to provide a home for Susie. It would appear an ideal solution for them both and that is why I cannot understand why you are so adamant Susie should go to Westfield.'

Leo gritted his teeth. 'I am *not* adamant she must go there. I merely wanted Miss Allen to consider all the facts before making her decision. You have just confirmed my belief that she is using Susie to make herself feel useful rather than thinking about what is best for the child.'

'But even Dominic admits it is preferable for a child to live in a real home rather than in an orphan asylum. Are you certain your real reason is not that you do not want Susie in your household if you and Miss Allen marry?'

Leo scowled. 'Of course it is not. And who said anything about marriage?'

Cecily smiled. 'You have—as you very well know—made your intentions towards Miss Allen abundantly clear.'

The door opened and Grantham approached, carrying a bottle of brandy.

'Leave it,' Leo snapped as the butler began to pour the spirit into the decanter.

Expressionless, Grantham bowed and left the room, leaving Leo feeling even more wretched and guilty than he did already. He grabbed the bottle and refilled his glass.

'Well?' Cecily asked as he lifted the glass to his lips.

He eyed her over the rim. 'It is your question that is unnecessary, Cecily. There will be no marriage.'

'I do not believe you. You never give up when you have set your mind on something.'

'Unless I change my mind. I refuse to further humble myself.'

'Take care your pride does not blind you to the truth, Brother. You may change your mind but, when it comes to love, can you so easily change your heart?'

Leo leapt from his chair and took a hasty turn around the room. 'Who said anything about love?'

Cecily raised her brows, and stood, smoothing her skirts. 'You did not have to *say* anything, my dear.'

She glided from the room, leaving Leo ready to punch the wall. He stood in the middle of the room, fists clenched, eyes shut, breathing hard.

Damn her. She knows nothing about it. I can do anything I set my mind to.

After several minutes, he returned to his desk and sat down.

And there it was.

The letter.

He had forgotten it. He could simply throw it away, but he reached for it anyway and read the words on the outside: *The Duke of Cheriton.* Two smudges attested to the haste with which those words had been written. Leo broke the seal. As he unfolded the letter, a second sheet of paper fluttered to the desk. The first sheet, apart from his name, was blank. He reached for the second, his pulse quickening as he recognised Anthony's writing. It was the letter he had seen at Lady Glenlochrie's house.

He read the words and his fist clenched without volition, crumpling the paper. A vicious curse was torn from his lips as he hurled the ball of paper at the wall.

He had told Rosalind to come to him for help.

She had done just that and he had denied her.

Chapter Twenty-Four

Why did I not tell Leo the truth?

It was too late to regret her hasty decision, made to conceal Susie's absence and to protect herself.

She had thought Susie had run away. She was wrong. The words Lascelles had penned were seared into her brain. He had taken Susie and he was confident Rosalind would now see the wisdom of accepting his earlier proposal. If she failed to come to his house by five o'clock, she would never see Susie again. If she told anyone, she would never see Susie again.

She had no one to turn to. Leo had rejected her. He was at home, but he refused to see her and that snooty butler had ensured she was aware of that fact.

'His Grace does not wish to be disturbed.'

In desperation, she had asked for Freddie—although she was loath to embroil him in anything to do with that snake, Lascelles—but he, it seemed, was genuinely absent. Her only hope was that the butler would deliver Lascelles's letter to Leo before it was too late. She had no illusions about Lascelles's intentions. He would not hesitate to preempt their wedding—if it was indeed his intention to wed her at all.

She'd had no choice but to leave. Her spirits had lifted

when she met Cecily on the front steps, but plummeted again almost immediately. She would not burden Cecily with this when there was nothing she could do. She crossed Grosvenor Square in a daze, desperately searching for a solution, scanning the faces she passed by, but they were all strangers. She knew nobody else in London. She had never felt more alone. Rosalind hurried down South Audley Street, ignoring the curious looks of those she passed. She was beyond caring. She arrived at Lady Glenlochrie's house and hesitated on the step, catching her breath. She had to answer Lascelles's summons. The thought turned her bowels to water, but she could not abandon Susie to that rogue. Who knew what might become of her.

Keating opened the front door for her and the first inkling of a plan glimmered in her brain. She had thought of taking Hector, and dismissed the idea, knowing Lascelles would never allow him into his house and fearing the consequences for Susie if she tried. She watched as Keating closed the door by rote, not really paying attention to his actions, his focus upon her.

What if...?

'I shall take Hector for a walk, Keating. Please have someone bring him upstairs.'

'I believe he has already been exercised, miss.'

'Then I shall take him again. If her ladyship or Lady Helena should ask, please tell them I shall not be very long.'

Helena would be expecting to go to the park. Well, that must wait. Keating disappeared towards the servants' stairs and Rosalind slipped into the dining room. There. A fruit knife. Perfect. Not too big, but sharp. She tugged open her reticule and put it inside, then she hurried upstairs to her bedchamber, where she grabbed hold of a parasol, and smiled grimly when she realised it was the very one Nell had bought for her when Lascelles had escorted them to the shops.

She stood in the centre of her bedchamber for a moment, thinking through her plan, looking for flaws. She grimaced. There were many. But she had no choice. Susie needed her. She left her bedchamber and hurried down the two flights of stairs to the ground floor, where Keating held Hector's leash at arm's length, his nostrils flaring in distaste. Rosalind took the leash and made a fuss of an overjoyed Hector.

Keating eyed Rosalind's parasol as he opened the front door.

'You will have no need of that, miss. It is cloudy.'

'I am hopeful the sun will break through,' Rosalind said. 'At least I shall be prepared.' She paused on the stoop. 'Which direction is Curzon Street, Keating?'

'It is just around the corner, miss.' The butler pointed down the street.

'Thank you.'

As she neared Lascelles's address in Curzon Street, her steps faltered. There was a black travelling coach outside, with a team of four harnessed to it and a coachman and groom standing at their ease on the pavement. The team looked fresh, as though they were about to go on a journey. Rosalind swallowed nervously, but the two men studied her with casual, non-threatening interest as they doffed their hats.

She bent to Hector, unclipped his leash and moved him into a position where he could not be seen from the front door of the house.

'Sit, Hector. Stay.' She held up her hand, fingers splayed, and the great hound sat, cocking his head to one side as she walked to the front door.

''Ere, lady. You ain't leaving that brute there without tying him up, are you?'

'I am, but do not worry. He will not hurt you unless I tell him to.'

The two men shuffled around to the far side of their horses, muttering. If only it might prove as easy to deal with Lascelles. Rosalind hauled in a deep breath, lifted the knocker and let it fall. Then she waited, breathing slow and steady, her back straight and her chin up. She would not allow him to intimidate her. Not again. She clutched her parasol, hiding it down by her side in the folds of her pelisse and she took comfort in knowing Hector was close by.

The door opened. She had steeled herself for Lascelles himself to answer it, but it was a young maidservant. This was an unexpected bonus.

'I have come to collect my little girl, Susie,' Rosalind declared. 'Would you kindly go and fetch her?'

The maid chewed her lip. 'The master said you were to come inside first, ma'am,' she said.

'But she is here? You have seen her?'

'Yes'm. She's upstairs. But you must speak to the master first. His orders, ma'am.'

'Very well.' Rosalind put as much hauteur as she could muster into her speech. 'Lead the way.'

The maid did as she was bid, leaving Rosalind to close the front door. She placed the parasol over the sill and pushed the door to. If the maid looked round she might notice the door was not properly closed, but it was the best Rosalind could contrive. She followed the maid, prepared to distract her if necessary.

The stairs were in the middle of the house, between the front and back rooms. They dog-legged out of sight and Rosalind followed the maid up to the first floor and to the open door of a room at the front of the house.

The blood tore through her veins in a torrent, driven by her pounding heart. She stepped through the door into a parlour. Standing by the unlit fireplace, a satisfied smirk on his face, was Anthony Lascelles.

The maid disappeared.

'Where is Susie? Bring her to me.' Rosalind clutched her reticule, surreptitiously working the drawstrings loose, ready to reach in for the knife if necessary.

'My dear Rosalind. Is that any way to greet your betrothed? Come, surely a celebratory kiss is warranted?' He crooked one finger.

Rosalind did not move and his expression hardened.

'Is it possible you did not fully understand my little billet-doux? Susie is quite safe, but her continued well-being depends upon you, dear heart. If you please me, Susie will benefit. But…if you should prove *overly* difficult…'

He shook his head regretfully and nausea threatened.

'This is…madness.' She forced the words through dry lips. 'Allow me to take Susie and we shall say no more about this. Why would you wish to marry a woman who does not want you?'

His smile chilled her. 'Can you really not guess, my sweet Rosalind? Do you expect me to pass over this perfect opportunity to have ownership of the woman my dear cousin desires? Besides…' his voice softened menacingly '…you may recall, dear heart, that I did warn you I enjoy a degree of resistance in my women. Docility, I find, has little to recommend it.'

Rosalind licked her lips, then wished she hadn't as his eyes fixed on her mouth. Her insides churned with disgust as his grin widened.

'Come to me,' he said.

She removed her glove and raised her hand to put two fingers in her mouth and his grin vanished. He lunged towards her, but she spun on her heel, emitted a piercing whistle and then rushed out on to the landing, delving into her reticule for the knife. She faced Lascelles, her back to the balustrade, holding the knife before her as a deep-throated bay sounded from below, punctuated by the scrabble of claws against the front door.

Lascelles hesitated in the doorway, his gaze flicking to the stairs. Then he bent, fumbled at the top of his boot and withdrew a knife that made Rosalind's fruit knife look like a child's toy. Sick horror invaded her. She had not bargained for him having a weapon.

Hector bounded up the final stair and stood to attention, lips drawn back to bare his teeth. One word from her and he would attack.

'You had better control that animal or...' Lascelles thrust the knife forward. 'And you will never see the brat again.'

She could not do it, could not risk losing Hector.

'Susie! Where are you?'

Her shriek echoed up and down the stairwell.

'She is not here,' Lascelles said.

'You are lying.' She must play for time—wait for him to drop his guard. 'The maid told me she was here.'

'The maid's a fool. The child was here, but no longer. My coach is outside, ready to take us to Halsdon Manor. Come without a fuss and you shall see Susie there.'

'You cannot get away with this,' she said.

'Can I not?'

Lascelles stepped towards her. Hector snarled, tensing, and Rosalind put her hand on his collar.

'Who will stop me? Not you, with that joke of a weapon. Not him...' He pointed his knife at Hector. 'He is no match for this and you know it. It would be but a second's work to gut him if he attacks.'

'Your cousin knows what you have done,' Rosalind said in desperation. 'He has read the letter you sent to me.'

Lascelles laughed. 'My all-powerful cousin? And, so... where is he? Why is he not here to protect you?'

He took another step, narrowing the gap between them. Rosalind shrank back, the hard rail of the balustrade pressing into her back.

'Lascelles!'

The roar boomed from below, followed by the thunder of boots on the stairs, distracting Lascelles. Rosalind released Hector.

'Get him!'

Hector leapt, his jaws closing around Lascelles's arm. Lascelles screamed, staggering back into the drawing room. His knife clattered to the floor as he fell back and he lay still as Hector planted his front paws on his chest.

And then strong arms encircled Rosalind and she was pulled into Leo's embrace, her head clamped to his chest, his heart thundering in her ear. She melted against him for a few treasured seconds, then wriggled to free herself.

'Susie,' she gasped. 'I must find her.'

'Do not fret, sweetheart. I shall find her. You have exhibited quite enough bravery for one day.' He tilted her chin to look deep into her eyes. 'Enough for a lifetime.' He pressed a kiss to her forehead and whispered, 'I am never going to let you out of my sight again, you stubborn woman, you. My nerves are in shreds.'

He released her and only then did Rosalind see Alex reach the top of the stairs. He ran towards the open doorway and stopped.

'Is that Hector?' Delight rang in his voice. 'Hi! Freddie! That wolf dog of yours is a hero!'

'Freddie? How…?'

Freddie negotiated the final flight of stairs and grinned at Rosalind. 'Soon as I saw old Hec outside, I knew you'd be a match for that blackguard. Brava, my dear.'

'Frederick, be a good fellow and call off your dog,' Leo said. His voice hardened. 'I wish to have a word with my cousin.'

He stalked over to the parlour door as Hector responded to Freddie's whistle with a wagging tail. Rosalind glimpsed Lascelles scrambling to his feet as Leo entered the room and banged the door behind him, choking off Rosalind's warning cry.

She caught the meaningful looks Freddie and Alex exchanged and ran to the door, dodging Alex's attempt to stop her. She thrust it wide as Leo punched Lascelles, who staggered sideways before dropping to his hands and knees, close to where his knife had fallen.

Leo turned to the door, scowling. 'Out!'

Rosalind's breath seized as, behind Leo, Lascelles regained his feet, lithe as a cat, the knife in his hand.

'Leo!'

Lascelles lunged at Leo. Rosalind leapt, hands outstretched, and shoved Leo aside with all her strength.

There was a jolt. A burning pain. Her legs crumpled.

Chapter Twenty-Five

Silence shrouded Beauchamp House as the occupants slept. Apart from Leo. He longed for the relief of slumber, but when he sought his bed it was only to pitch around until his sheets were in a hopeless tangle and saturated with the sweat of his fear. He could only be soothed by having Rosalind within his sight, by knowing she was safe, by hearing the soft sough of her breath and knowing she lived.

He shifted in the chair, smothered a yawn, scrubbed his hand over his bristled jaw and continued his bedside vigil. She was all right. Doctor Kent had confirmed it, after he had cleaned and dressed the shallow slash across her ribs. 'Rosalind must rest,' the doctor had said, administering a few drops of laudanum to calm her mind and prevent her dwelling on what might have been.

A solitary candle flickered on the bedside table, dancing over her features. She muttered, moving her head on the pillow, her forehead wrinkling as unknowable memories chased through her dreams. Leo reached out and covered her hand with his. She quieted.

His mind *knew* she was not gravely injured yet his heart could not quite believe she was safe. The events of the previous day returned again and again to harry him. And not only *what* had happened, but how they had made him *feel*. Feelings and emotions that he never, never wished to experience again: the sick dread on reading Lascelles's letter, the guilt of knowing he had turned her away when she needed him, the terror that he would not reach her in time.

He had sprinted from his office and out to the street, prepared to commandeer the first conveyance he saw. And there, having just drawn up, was Alex's curricle, with Freddie in the passenger seat. The relief had very nearly unmanned Leo. He'd had to blink to clear his stinging eyes as he dragged the groom from his perch at the back and leapt up to take his place. And Alex—thank God—had not asked why, but had responded with speed, whipping up his horses. They had reached Lascelles's house in minutes.

And he had not been too late and love had exploded in his heart, filling him with relief and overwhelming him with gratitude.

Leo cradled Rosalind's hand between his as the following events unfolded in his memory, reliving that sickening moment when Rosalind shoved him aside—taking the knife thrust intended for him—and his deadly fury as he had launched himself at Lascelles, landing a hefty punch on his nose with a satisfying crunch of bone. He had followed Lascelles to the floor and wrapped his hands around his throat. Thank God Alex had stopped him.

Back in the present, Leo stared down at Rosalind's fingers, caressing them. So delicate, compared to his. And yet *she* had protected *him*. And he might have lost her. And he might *still* lose her, if she would not have him, if she still refused to marry him. No. He could not fail. He *needed* her. Only her. She, and she alone, had the power to reduce him to nothing. His title? His wealth? They were nothing without her.

She stirred, and her fingers curled around his.

'Shhh. Sleep.'

Her eyelids opened, the merest crack. 'Leo.' And she smiled and slept again.

He leaned over to press his lips to her brow, then settled back into his chair to listen to the reassuring sound of her breathing and to continue his vigil.

'You're awake. May we come in?'

Nell peered around the bedchamber door. Rosalind smiled and then frowned. It was barely ten in the morning.

'What are you doing here so early?'

She had breakfasted on hot rolls washed down with a cup of chocolate, and was feeling surprisingly well, despite the soreness of her injury. Nell entered the room, leading Susie by the hand. Penny followed, her round face beaming.

'Susie!'

Rosalind held out her arms. Susie needed no further encouragement and clambered on to the bed, cuddling next to Rosalind, who hugged her as she blinked back her tears.

'Lady Cecily told me Susie was safe, but I longed to see her for myself,' she said. 'Thank you for bringing her.'

Cecily had also told her how Lascelles had come across Susie on the landing at Lady Glenlochrie's house and had lured her outside with the promise of a ride on his horse. Keating's absence from the hall at the time they left had proved a lucky coincidence for Lascelles and an unhappy one for the rest of them.

Nell grinned. 'There is no need to thank me. We have been here all night.'

'All night? But…why?'

'The Duke insisted. Aunt Susan is here, too. He would not take no for an answer. Oh, and Aunt Susan has dismissed Keating for taking Lascelles's bribe.'

'Well, I cannot be sorry for *that*,' Rosalind said. 'What happened to Lascelles?'

At his name, Susie pressed closer to Rosalind. 'He is a Bad Man.'

'He is a very bad man, Susie,' Nell said, 'but you will not have to see him again, I promise.'

Rosalind hugged the little girl as Nell said, 'He is gone, but that is all I know. The men are very tight-lipped over the details.'

'I shall ask the Duke when I see him,' Rosalind said.

As they chatted, part of her mind picked over vague memories from the day before. And the night. Had she dreamt it, or had Leo really been sitting beside her bed when she roused in the middle of night? She had a vague recollection of candlelight playing over his roughened, unshaven features.

'Where is the Duke?' she asked abruptly.

'I am not certain.'

She had questions to ask, and one question—a very important question—to answer. Besides. She *wanted* to see him. She pushed back the bedcovers.

'Ros. What are you doing? You should stay in bed.'

'Nonsense. I am quite well apart from a little soreness. Will you ring for hot water, please, Penny?'

A short while later, washed and dressed, her hair brushed and pinned up, Rosalind descended the stairs to the ground floor. Nell had taken Susie to visit Lady Glenlochie—happily holding court in the best guest bedchamber—and the rest of the family and Freddie were nowhere to be seen. Only Hector was there to greet her with gently swinging tail as she crossed the staircase hall, his claws clicking on the floor tiles. Her heart sank as she passed through the doorway into the entrance hall. The butler stood guard outside the door of Leo's study.

Rosalind tilted her chin. 'I should like to see the Duke, please.'

The butler bowed. 'Certainly, Miss Allen. I shall announce you.'

Rosalind bit back her impatience at such pomp. He was only doing his job.

'Miss Allen, Your Grace.'

He stood aside. Rosalind glanced at him as she passed. Was that a glint of approval in his eye? He certainly appeared to have lost his former condescension. He hadn't peered down his nose at her once.

And then she forgot all about the butler, for there was Leo, coming towards her with hands outstretched, a troubled frown creasing his handsome face.

'Should you not be resting, sweetheart?'

She read concern in the fine lines surrounding his mesmeric silver-grey eyes. He was clean-shaven now, but dark shadows attested to a broken night.

'I am well-rested, Leo. It is you who looks in need of sleep.'

She cradled his cheek and he turned his head to press his lips to her palm. Then he laughed as he noticed Hector, who wandered over to the fire to curl up with a contented sigh.

'Protection?'

'Am I in need of protection?'

One corner of his mouth quirked up. 'What do you think?'

He dipped his head to brush her lips with his, then gathered her into his arms, gazing into her upturned face.

'I think...' she slipped her arms around his shoulders, interlocking her fingers at his nape '...that it may be you who is in need of protection, Your Grace.'

She pulled his head down and pressed her lips to his, the now familiar tug at the secret place between her thighs reminding her of pleasures to come. With a heartfelt groan, Leo hauled her to him as their mouths and tongues conveyed the feelings that words, for the moment, could not.

Her legs quivered with need and she clung to his shoulders, relying on his strength to support her. When he ended the kiss though, she felt the tremble of his hand as he stroked her cheek, a look of wonderment on his face.

'I *need* you, my sweet Rosalind.' His voice, normally so assured, shook. 'Put me out of my misery. Say you will marry me.'

She opened her mouth, but he stopped her with one finger to her lips.

'I know you have questions, as do I, but I can barely think straight with the dread of losing you hanging over me. You think me powerful, but you do not realise that it is *you* who truly holds the power...the power to make me the happiest of men or the most wretched...the power to bring me to my knees. I cannot bear to think of my life without you.

'I love you, Rosalind Allen, with all my heart. I ask you again...will you marry me? Please?'

All doubt fled her heart at his words.

'I love you, too—' how she had longed to say those words '—and, despite the fact you are a duke, my answer is yes. I will marry you.'

He stared at her, then burst into laughter. 'Of all the answers I dreamt you might give, I never imagined you would accept me *despite* my title.'

He framed her face with long fingers. 'Oh, my precious love...' His mouth descended on hers and she lost herself in his kiss, but still doubt nibbled at the corner of her mind. She pulled away. He looked down at her questioningly.

'You are certain you will not regret marrying a nobody like me?'

'A *nobody*?' His brows drew together in a fearsome frown. 'Why would you—oh! I see: your mother's family. Sweetheart...' he hugged her close '...they are fools. You are the bravest, wisest, most compassionate woman I know.

And I am certain if your father were alive he would be very proud of you and the way you have cared for your brothers and sister. I shall never regret marrying you, I promise.'

Tears welled, and Rosalind swallowed them back.

'Is that what you feared?' He tilted her chin. 'That I should grow weary of you?'

'Mama fell out of love with Papa.'

'Come...' he led her to a wingback chair by the fire '... and tell me all about it.' He sat and pulled her to his knee. 'Is that why you said "I cannot" the other day? Because of what I am, not who I am?'

She told him about her mother's dissatisfaction and her parents' constant arguments. 'It is the last thing I remember before Papa died.' She gulped back her tears, reaching for the comfort of her locket. 'Them arguing. Mama crying. And then the crash. And afterwards...afterwards... she was happy again. And she met Lord Lydney and they were happy together. Our marriage will be unequal, like theirs. People will look down on me, like Mama looked down on Papa and on Grandpa. Like my aunts look down on me and Freddie.'

She cried into his shoulder as he rubbed her back.

'Your grandpa is still alive?' he asked, when the tears stopped.

She sniffed and he handed her his handkerchief. 'I know not. We visited him. He made me this...' she showed Leo her locket '...for my sixth birthday, but Mama refused to stay any longer and so we travelled home a day early, on the day of my birthday, and that is when...when...'

'Oh, sweetheart.' Leo held her close as her voice tailed into silence. 'No wonder you are afraid, but there is no need to be.'

He wiped her eyes, then tilted her face to his. His dark brows rose as he said, 'Do you really believe *anyone* would dare to shun my Duchess? Your mother was a young girl when she eloped with your father and her reputation was bound to suffer. Like it or not, that is the world we live in. It will be different for me and you, I promise.'

She knew he was right. Who, indeed, would dare to stand against him?

'Will you tell me about your wife?'

A muscle bunched in Leo's jaw, then he sighed. 'I promised myself I would learn to confide in you and to trust you.'

He told her how he had married at eighteen to set his father's mind at rest.

'Although it was not a love match, I thought we would be content, but once Margaret had done her duty, she lost all interest in me and in the children. All she cared for was being the Duchess of Cheriton. I later discovered she'd taken many lovers, but all I cared about by then was protecting the children from the truth of their mother's character.'

Rosalind kissed his cheek, stroking his hair, knowing how hard it must be to expose the hurt he had suffered with Margaret's lies and deceit and, worse, her casual dismissal of her own children.

'How did she die?'

'She was killed, at Cheriton Abbey.'

'Killed? How?'

'We think by a passing vagrant. Alex found her body in a summerhouse where there were signs that someone had been sleeping rough. Margaret...' his voice cracked with emotion '...she had been violated and strangled.'

Rosalind hugged him close.

'Oh, my darling. And poor, poor Alex.'

'He was only seven. He lost his speech for almost a year.'

'Your poor children, to lose their mother in such a way. Thank goodness they had you and Cecily to support them.'

'And now they will have you. Us. As will Susie.'

'Leo! Really? Susie may stay?'

'Of course she may.'

Rosalind kissed him, pouring all of her love into her embrace.

'Thank you,' she whispered when she finally took her lips from him. She traced his eyebrow with her forefinger. 'Leo, what happened yesterday? Did you have Lascelles arrested?'

'Ah. No.'

Rosalind stiffened, pushing away from him. 'No? But… why not? He kidnapped Susie and he would have done far worse to me if you had not come.'

He sighed and thrust his fingers through his hair. 'That was my intention, but he made it very clear that if I involved the law, he would drag both the Beauchamp name and yours through the courts for the newspapers to slaver over.

'So I came up with an alternative punishment for him.'

Rosalind shivered at the wolfish grin that crossed his face.

'I had him hauled off to the docks and chucked on board a ship about to set sail for China. I sent plenty of coins as an incentive for the captain to work him hard.'

Rosalind refused to feel pity for Lascelles.

'Now…' Leo peppered her face with kisses '…I have it in mind to apply to the Archbishop for a special licence, so we can wed as soon as possible. What do you think?'

A warm glow suffused Rosalind. Here was more proof of his change. Proof he would ask for and listen to her opinion.

'Could we not have the *banns* read in the normal way and marry in church?'

'That will take weeks. I do not know if I can wait that long to claim you as my own.'

She pushed her fingers through his hair and kissed his lips. 'Patience is a virtue.' She smiled at him, then feathered kisses along his strong jawline. 'I was thinking more of Olivia and Nell. We do not want to steal attention from their come-out balls, do we?'

He narrowed his eyes at her. 'Hmm. That is a good point. I shall agree on one condition.'

Rosalind lifted her brows.

'You remain here. At Beauchamp House, where I can be certain you are safe.'

Two days later

The instructions were clear. She was to wear her riding habit and meet His Grace by the front door at five that afternoon. Mystified, Rosalind did as she was bid and arrived in the entrance hall as the longcase clock opposite the staircase struck five. Leo, dressed in immaculate breeches and tailcoat, waited at the front door.

'Where are we going?'

Leo crooked his arm and escorted Rosalind to the pavement, where Conqueror and Kamal, coats gleaming, were held by a groom.

'To the park.'

She looked around as they halted next to Kamal. There were no other horses.

'Alone?'

Leo set his hands to Rosalind's waist.

'Together. It is time to introduce my future Duchess to London society.'

Chapter Twenty-Six

5 May 1812

The open-topped barouche, drawn by six gleaming chestnuts, turned the corner from Conduit Street into St George's Street. The portico of St George's, with its vast pediment atop six Corinthian columns, came into view and Rosalind's heart thumped in her chest at the sight of the crowd that had gathered. Inside the church, Leo waited. And, when they had said their vows, they would be man and wife. And she would be a duchess!

Freddie, handsome and debonair in his dark grey tailcoat and light grey trousers, squeezed her hand.

'Nervous?'

Rosalind smiled. She could not speak, her mouth was too dry. The horses came to a standstill and the crowds parted to leave a clear path all the way to the huge church door, before which waited her bridesmaids: Nell, Olivia and Susie, dressed in lilac satin and clutching posies of white jasmine and violets.

Another figure waited with them. He was also dressed in a dark grey tailcoat and light grey trousers, but he was a stranger—stooped and elderly, tweaking at his white neckcloth as though unused... Rosalind gasped, her hand to her mouth. Freddie had already alighted from the coach, with the help of a footman, and he now waited to assist her to the pavement.

'Freddie? Who is that man?'

Freddie tucked her hand into the crook of his arm and, slowly and steadily, with Freddie leaning heavily upon his crutch, they ascended the steps. Rosalind forgot the crowds, forgot the occasion, even momentarily forgot the love of her life who awaited her inside the church. She had eyes only for that stooped figure.

As they drew nearer she knew.

'Grandpa!' Tears swam, blurring her vision. 'It *is* you.'

The old man hobbled forward and took her face between his gnarled hands.

'My beautiful bab.' His voice caught and his own eyes grew moist. 'I never thought to see you again.'

'But, how… Where…? Freddie! How did you find him?'

'Not me, Ros. The Duke. In Birmingham. He wanted to give you something money can't buy.'

Rosalind threw her arms around her grandfather and hugged him tight. 'Oh, I am truly the happiest woman alive. I did not even know if you were alive or dead, Grandpa. Look…' she stepped back '…I still have the locket you made for me.'

He smiled, shaking his head. 'And you're wearing it on your wedding day, bab. You should be wearing precious jewels: diamonds and pearls.'

'This is more precious to me than all the diamonds and pearls in the world, Grandpa. I promise you that.'

'The Duke thought you might want Grandpa to walk you down the aisle, Ros. Speaking of which…it is time we went inside.'

'Oh, you don't want an old man like me spoiling the occasion,' Grandpa said.

'You will *make* the occasion, Grandpa, truly you will… but… Freddie, what about you?'

'Don't you mind about me, Ros. I shan't mind.'

'I shall have you both,' Rosalind declared. 'One on each side of me to walk me down the aisle. My family. I shall be so very proud of you both, but I should still like Freddie to give me away.'

Freddie beamed and Grandpa nodded his approval.

They entered the church, arms linked. And there, waiting, was Leo. Tall, handsome and ducal, with Vernon by his side, both of them clad in the same dark and pale grey combination as Freddie. He turned as she walked up the broad aisle between the wooden box pews. A smile of pure joy lit his face.

I shall be the proudest man alive when I see you walk down the aisle to me, my sweetest treasure.

And she could believe every word he had whispered the night before, when they had kissed goodnight before going, for the last time, to their separate bedchambers. A low cough from a pew distracted her. Aunt Tring, her mouth pursed, as though she had swallowed a wasp. Rosalind hadn't wanted to invite any of her mother's family, but Leo had persuaded her that she would gain far more satisfaction from rising above their petty behaviour than in emulating it. And he had been right.

Her wise, handsome husband-to-be: Leo.

To her, he would always be Leo. The Duke was for others. Leo was for her.

She arrived before the altar and smiled into his eyes, love flooding every fibre of her being. Freddie remained at her other side, but Grandpa shuffled across to sit in the front pew and Rosalind checked over her shoulder to make sure he was safely seated next to her stepbrother, Jack, Lord Lydney, who beamed at her. She drew in a deep breath and turned back to face the Reverend Hodgson.

The ceremony passed in a blur of questions and responses, and then they were declared man and wife, exchanging a chaste kiss at the behest of the rector. Heart near to bursting with happiness, Rosalind took Leo's proffered arm, ready for the long walk back down the aisle and to the rest of their lives.

She looked up at him, and their eyes locked. With a slow smile, he straightened his arm, his hand sliding down her silk sleeve to hold her hand. He turned and reached across her to capture her other hand. He tugged her round to face him.

'I love you.'

No whispered declaration, but bold and assured—a proclamation for all to hear and to marvel over and to report back to those not present.

'You have brought serenity and joy, happiness and passion into my life.

'My friend, my love, my Duchess.'

* * * * *

*If you enjoyed this story, you won't want to miss these
other great reads from Janice Preston*

*MARY AND THE MARQUIS
FROM WALLFLOWER TO COUNTESS
RETURN OF SCANDAL'S SON
SAVED BY SCANDAL'S HEIR
THE GOVERNESS'S SECRET BABY*

HOMETOWN HEARTS ♥

YES! Please send me **The Hometown Hearts Collection** in Larger Print. This collection begins with 3 FREE books and 2 FREE gifts in the first shipment. Along with my 3 free books, I'll also get the next 4 books from the Hometown Hearts Collection, in LARGER PRINT, which I may either return and owe nothing, or keep for the low price of $4.99 U.S./ $5.89 CDN each plus $2.99 for shipping and handling per shipment*. If I decide to continue, about once a month for 8 months I will get 6 or 7 more books, but will only need to pay for 4. That means 2 or 3 books in every shipment will be FREE! If I decide to keep the entire collection, I'll have paid for only 32 books because 19 books are FREE! I understand that accepting the 3 free books and gifts places me under no obligation to buy anything. I can always return a shipment and cancel at any time. My free books and gifts are mine to keep no matter what I decide.

262 HCN 3432 462 HCN 3432

Name	(PLEASE PRINT)	
Address		Apt. #
City	State/Prov.	Zip/Postal Code

Signature (if under 18, a parent or guardian must sign)

Mail to the **Reader Service:**

IN U.S.A.: P.O. Box 1867, Buffalo, NY. 14240-1867
IN CANADA: P.O. Box 609, Fort Erie, Ontario L2A 5X3

* Terms and prices subject to change without notice. Prices do not include applicable taxes. Sales tax applicable in NY. Canadian residents will be charged applicable taxes. This offer is limited to one order per household. All orders subject to approval. Credit or debit balances in a customer's account(s) may be offset by any other outstanding balance owed by or to the customer. Please allow 4 to 6 weeks for delivery. Offer available while quantities last. Offer not available to Quebec residents.

Your Privacy—The Reader Service is committed to protecting your privacy. Our Privacy Policy is available online at www.ReaderService.com or upon request from the Reader Service.

We make a portion of our mailing list available to reputable third parties that offer products we believe may interest you. If you prefer that we not exchange your name with third parties, or if you wish to clarify or modify your communication preferences, please visit us at www.ReaderService.com/consumerschoice or write to us at Reader Service Preference Service, P.O. Box 9062, Buffalo, NY. 14240-9062. Include your complete name and address.

HHBPA17

Get 2 Free Books,

Plus 2 Free Gifts—
just for trying the Reader Service!

Get 2 Free Books,
Plus 2 Free Gifts—
just for trying the Reader Service!

Get 2 Free Books,
Plus 2 Free Gifts—
just for trying the Reader Service!

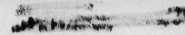

Get 2 Free Books,
Plus 2 Free Gifts—
just for trying the Reader Service!

♥ HARLEQUIN
SPECIAL EDITION

YES! Please send me 2 FREE Harlequin® Special Edition novels and my 2 FREE gifts (gifts are worth about $10 retail). After receiving them, if I don't wish to receive any more books, I can return the shipping statement marked "cancel." If I don't cancel, I will receive 6 brand-new novels every month and be billed just $4.99 per book in the U.S. or $5.74 per book in Canada. That's a savings of at least 12% off the cover price! It's quite a bargain! Shipping and handling is just 50¢ per book in the U.S. and 75¢ per book in Canada.* I understand that accepting the 2 free books and gifts places me under no obligation to buy anything. I can always return a shipment and cancel at any time. The free books and gifts are mine to keep no matter what I decide.

235/335 HDN GLWR

Name	(PLEASE PRINT)
Address	Apt. #
City	State/Province	Zip/Postal Code

Signature (if under 18, a parent or guardian must sign)

Mail to the **Reader Service:**
IN U.S.A.: P.O. Box 1341, Buffalo, NY 14240-8531
IN CANADA: P.O. Box 603, Fort Erie, Ontario L2A 5X3

Want to try two free books from another line?
Call 1-800-873-8635 or visit www.ReaderService.com.

*Terms and prices subject to change without notice. Prices do not include applicable taxes. Sales tax applicable in N.Y. Canadian residents will be charged applicable taxes. Offer not valid in Quebec. This offer is limited to one order per household. Books received may not be as shown. Not valid for current subscribers to Harlequin Special Edition books. All orders subject to approval. Credit or debit balances in a customer's account(s) may be offset by any other outstanding balance owed by or to the customer. Please allow 4 to 6 weeks for delivery. Offer available while quantities last.

Your Privacy—The Reader Service is committed to protecting your privacy. Our Privacy Policy is available online at www.ReaderService.com or upon request from the Reader Service.

We make a portion of our mailing list available to reputable third parties that offer products we believe may interest you. If you prefer that we not exchange your name with third parties, or if you wish to clarify or modify your communication preferences, please visit us at www.ReaderService.com/consumerschoice or write to us at Reader Service Preference Service, P.O. Box 9062, Buffalo, NY 14240-9062. Include your complete name and address.

HSEI7R2